The NOT
DIARY of a
PAWNBROKER

Elliot Stanton

Michael Terence
Publishing

First published in paperback by
Michael Terence Publishing in 2017
www.mtp.agency

www.elliotstanton.com

ISBN 978-1-521-10259-6

To my wife, Melanie and my children Abigail and Bradley, and my family and friends for their encouragement and support.

The NOT SO SECRET DIARY of a PAWNBROKER

Elliot Stanton

Preface

My name is Elliot Stanton and I have been a pawnbroker in East London. It is a job that I have been performing for 21 years. I am married with twins and live on the outskirts of North London.

For years I have been relaying stories and amusing incidents to family and friends about my job and the people I come in contact with, and on many occasions, I have been urged to write these down in some format. Eventually, after many years of apathy I decided to do just that, but within the confines of a fictional story.

I have seen the area and the community change a lot over this time, but I still find a lot of humour and humility with the people I deal with on a daily basis. All of the incidents with the customers that take place within this book are absolutely, well, at least 90 percent true - after all, one needs a *little* poetic licence. Only the names have been changed to protect the guilty. Everything else, however, is purely fictional.

Contents

Introduction

Three, four... five, six... erm, seven, eight. No, hold on, that's a hair. Seven. How can I have *seven* wrinkles around my eyes? It's uneven. Six or even eight, yes, but seven? Perhaps that stray hair was a wrinkle that fell off. It seems like I'm becoming very vain, but it's not like I regularly spend any length of time staring at myself in the bathroom mirror. Not normally, anyway. "The years are catching up with you, Pete", I thought out loud. The bags under my eyes had become a little more prominent and now I clearly had more grey hair than brown... much more. There's no going back now. A couple of years ago I could have dyed it when the number of grey hairs was more of an infiltration rather than a full blown proliferation. Now, it's too late. Paul McCartney, amongst others, should share my thinking. Why do men who have already gone grey, decide to dye their hair... and their eyebrows? Oh, the eyebrows. Who do they think they are kidding?

When I was young, Mum would often tell me `if you have nothing nice to say about someone, don't say anything at all'. If that was a mantra for my life, then this would be a very dull diary. It might *still* be a very dull diary. In fact, it would be little more than an ill-judged pamphlet. Is that a good opening? It sounds reasonably witty, but perhaps a little trite.

I haven't written a diary since my teens, and I am only writing it on the recommendation of my psychotherapist, but more about him later. He suggested it as if to prove to myself that my life isn't as humdrum and tedious as I imagined, so I thought `why not?' I feel that I have something to say and occasionally it's worth hearing, or reading. Sometimes it's poignant; sometimes it's comical, and sometimes it just plain doesn't make sense. I'm not infallible. Because, after 35 years of dealing with the Great British public, I have concluded that you either meet them on their level and play them at their own game or you let them walk all over you.

Thursday 16th February 2012

Start Me Up

(11.00 a.m.) To be honest (and that's a phrase which often precedes a bare-faced lie), I'm not even sure how an adult person's diary is supposed to be written. Perhaps I should have started with:

Dear Diary,

Allow me to introduce myself. My name is Pete Dawson and I am 50 years old. I am married to Kathy, and we have three children; Melissa, who is 27, is an artist with a family of her own, Simon, who is 24, divorced with no children and is a stockbroker, and Leanne, my baby, who is 19. Two of my children have now flown the family nest and the youngest is currently travelling around Australia. They say that when your kids leave home you feel empty and you wish you had them back again. Don't believe a word of it. It's bloody wonderful! Don't get me wrong, I do love them, but love can just as easily travel great distances as it can to their friends' houses or the bedrooms upstairs, where they spent so much time.

I live in a leafy North London suburb. In fact, are there any suburbs that aren't 'leafy'? I'm part-owner of an East London pawnbrokers, jewellers and cheque cashers and this has been my career for most of my adult working life. My business partner of the last seven years, Phil Bryan, perhaps comes into work two or three times a week. He has plenty of irons in many fires and his optimistic gung-ho attitude to life is something that some people find refreshing and admirable. His glass is always filled to the brim. There's none of that 'half full' nonsense for him. Personally, I find it quite sickening at times. I am, what they (or at least I do), call a realist/pessimist. My theory on having this state of mind is that one can never be too disappointed; even though I so often am. However, my glass is not *always* half empty, as I normally prefer to drink straight out of the bottle wherever polite company allows.

In my late teens and early 20s, I flirted with the back-stabbing world of estate agency for a few short years, before I packed it in. Finally, being my own boss seemed appealing, but I soon learnt that it wasn't all about clocking off when I wanted or taking month-long Caribbean cruises. I would suggest that I have spent more time within the confines of my small business than I ever did in as an employee in someone else's. However, it is (half) mine and it provides me and my family with a good lifestyle, but it also gives me an insight into the minds of the people who I deal with on a daily basis. Some have no morals or no dignity or no self-control or no underwear, and sometimes all four. Occasionally, however, they can be quite pleasant and even charming. I realised fairly early on that my pawn customers generally fall into four categories. They are:

The Normal Ones. Honest, understanding and pleasant folk. Happily, this made up for about 80 percent of my customer base.

The Disillusioned Ones. These are the people who believe they are always right in any situation. These are the ones who are usually actually wrong in every situation.

The Stubborn Ones. These are the people who understand they are wrong, but will not concede to reason or fact. An offshoot of the 'disillusioned'.

The Funny Ones. These are the ones who make my job worthwhile. Whether it is through drunkenness, misunderstanding, attempting to catch me out or trying to enter me into any extra-curricular non-pawn broking forays.

Occasionally, I leave my business premises at the end of the day with a heart redundant of compassion, but from my formative years, entering into adulthood, I have always tried to find the best in people. Essentially, I believe that most people in any given situation are basically good, honest and interested in doing the right thing. Now, I realise that I might be coming over extremely self-righteous and self-absorbed, but I don't think there is anything wrong in believing this. Of course, as one travels along the highways and byways of life, one becomes very much aware that not *all* people are interested in being fair and balanced, and some are simply irredeemable in every way. Yes, I'm quite a cynical old bastard, but I do believe that most of us fall in between those two stools.

There are people who won't say anything and will always keep their mouths shut to avoid confrontation. These people tend to become mass murderers. We have read many times about the serial killer who, according to his neighbours and (ahem) friends, "was so polite. He would never say boo to a goose." This is exactly the type of person who I'm talking about. This is the person who would live years in virtual silence, building up such anger and resentment, for one day to snap and, 'bang' or slice or thump or crush... And there's your serial killer for you.

Then there are those who will give you their opinion at the drop of a very large hat to fit their very large head. These people normally become leaders of extreme right-wing political groups and demand the repatriation of every racial group they are not part of, even if they are not indigenous to these British Isles themselves.

Then, of course, you can just be 'nice'. Let's face it; there is something a little odd and off-putting about someone who tries so hard to be everything to every man (or woman). I mean who likes 'nice', outside a local village vicar, Michael Palin and pre- "Let's be 'avin' you," Delia Smith, eh?

I believe that one needs to be a little of all three. Keep one's mouth shut when one needs to; be outspoken when one has to and be nice if the situation warrants niceness. I always try to be as pleasant as I can, but depending on the attitude of the customer in front of me, my responses will be deployed accordingly. After all, there are only so many times I can try to reason with someone's ill-judged assumption of what my job should entail.

The old saying, 'The customer is always right' is really just for the customer. In actual fact, how can they always be right? I know exactly what I'm doing and I have a computer that works out all the interest charges and redemption costs of their pledges.

Sometimes though, the temptation is too great not to correct them of this very basic, but all too often erroneous and counterfactual retail fallacy. Unfortunately, many people, especially ones of the younger generation see it as their mission in life to always be right, to 'always be themselves', and to 'say it how it is', however incorrect whatever they are saying is. In my view, and this is just *my* view, it is a very simplistic and naïve way to live your life. TV's Big Brother is very much to blame for this.

"You're fat, you're ugly, and you smell... but I'm only saying how it is, mate. Could you move along the bus, please?"

"Thank you so much for your most honest assessment of me, Mr Bus Driver. Oh, and I've lost my Oyster card too, so I'm using one that I stole off that woman in the queue - you see the one frantically rummaging around her unnecessarily oversized bag at the bus stop?"

Okay, that's a bit extreme, but if we are led to believe that being honest and truthful in every aspect of one's life is the only way forward, then how many divorces would result from the kernel of a simple, yet loaded question? To coin a well-known sketch show catchphrase – "Does my bum look big in this?" For a man to answer in the affirmative because he's 'only being honest' is surely the road to disaster; so we learn to live with little white lies. We have to. After all, 100 percent honesty can be hurtful and harmful. With friends and family though, one's personality and character should be understood, so the occasion for these little trick questions should, hopefully, rarely arise.

In business, as in one's personal life, a white lie can be lifting, encouraging, relieving and nourishing. It's true, and we all know it. After dealing with the great and not-so-great British public for a not too inconsiderable length of time, I can confirm that it is essential. There is a fine line between being economical with the truth and out-and-out bullshitting. Although, I say 'fine line', but from the mouths of some, it's a trench, a ravine, a chasm even.

People can be infuriating, but they can also be amusing and entertaining. Occasionally being lied to, certainly has certainly made my job a little more entrancing. It is not *all* about lies, though. Many people seem to live in a fantasy world, and far from me thinking them foolish or stupid, in many cases, I find them quite endearing and honest. One man's deranged old nutter is another man's idealistic dreamer. You pays your money;

you takes your choice.

People who have spent all their lives working in an office situation really have no idea what a trial, and indeed pleasure it is to meet and deal daily with the general public. One has to try to understand their various foibles and idiosyncrasies. It's not something that I always find easy, but I do try to start the day with an open mind and a pleasant disposition. However, so often the light has diminished and the goodwill spent by my midmorning coffee. There's nowt as strange as folk. Indeed, some folk might say that there's nowt as strange as me, and that is a statement that actually sits quite comfortably with me, thank you very much.

So, dear Diary, this is me. You are an inanimate object housing my thoughts and activities, so what do you care? Does this count as talking to oneself? I really must mention to my shrink that I may have developed mild schizophrenic tendencies.

Friday 17th February 2012

Food For Thought

(7.00 a.m.) It's another Monday morning. Well, it wasn't, but it might as well have been. It's all a bit Groundhog Day at the moment. Friday, Monday, Saturday, it's all the bloody same. I know it wasn't the third Wednesday of the month as that is my 'shrink night'. I eagerly look forward to my monthly meeting. I can get things off my chest and receive modest succour from someone who barely knows me, but appears to be interested in me, or at least my marital life and my private insurance payments. He is very convincing though, and I've been seeing him for about three months now. Because I had been feeling very low, and I had been finding my wife had become increasingly difficult to communicate with, it was felt that I needed someone to vent my concerns to. My GP referred me to this guy and I must say it's helped.

(7.30 a.m.) I left home at the normal time and, as usual, found myself part of an ever-extending line of dirty, exhaust-expelling metal and glass. I got a very funny look from a woman in a Vauxhall Astra, for coughing. Yes, coughing. I didn't cover my mouth, but she looked totally disgusted. I might as well have held up a baby and spat in its face, such was her discernible derision.

(11.30 a.m.) This morning really dragged. The day had

been slow, but lo and behold, in walked my 'Superfan'. Well, not so much a fan, more of a disgruntled antagonist really. She always wants me to take her out to lunch and 'discuss stuff'. I get the feeling when she makes these demands – because they *are* demands –like I'm being put on the spot. I don't want to be rude, but being blunt is the only way I can get through to her. Today, she didn't just plainly ask, "When are you taking me out to lunch?" but was a little more confrontational. "*Why* won't you take me out? What's wrong with me? What's wrong with you?" I was a little concerned (in a 'trying to get out of a frightening lunchtime scenario' kind of way). "I am married, and I don't think it's appropriate," I told her in no uncertain terms.

So, this time, she really stepped up her game, and told me, "If you're not going to take me out then give me some money for lunch." This caught me on the back foot somewhat and the realisation that it wasn't me she was interested in, but a free lunch, gave me a strange sensation of blighted hope and extreme relief, but mainly relief. However, it gave me the confidence to 'see what I could have won', so I asked her where we would have gone for lunch. Knowing the area not to exactly be an oasis of fine dining, the choice of restaurant mainly consists of Indian and Sri Lankan cuisine and not much else, unless you wish to visit one of a dozen or so fried chicken outlets, so I was expecting one of these. I was a little surprised when all she wanted was a simple Big Mac meal and a McFlurry.

"Are you sure that's all?" I enquired.

Now seeing the chance to fleece me, she added "Yeah, and *two* apple pies," nodding defiantly in an Oliver Hardy fashion. She held out her hand for some money. I was clearly at a disadvantage.

The whole thing then developed into a Cuban Missile Crisis type standoff. I wasn't going to hand over any cash, and she wasn't going to put her hand down. As luck would have it though, an extremely loud friend/sister/mother person shouted through the open door to her, "Are you coming or what?" So, at the very brink of World War III, as the entire world held its breath, the Soviets backed down at the last moment and... hang on, that *was* the Cuban Missile Crisis. It still could have been a very nasty situation for me though.

With a sneer and a suck of her teeth (oh yes), she departed my shop for what I assumed was her dream Big Mac meal and McFlurry, but I very much doubt, *two* apple pies.

(12.25 p.m.) A rather sharp-nosed, angular Northern Irish gentleman marched up to the counter and asked me if I'd be interested in buying his Citizen watch. I told him that it wasn't the sort of thing I was interested in and politely declined. He put it back on his wrist and told me in no uncertain terms, "I've seen you before. You're a member of my Lodge." He announced this in a very brusque, broad Ulster accent, whilst his steely gaze was fixed on me, very sternly. I told him I wasn't, but his extraordinarily menacing presence made me even doubt myself.

He then leant over and looked behind me into the back office. "Are you sure?" he persisted without apparently picking up on my non-Ulster accent.

"Quite sure," I replied. He was still trying to look around and behind me. I don't know what he was expecting to see - perhaps a bowler hat, an umbrella, and an old 7-inch single of 'The Sash My Father Wore'?

He completed his interrogation with "Nah, I suppose you're too young anyway." With that, he sniffed, frowned, and marched out of the shop. I doubt if he'll be seeing me down the Shankill anytime soon.

(12.45 p.m.) Lunch consisted of part of a day old tuna mayo sandwich and a lucky dip into a six-pack of crisps. Oh goody - ready salted. There were only two packs left anyway - both ready salted. Someone else had taken my last packet of cheese and onion. At least I had the choice of a Diet Coke or Pepsi Max. Decisions, decisions... I took a Diet Coke from the fridge and sat down at my desk. Phil wasn't in today, so Sabrina (my former Saturday girl who now comes in most days, because her life is even more moribund than mine), was my assistant. She sauntered over to me from the counter where she had just been serving and asked if she could have a packet of crisps. Her knee-length skirt and bare legs were more befitting the summer months than the icy conditions that we've been having recently.

"There's only ready salted left," I said, trying to draw her into a conversation. Nothing. "Have you done something with your hair?" I asked in desperation. She raised her head and instead of answering me, just touched her fringe as if to confirm my suspicions without uttering a single word. I think she probably knew that I really didn't care either way. At the time, I assumed that her request for the crisps was probably all I'll get out of her today; such is her stealth and laconism. She shimmied over to Phil's desk and to what was left of the six-pack and gingerly reached in as if to avoid a carefully placed mousetrap. Her brown eyes opened wide and looked at me as she retrieved her prize. She pulled out a packet of cheese and onion - cheese and bloody onion. *That* wasn't in there before. It just wasn't. Evidently, I had miscounted the situation on the potato snack front. The look on her face suggested to me that I'd been an idiot not to check the options more carefully.

(1.00 p.m.) I switched on the old TV and I was informed that we're going to have the Olympic Games in London in a few months. Wow, who knew? It's not like every TV and radio station had been going on and on and on about it for years and years. I thought about how much money the local council will be spending on 'the Olympic legacy'. Here's your legacy - enough debt to finally bankrupt the country five times over. What a bloody waste of money. They might as well flush half of it and spend the rest on giving Dyno-Rod its biggest contract since Eric Pickles' 'Pie till you Die' marathon.

(3.00 p.m. – 3.05 p.m.) I found myself playing Agony

Uncle to Sabrina - not that she said too much. That's why it only lasted five minutes. She told me her boyfriend, Daz, has "not been at all attentive recently." I know for a fact that her on-off beau has been playing away from home again. Will she ever learn? Unlikely, as she's gone back to him more times than Boris Johnson has been on television this week... which is a lot. This time, he's been on an overnight patio laying job in Crawley. "Apparently, she does have garden lighting though," Sabrina tacitly reassured me. He couldn't do it during the day as he was laying something else in Esher, I thought. Still, she's (sort of) happy. Well, she's not exactly happy, but she's not *too* miserable either. Actually, I don't think I've ever seen her happy for any length of time. I think that's why we work so well together.

(4.20 p.m.) The conditions outside were very windy and blustery and it swept in a family who, at first contact, I could tell would bring a certain comic relief to my ready salted day. A Polish family of five males, known to me as the Kowalski's, came in wanting to pawn some gold. The lead Kowalski, who was a lot older that the other four, handed over the assorted bracelets and chains and asked me, "Please boss the maximum." First of all, I informed him that the price of gold had been on a downward tilt for some months, for I knew that whatever I offered would be met with a "No, please boss... more..." I then weighed the gold items and made him an offer. Along with the predicted response, coupled with a sneer, I was met with a fair deal of 'tuttage' and a soupcon of under-the-breath muttering. "Last time you gave more," he said. I was sure he'd never been in before, but I might have been wrong. I decided to take the calculated risk of lending them a little extra as I was feeling particularly generous. I began to check the individual pieces for their authenticity and before long, two of the family began a heated discussion. This was not unusual, as shouting at one other is a favoured choice of communication for much of my Eastern European clientele, but this soon escalated to pushing, and dare I say, a fair bit of shoving too, which resulted in Kowalski the Younger being pushed over a chair by Kowalski the Monobrow. The Kowalski patriarch then spun around, yelled at them and clipped the fallen one around the year. Order was restored.

I continued to check everything when all hell broke loose again. Even Sabrina looked up from her Heat magazine. Kowalski the Younger and Kowalski the Monobrow were at it again; this time joined by Kowalski the Brave (for he was wearing an Adidas vest top on this rather cold and windy afternoon). He was mainly goading the other two and just chipping in with the odd shriek. Pa Kowalski once again turned around and read them the Polish Riot Act, which I expect was still at The White Paper stage as it didn't seem to hold much gravitas. All this time, the quiet one, Kowalski the Appeaser just stood observing the brouhaha - I love that word. By now, I had weighed and checked every item of jewellery and made an increased offer which was accepted by the now exacerbated elder. Peace had now broken out.

It was then when a little old lady walked in and pushed a contract through to me from an adjacent window, and asked if she could come next week to collect it. As the Kowalski's contract was being signed, I briefly saw to her and told her 'yes' and she left the shop. Unfortunately, she had a rather pungent hygiene problem - a fact that Monobrow was all too ready to raise as soon as she left the shop. "She smells of animal" he delighted in shouting at me.

"Cats," I jokily replied. He laughed. Kowalski the Younger did not laugh.

"Not cat... wet dog," he concluded angrily. And so they started arguing again, followed by the rest of the clan. Could they really be arguing about the kind of stench that emanated from the old lady? I wouldn't be at all surprised. The old man took his contract and money and ushered his disgruntled mob out of the shop, just turning to offer a cheery "thanks, boss," before lamping poor Kowalski the Younger once more. Maybe it's me, but I do like to do things in a simple and straightforward fashion. Still, people are people as Depeche Mode sang and business is business – which I think was their follow-up single.

(6.45 p.m.) The journey home was another miserable one because the North Circular was snarled up again. I'm not saying that seeing the carnage of a car crash isn't vaguely interesting, but why do people have to slow down to a snail's pace to get a good eyeful? Once you've seen one...

Supper was last night's leftovers. Roast lamb. I do love leftovers and there's nothing wrong with twice or thrice cooked meat. That's what Kathy says anyway, and my wife always knows best.

(8.00 p.m.) I sat down to watch some instantly forgettable garbage on ITV. The news was exciting though. Apparently, the country is gearing up the lavish (but highly secretive) Olympic Games opening ceremony. I wonder how the certain debt will affect me. Higher taxes, higher rates and higher blood pressure, probably. What is there to celebrate, another year older and deeper in debt? Thanks, Tennessee Ernie Ford. I wonder if that was his real name, like James Earl Jones or Jumping Jack Flash.

Oh well, tomorrow's another day. Another Monday morning awaits me.

Saturday 18th February 2012

The Candy Man Can

(7.45 a.m.) I left a little later for work today, just because I could. I like being my own boss. I allowed myself an extra 15 minutes before the trudge into work. I'm living the high life. The house is quiet on a Saturday morning. Kathy was up before me and put the washing on. Even if there is nothing to wash, Kathy will find something. My wife is a real creature of habit. The weather was in stark contrast to yesterday. It was a most pleasant, crisp late winter's morn with a few wispy puffs of cloud in the sky. I sipped my hot coffee and looked out of the kitchen window at this lovely, peaceful image. Surely, this was the first time the blue sky had been seen in this part of the country for three months or more. I found myself feeling unusually chipper for some bizarre reason and not even wondering who or what will conceal my new found contentment into an all too familiar cloak of seething cynicism when I got into work.

(8.10 a.m.) No traffic on the North Circular today as I sang along to my 1970s rock and pop compilation. The road ahead was clear, almost spookily empty when the traffic lights on a pedestrian crossing turned red - just for me. There were no pedestrians in sight. Even this blatant mocking of me by this set of lights didn't vex me like it probably would most other times. I stopped and before I could reach the chorus of Bonnie Tyler's *Lost in France*, I could sense I was being watched. I looked to my right and a stationary police car with a pair of grinning officers cut short my rendition immediately. I hoped to God that they weren't able to lip read. The previous song was *White Riot* by The Clash. I would have been almost proud to be gazed upon blasting out a punk classic. Damn the shuffled order of my playlist. I mean, Bonnie Tyler! Bonnie bloody Tyler!! As the amber light began to flash, I cautiously waited for the police car to move off. He did very slowly, keeping my pace as if to mock me for my music 'choice'. I wanted to put the window down and explain "Tyler wasn't my decision. The mp3 player chose it. The one before was The Clash you know! White Riot!!" They then sped off thus slightly alleviating me of my embarrassment.

(**8.45 a.m.**) I parked up around the corner and made my way, still in good spirits, to the shop where Sabrina stood outside waiting for me. She had her mobile phone in hand, frantically texting away. She looked up sheepishly and offered me a little nod of the head and a barely audible "Good morning, Pete." I acknowledged her before I opened up the shutters and crossed the boundary into the world of the strange and peculiar. There was a rather unpleasant aroma to the shop this morning. It was an unpleasant whiff, which grew stronger as we made our way into the office. Then it dawned on me – it was the other half of that now two-day-old tuna sandwich. Just then, Sabrina sprang into action. Without prompting, she rushed into the kitchen, took a black rubbish sack from underneath the sink, danced back to the office and picked up the offending item still in its packaging a top of the overflowing rubbish bin and dropped it into the sack. Not only that, she emptied the rest of the bin, which featured all amounts of unknown unpleasantness, and dumped the refuse outside the back of the shop before cleaning the surfaces and Febreze-ing the area. "Coffee?" she cheerfully enquired. Her demeanour and efficiency amazed me. It must be the weather.

(10.45 a.m.) A reasonably ordinary looking guy in his late 40s came to pawn a ring. He understood the terms, accepted the offer without argument, and even knew where to and how many times he had to sign the contract. He was a dream punter. I handed over the money and he folded his contract up neatly and carefully put it away in his wallet along with the money. As he was just about to leave, he turned and said to me "I can buy a lot of Cadbury's chocolate with that. I love Cadbury's chocolate. I like Toblerone too, but you can't beat the taste of Cadbury's chocolate. Do you like it?" He said it in such a wide-eyed, excitable, and childlike way too. It was so strange that I genuinely looked for the tiny hidden camera about his person. I'd seen these sorts of things on YouTube. He continued, "There is something about Cadbury's chocolate that is unlike anything else. It's smooth, yet has an edge - unlike Galaxy. That's much too smooth." I imagined the guy must have believed that he was a marketing man for Cadbury's. Perhaps he was before he 'lost it'.

"Yes, I like Cadbury's," I conceded.

"That's good. Very good." I wondered if I passed the test. Was he really a modern day, real-life Willy Wonka? What did I win? Was he going to hand over his fabled chocolate factory to me? A year's supply of Dairy Milk? A briefcase full of Wispas? A pocket full of assorted Roses, maybe? Perhaps then, a single, dented Crème Egg? No. Nothing was forthcoming. He just nodded, smiled knowingly and left me with a loud and proud, "Everybody loves Cadbury's chocolate," and went on his way. It turned out he was not at all normal, but he fitted in perfectly with this place.

(1.15 p.m.) I splashed out on a McDonald's for lunch and treated Sabrina. At the moment, she is a vegetarian. It's the third or fourth time she's gone through this 'phase' in the last few months, so she bought herself a Fillet-o-Fish. What is the bloody point of a Fillet-o-Fish? I can honestly say that I can't remember the last time I witnessed anyone buying one of those. Really, I can't. She'll be back on the old Big Macs within a week. Having McDonald's for lunch would assure me that nothing would end up lurking in the trash to greet us on Monday morning. I don't even leave the gherkin.

We enjoyed lunch and even managed a nice, but brief little conversation about various aspects of the business. Things were going well today - probably too well.

(2.15 p.m.) The phone rang. It was Phil. He joyfully informed me that he was going away for a few days at the back end of next week. I was very much looking forward to a couple of days off myself, but he put the kybosh on that. That call was the catalyst for a distinct downturn in the overall level of calmness and serenity of the day, because not a minute after I put the phone down...

(2.17 p.m.) A woman came in who hadn't pawned with us for a while and I explained we now charge interest daily instead of monthly, as the law of money lending had recently changed. I explained this and the fact that it was still a six-month contract, but the customer had great difficulty in understanding this. I really wish I hadn't bothered. At first, she thought she would have to come in every day to pay all the interest. Then, she thought she had to come in every six weeks to pay the lot, and finally, she expected she'd have to pay *all* the interest the next day. This is all standard fare and I shouldn't really have been surprised, but after (I thought) she understood everything, and I handed her the £75 loan, I watched on in disbelief as she went through the following sequence:

She put the money in her purse, shut it, put the purse back into her bag, nodded, reached back into her bag, nodded, took the purse out again, opened it, took the £75 out with an extra fiver and put it on the counter in front of me. "There you go. That should cover it." This happened verbatim.

"No, you don't pay it back now," I spluttered.

"Oh yes, of course. I didn't want to fall behind with my payments," she said pushing the money further towards me.

"No dear. Not yet. When you come to collect your jewellery," I reassured her.

"Oh, I'm a bit of an idiot, aren't I? " Believe me; the temptation to concur was almost too much.

"A *bit*?" I questioned, "Not at all, madam." A '*bit* of an idiot' might have remembered why she needed a loan in the first place," I thought to myself, although if I had said it out loud she probably would have just nodded in agreement. She was in a whole different league.

This woman spoke perfect English and she looked like she had her faculties. I do know appearances can be deceptive, but come on...

(5.30 p.m.) We left the shop and all in all I felt it was a really good day. It could have been so much worse and that would not have been surprising to me. Sabrina showed more initiative this morning than she had done in the previous year or so since I took her on as a Saturday girl. She now knows how to dispose of a rank two-day old tuna sandwich. She can add that to her résumé. Hold on, she didn't actually give me my change from lunch. Also, I can't remember if I gave her a £10 note or a £20 note. Perhaps, it's me who is losing his faculties.

(8.15 p.m.) In the car with Kathy trying to find a parking space in the exorbitantly priced NCP car park off Brewer Street in London's 'glittering' West End. We decided to go up West for a meal at a fish restaurant we hadn't been to in donkey's years. As we drove around and around and up and up the spiral ramps, being careful not to add to all the scrapes and scratches on the walls left by other, not so diligent drivers, Kathy suddenly informed me that she was feeling quite bilious and wanted to go home. I told her it was just the car park dance that we were partaking in and that she would feel alright as soon as we parked up. "No Pete, I feel ill. Very ill. Take me home please." It was bloody unbelievable. For the first time in ages, we've ventured into London for a nice night out and she wanted to cut it short before we even parked up. I had really looked forward to it topping off a pretty good day, but I knew I wasn't going to change my wife's mind by promising am almost vomiting woman, fresh-baked sea bass in garlic, lemon and butter sauce; so round and around and down and down we drove to the exit, noticing, even more, scuff marks and dents on the walls in the descending spiral.

I approached the barrier and quickly realised that I might have an issue. Even though I had not been in this twisty-turny hell for even five minutes, I expected (quite fairly, I thought), to get out of it without paying the £8 minimum charge. Luckily, it was one of those manned barriers and not an electronic one, so I thought I would be able to reason with the attendant. I drove up to the barrier and the man sauntered over. The ensuing conversation went like this:

Me: Excuse me, but I just drove in five minutes ago, my wife doesn't feel well, so we didn't even park up. Can you just let me out, please?

Attendant: No sir, you'll have to pay the minimum £8.

Me: But, my wife doesn't feel well and I need to get her home.

Attendant: Sorry, but you still have to pay. That's £8, please.

Kathy: Just pay him please Pete, and get me home.

Me: Hold on Kathy, I'm not paying an eight quid parking fee when I didn't even park. (By this time there was another car behind me waiting to exit).

Me: Look, you know I didn't even park in here and the charge is for parking, right? Parking... but I didn't park.

Kathy: Pay the man, Pete.

Attendant: Sir (said in a very condescending way), you'll need to pay the fee before I raise the barrier. (The driver in the car behind honked his horn.)

Kathy: Just, will you pay the man, Pete?

Me: No I won't, Kathy. I'm sorry, but this is a matter of principle... and probably law, too. The charge is for *parking*, not for driving around a building aimlessly. (The impatient git behind me honked thrice more,)

Me: Just let me out, will you?

Attendant: No mate. ('Sir' had now become simply 'mate'). Not until you pay. You're holding up other people now. (A 10-second horn blast belts out from behind.)

Kathy: (shouting): Peter, will you just pay the man and get me home?! (The difference between Pete and Peter might only appear to be one letter, but in actual fact, it's an enormous ocean between slightly agitated wife and extremely annoyed wife. It indicated in no uncertain terms that the chance of winning any argument was almost non-existent).

I paid. The barrier was raised. We left.

After about 20 minutes of silence, we were almost home and I piped up, "How are you feeling now love?"

"Oh, I'm alright now. In fact, the sickness went soon after we got out of the car park. It was probably all those winding ramps that made me feel ill. I just want to go home now anyway. They'll be something in the fridge for you if you're hungry."

If I'm hungry? I was bloody famished, but I decided it was probably in my best interest to keep my thoughts on the whole matter to myself.

As I waited at a set of red traffic lights, I noticed a McDonald's across the road on my right. Suddenly, the notion of Sabrina's Fillet-o-Fish was mighty enticing as the image of that piscine and processed cheese treat might be the closest thing I was going to get to a nice fish supper tonight.

Friday 24th February 2012

Piano Man

(8.35 a.m.) I'm still playing my 70s compilation in my car and being very careful to look around me when sitting in traffic as not to be caught singing along to anything along the lines of *We're All Alone* by Rita Coolidge, *Angel In The Morning* by Juice Newton or *Shang-a-Lang* by The Bay City Rollers, but I let myself down and dropped the ball at the last moment this morning. At the last set of lights, just after turning off the North Circular, a paramedic inside an ambulance witnessed me in full *Wuthering Heights* mode. Strangely enough, I didn't feel as embarrassed as I might have, as I was tempered by the thought that it so easily could have been *Yes Sir, I Can Boogie*. I think that would have been worse.

(10.00 a.m.) The thought that I really should be having a few days off was playing on my mind a bit, teasing me, but if I had been off then I would not have been part of one of the funniest comedy routines ever seen in these parts.

One of my longest-serving patrons, Mr Bridger, a more than slightly drunken gentleman, and his slightly less loud, and less drunken sidekick, walked into my emporium. Mr Bridger (who used to be a member of the local council until alcohol took hold of him), had a large keyboard under his arm. This rather unkempt figure of a man placed his instrument very carefully on the counter. It was a Yamaha DX7 synthesiser and apparently, (I quickly learned), belonged to 1970s synth-pop pioneer Gary Numan. I knew this because his opening line in a booming, raspy voice was "There you are, son. This was in Tubeway Army." That's a quote I shall never forget. "It was played on 'Cars'." Although I was impressed with his knowledge of late 1970s electro-pop, his story fell down a bit because Cars was not by Tubeway Army, but by Gary Numan as a solo artist. If he had said 'Are Friends Electric?' well, then that would be a different story. I'm such a pedant.

He ordered his smaller and quieter friend to get out the power cable from the bag he was held so he could 'show vees people ow it works'. Sabrina took a step back and had a look of concern about her. This was all before he'd even asked me if we even took musical instruments, let alone how much he could borrow. Anyway, I knew this was good comedy value and I duly plugged in the power pack and off we went. Now, as it was the synth 'supposedly' played on Cars, he continued to try and play said song. I quickly realised he was probably even drunker than I thought. He made Les Dawson sound like Sergei Rachmaninoff.

After about 20 seconds and trying to hold back the laughter, I said "That's okay, Mr Bridger. I can tell it works."

"No, I 'ave to get it right," he reprimanded me. His search for the opening few chords of this song went on for some time and all the while he was getting more and angrier, punctuating his attempts with slaps to the hardware and hefty blows, disturbingly, to his head.

It was now plainly obvious that he was a lot drunker than I thought. His friend tried to interject by telling him to stop, but he wasn't having any of it, and told his sidekick, "Shut up or this is going straight up your..." He stopped. That probably wouldn't have increased his chances of getting money from me but would have made me a couple of hundred quid from *You've Been Framed.* Finally, after about five minutes, and a great deal of stifled laughter from my side of the counter, he got it right and screamed a triumphant "Yeahhh!" We thought that would be that, but he continued on to the first verse.

Risking his wrath, I just pulled the power cable and said, "Yes, that'll do. You're very good. Were *you* in Tubeway Army, by any chance?" The look on his face told me that he was certainly thinking about lying to that question, but he just exhaled, and admitted "Er... no son." Son? He's younger than *me*!

So, now we had to figure out how much we could lend on this piece of supposed pop memorabilia. "How much do you want to borrow?" I asked.

"Just a tenner will do," he said. "I'll show you my ID as I've moved since last time. I've got a driving licence in my old address," he replied. I was surprised he still had one, as I assumed that someone who had imbibed so much so early on a Monday morning would probably not be the sort of person to still be in possession of one, even if it was in an old address.

"So where are you living now?" I enquired.

"The pub," he blurted. I paused. "The Cock pub, on the corner." This could go some way in explaining his early morning inebriation. I took his details and did the business.

After he left, out of curiosity, I looked up on the internet to check if ex-councillor Bridger's instrument was possibly the synthesiser that Gary Numan could have used. I found out it was first produced a year after the hit it was supposed to have been played on, but it was only for a tenner and he'd always come back for his stuff before.

A few minutes later, my alcoholic friend came back and sashayed to the counter. "Er, I've got a guitar, too. It's an early 80s Stratocaster, which belonged to Don Henley from The Eagles. It's the one which he played on Hotel California in 1973." Yes, Don Henley, the *drummer* from The Eagles who played on the *1977* hit, Hotel California. I told him we don't take guitars. He sighed and muttered, "Oh well. I'll be seeing ya then," and left.

On a dark desert highway. Cool wind in my hair...

(**3.30 p.m.**) If this morning's encounter was comical, what I was confronted with this afternoon was perhaps more stereotypical of what I normally have to deal with. I've seen a hell of a lot of fake jewellery recently. Gold plated, gold filled with lead or resin, brass posing as gold; all sorts. Even more prevalent is the plethora of fake 'prestige' watches that have been bought in. It's open season for faux jewellery at the moment. In particularly, I've had a lot of counterfeit Rolexes in. Some of them are good fakes; very good indeed. Many of the current hauls of fakes have even been made of gold with genuine diamonds set on the face and bracelet, but on very close inspection, they have did not have bona fide Rolex parts inside the watch.

It's not always the items themselves, but the individual that brings them in. I know I shouldn't judge every book by its cover, but sometimes one instinctively marries up the age, race and urgency of a person and the items they bring in. If an 18-year-old, white male comes in with a handful of old-fashioned, 22 carat Asian jewellery, you really have to wonder if it's his or not. Similarly, if an Asian youth came in with a pocket watch inscribed with 'George Anderson. For 50 years of remarkable service', you have to ask questions, too. The errors are so obvious, it makes one wonder what these people are thinking.

I've been shown watches for pledge or sale over the last couple of decades that would not fool a comatose Stevie Wonder. Today's effort took the biscuit, though. If there was a checklist of concerns regarding the validity of a genuine Rolex, it would have ticked every box in the 'fake' column.

Three young, hooded individuals wanted to sell me a 'Rolex'. At least two of them were human and one I believe had the male gene, but any more than that, I couldn't confirm. The leader, who was undeniably male, for he had a magnificent tuft of ginger hair sprouting from his chin, shuffled up to the counter after being coaxed into it by the others *(Tick 1)*, and asked, "Do you buy Rollex?" I say 'Rollex' because he pronounced it more like 'bollocks' than 'Roeleks'. *(Tick 2)* I told him we did and I asked to see it. The watch was placed not too carefully into the draw under the counter window and on brief inspection immediately ticked a few more boxes.

It weighed as much as an under-endowed field mouse. *(Tick 3)*.

The 'dual metal' bracelet was comprised of varying degrees of fading gold colouring and featured several chipped areas of grey metal. *(Tick 4)*.

The name 'Rolex' on the face had at least 60 percent wonky lettering. That's severe wonkage! *(Tick 5)*.

The date window was clearly rudimentarily glued on at a unique jaunty angle. *(Tick 6)*.

The box that came with it was a 'Blue Peter - one we prepared earlier' special. *(Tick 7)*.

Humouring them, I asked them how much they were looking for, and was told "Whatever we can get for it. It's an unwanted birthday present. Generally, people only say 'we' and 'unwanted present' if something is knowingly fake or nicked). *(Ticks 8 & 9)*.

"I can probably go two on this," I told them. The leader of this little posse's eyes lit up. He must have thought 'Bingo, it's my lucky day.'

"Yeah, I'll take two grand," he excitedly announced.

"No, you misunderstand," I replied, somewhat bursting his bubble. "I'll give you two-pence. This is, without a doubt, the worst fake I have ever seen in my life and I have seen a lot."

"It's not a fake," he insisted, with a very puzzling look on his spotty, hairy-chinned, young face. I set out listing several, but not *all* of the little 'errors' I picked up on. When I finished, the look of disbelief on his boat race suggested to me that the poor lad believed it was a real watch, and he only wanted to sell me something that he knew was just stolen... but, not fake. He wasn't *all* bad. This pause led me to believe that perhaps he was contemplating my generous offer. However, he came back with what so many say when trying to sell something of dubious genuineness or ownership. 'I'll take it back to where I bought it from'. *(Tick 10)*. The unwanted present was now an unwanted purchase.

Scooping up the watch and box, (which immediately collapsed on itself due to the incorrectly applied sticky back plastic), the three individuals left the premises in virtual silence. I watched them as they had a short confab outside before making haste to the jewellers across the road to no doubt test their mettle and knowledge of things that look shiny, but in fact are just crappy.

(8.15 p.m.) Leanne called from Melbourne, Australia, not that there's another Melbourne she's visiting that I'm aware of. She reversed the charges, of course. I can't believe that she's been travelling in the Far East and

Australia for almost a month now. She informed me that she was having a wonderful time and meeting lots of interesting people. Oh, and she was running low on money and wanted Daddy to wire some over. I said I would. In actual fact, her brother and sister milked me for far more cash over the years as their university education and entertainment costs far exceeded Leanne's requests. Anyway, she's still my little baby girl and she spoke at least last three sentences before requesting the dosh. That, as far as my children are concerned, showed a great deal of restraint. Still, it was lovely to hear from her.

(10.20 p.m.) News night tonight focussed on... the sodding London Olympics and featured Lord Sebastian 'frigging' Coe telling us what 'a wonderful experience it will be for the whole country'. I bet they're dancing in the streets of Kirkcaldy (to steal a line from the late Rugby League commentator Eddie Waring), at that particular statement from the ex-Tory MP. Next, was the Minister for Sport and Recreation, Hugh Robertson, who expressed the belief that the London Olympics will leave us with... wait for it...'a fantastic legacy for us and our children'. Thank goodness for that. It must have been five minutes since someone from the Government mentioned the word 'legacy'. They really should trademark that word.

Tuesday 28th February 2012
Crime Of The Century

(9.15 a.m.) Phil came back today and couldn't help himself, but to regale me of his latest business venture. He's investing in a yacht making company. I'm not even going to go into any details about how he got involved in this. I can't - my mind turned off as soon as he started waxing lyrical about all the terribly interesting folk he met last week down in Weymouth. He did ask me if I was aware that the Olympic sailing events are going to take place in Weymouth, and he could get tickets for any of the events taking place there.

I think it was the first mention of 'The Olympics' that turned my mind off his 'wonderful' news. I began to think how one would be charged to watch bloody sailing and why you would even need tickets? Are the organisers going to ban the plebs from walking along the quay and looking out to sea? Perhaps they'll erect a massive black screen a mile long and 100 feet high, to deny anyone without a ticket (therefore not entering into The Olympic spirit, of course), the privilege of watching any part of 'The Greatest Show on Earth' as Lord Coe tells us, at first hand, or first eye. There's always watching it free on television though. Sailing on television? I'd rather watch endless repeats of Loose Women.

(10.25 a.m.) We had a bit of a situation. For the first time in quite a while, some people came to the shop to cash some cheques. A group of five or six young men came in, but I became suspicious as they were all for the same amount, and in consecutive cheque numbers. However, the killer clue was that the first guy's signature ID matched perfectly the signature on the cheque. Oh yes. An idiot could see that this was a little dodgy, to say the least. I asked Phil to call the police straight away and I tried to stall them. I carried on filling in the details for the rest of them, very slowly. Another giveaway was that the head idiot, whilst sitting down waiting for his cash, took out the business chequebook he'd nicked from work and tore out another pre-written cheque for another of his iniquitous number.

Ten minutes went by and the police still hadn't arrived. I was worried that the gang would think they'd been rumbled. I needn't have bothered though as they were totally unaware of their impending arrest. Plod finally arrived – in force (which was nice of them), and they dragged down a couple of runners who tried to make their escape. But the leader, the diabolical mastermind behind this caper, in a final and brilliant piece of tactical villainy, chucked said cheque book under the chair he was sitting on and raised his arms as it to indicate 'It's nothing to do with me, guv', as one of the constabulary's finest looked on and simply shook his head. Within seconds, he was handcuffed and was led away, still protesting his innocence. It made a fairly uneventful morning a little more interesting.

(1.20 p.m.) I ventured over the road to Sainsbury's to

find some wondrous delicacies to thrill and excite my taste buds as luncheon approached. It's a rare occurrence that I can walk up and down the high road or do some shopping when someone doesn't say hello or nod at me in recognition – after all, I have been working here for the best part of 25 years. Recognition usually consists of a stuttered nod, a smile or a hearty Phil Mitchell style, "Oriiiight!!" Infrequently, I may be stopped to engage in a conversation which sometimes can be nice or sometimes, quite frankly, can be a right pain in the arse. It's usually the latter when I am meandering down the aisles of my friendly local Sainsbury's, as I was today.

When I'm in the supermarket though, not everyone who comes up to me to talk actually knows me - they just assume I work there. All you have to do, it seems, is wear a shirt and tie and this will give you instant gravitas and elevate you to Sainsbury's staff status. Recently, a fellow came up to me and asked, "What aisle is the condensed milk in?" Yes, condensed milk! That happened a few weeks ago. I was surprised that, 60 years after the war that this stuff was still being produced. It was probably on a shelf alongside the powdered egg and mock turtle soup. I told him politely that I didn't work there. However, sometimes I feel a lot more mischievous.

I remember one occasion when I was in a particularly cruel mood and a young woman (in her 30s – for that is what I call 'young' nowadays) asked me, "Where would I find the tinned fruit?" Now, simply because she did not say, "Excuse me" or more poignantly, realise that I didn't actually work there do to my 'uniform' looking unlike any other member of staff, I gave her the runaround.

"Why do you ask, madam?" I joyfully responded.

"I just want to know where they are," she replied, somewhat confused.

"Well, I'm not going to tell you," I replied.

"What? Where's your manager?" she fumed.

"Not telling you that either. Now go away." She looked around and spied the store manager. She then strode over to him and rather animatedly told him about her run-in with a rude, unhelpful pig of an employee. I watched him shake his head as he told her that I didn't work there. It serves her bloody well right. I winked at him and he acknowledged me with a sly grin. I may not be able to be rude to some of the more obstreperous people in *my* shop, but I sure as hell can in somebody else's.

On another occasion (when I wasn't even wearing a tie), a woman sidled up to me and asked if 'we' had any Easter eggs in. It was the day before Good Friday. Now, as we all know as soon as Boxing Day is over, the shelves are full of them. This person didn't deserve a straightforward answer for such a stupid question, particularly as we were standing at the front of the shop right next to a Special Offer stand with... Easter eggs on display.

"No madam, we're not permitted to sell Easter eggs here anymore, I'm afraid." I sorrowfully informed her. "We're just not allowed. New government regulations, you see."

"That's because of the loony left council, isn't it? I'm sick and tired of the council and the government doing whatever the immigrants and doing nothing for us. They come over here and expect to be given everything on a plate. It makes me sick," she informed me. I just stood back as her rant rapidly became a full on right wing tirade.

"Look, they've got all the bloody food from around the world here," she screeched. As she turned around to point out her observation to me, she noticed the display of Easter eggs next to her. She looked at me and I just smiled and shrugged my shoulders as a security guard asked her to leave the premises. Stupid, borderline racist *and* now without her shopping too. It did put a smile on my face.

However, to today's situation - (What seemed to be) a sweet old lady, for there are some left in these parts, asked me very nicely to fetch a packet of cereal from the top shelf (x-rated cereal). I said, "Of course!"

I handed it to her, and she looked at it, looked at the price on the shelf and exclaimed, "Do you honestly expect me to pay that much?"

I told her I didn't work in the shop, but she wasn't having any of it. "Oh, don't tell me that. You keep putting the prices up and up and up. You're just ripping people off."

I told her again that I didn't work there, but she

continued, "Don't try and get out of it now. I suppose you get a bonus for every packet you sell!" Now, even though I didn't work for Sainsbury's, I was pretty sure they didn't offer a commission for every packet of (own brand) Frosted Flakes they sold.

"Look," I told her," I don't work here. See, I am carrying a potato, a tin of beans and a tin of sweetcorn, which I bought for my lunch."

She clearly hadn't noticed them before. "Well, please go and get someone that can explain this for me. I am not happy."

I just nodded and walked away. Needless to say, I didn't bother to let any staff member know of this poor woman's strife and for all, I know she could have set up camp in front of the over-priced boxes of cereal, cross-legged and singing 'We shall overcome' until the local ineffectual Community Policeman arrived. I'd like to think that anyway.

(4.30 p.m.) I had a busy afternoon. Business is definitely picking up. Phil left early today. He always seems to leave early nowadays. (Note to self: Have a word with Phil about his time-keeping). Before he left, however, one of East London's brightest young fools challenged my sanity with a barrage worthy of a late Friday afternoon when the 'nasties' normally come out.

A West Indian woman thundered into the shop wanting to sell a small bag of 'gold'. This is what happened after she virtually threw the bag at me:

Me: Sorry, but this isn't gold.

Woman: What ya sayin' to me?

Me: None of this is gold. If fact, it's not even metal. It's plastic.

Woman: You lie to me!

Me: I'm sorry. (I wasn't sorry). This is definitely not gold.

Woman: I hate your lot.

Me: What? Men? Whites? Pawnbrokers? Humans? People, who tell you that you are wrong?

Woman: Yes. You is right. You's baaaad people.

None the wiser, I gave her back her bag of plastic crap and wished her a good day. She turned away and then uttered the word that instantly loses any argument in my book - "Whatever!"

(5.10 p.m.) As Phil had left for the day, I decided to shut up shop early and make my way home. I listened to Radio 4 in the car, which featured an interview with... Lord Sebastian Coe no less, although strangely enough, he didn't mention 'the L word'. He had probably exceeded his daily quota of 'legacies'. Bloody hell, I really need to be put in cold storage until all this nonsense is out of the way.

I switched over to my 70s compilation – David

Cassidy. I switched back straight away. This time and only this time, Seb Coe won. Ughhhhh!!

Saturday 3rd March 2012

I Swear

(8.55 a.m.) As usual, Sabrina, my little ray of sunshine, stood waiting for me outside the shop. I observed her as I turned the corner into the high road. Her head faced downward, staring at her phone and texting away as usual, probably to her boyfriend. I'm surprised he even had time to sleep around with other women with all that texting. She had her hair loose and the wind was blowing it all around her face, which caused her to hold it in position and halt her frenzied texting. I approached her and she raised her head to mutter, "Good morning." She had been away for a week, and I must say, I quite missed her being around. I'm really not sure why, as we don't really have much in common or have much to say to each other, but I probably spend more of my time with her than I do anyone else. It's actually quite comforting to have her around. She is very neat and tidy and *I* am not. Fortunately, she likes to tidy up all the time, and that suits me – and the customers like her too, which is a bonus. She's a calming influence and makes good coffee, albeit instant, but it's amazing how many people can't even get that right.

(10.45 a.m.) I had just returned from another disappointing jaunt to Sainsbury's, when I was alerted by Sabrina, to a couple of people sitting in the seating area of the shop. I was a little surprised to find two women of sub-continental persuasion, sitting opposite each other having a heated argument, both with a baby attached to their respective left breasts. They looked up, acknowledged me and then continued to feed and argue. I mean, what's a guy to do? I turned up the microphone volume from my side of the glass and spoke, "When you two are ready..." To which one sounded an apology and stopped arguing with her opposite number, but carried on feeding and within a few seconds, voices were raised again with increased volume. Now, there were three things I could have done:

1. With respect, ask them to leave, which is probably frowned upon now, bearing in mind the feeding situation.

2. Leave them to it, not knowing how long they'd take to finish (argument *and* feed).

3. Just stand there, wide-eyed, staring at them demonically.

I chose option 3 and it did the trick as they both immediately unattached their sprogs, mumbled something, no doubt disparaging about me, and left. Well, it worked.

(1.00 p.m.) Sabrina and I sat down together to have lunch. I had a Hoi Sin duck wrap, and she quietly nibbled away at an egg mayonnaise sandwich she'd bought from home. She was even quieter than usual today, and I assumed she's had another falling out with Casanova. I opened my mouth and was about to ask her if anything was wrong when she scrunched up and threw away the foil that once housed her sandwich, before asking me if she could step out for a few minutes. Naturally, I obliged, but it left me wondering if she knew I was going to ask her something and did not want to engage in conversation. However, I'm sure she'll get over it.

I watched the lunchtime news on TV and was flabbergasted to see that the second news story was about Angelina Jolie taking her children to the cinema. That is the second most important news item in the world? It beggars belief that an international news corporation like the BBC should deem this 'casual aside' to be newsworthy, let alone the second most important event taking place on planet Earth today. The realisation that it must be an incredibly slow news day was confirmed by the newscaster later in the bulletin when he announced that, the singer Adele has had an operation to cure her 'Rod Stewart' voice. Ah well, I'm sure that's great news to her millions of fans. After all, who wants to know what's *really* going on in the world?

(2.30 p.m.) As a member of Mensa, something happened today which I have been waiting for years to occur; and when it did, it didn't end quite the way I'd hoped, but probably did in the way I expected.

A bloke came in and literally flung a 'gold' chain under the window to me.

"How much will you give me to sell it?" he bawled. No finesse or manners. Immediately, I realised that it wasn't gold because it just didn't look or feel right. However, I wanted to be absolutely sure, so I performed an acid test on it and, of course, it foamed up like a rabid dog – proving that it was at best, gold-plated.

"I'm afraid it's not real gold," I told him.

"You're shitting me?!?" he responded.

"No, I'm sorry, but it's definitely not real."

"No mate, it's *you* who has got it wrong. I've had it for years and I know it's 18 carat gold," he shouted back, along with a fair bit of finger-wagging.

Now, after two decades of working here, I had a pretty good idea of the difference between gold and brass, so I knew that I was on quite solid ground. What he said next just made my day. "Oh no mate, I can tell you it *is* gold. You don't know what you're talking about. You're talking absolute rubbish. You're not exactly Mensa material, are you?" Ooooh, at last.

Putting aside the correlation between knowing what or what isn't precious metal and the ability to work out fiendish brain-teasing puzzles and conundrums, this was what I'd been waiting to hear for years.

"Actually, Sir (and a very sarcastic 'sir' I might add), I am," and I pulled out my membership card from my wallet to prove it. He looked at it, looked at me, paused, muttered something unintelligible and went to walk out. Score it 1-0 to me.

He paused at the door, turned and came back with, "Yeah, but you still don't know what you're talking about!" My Mensa membership revelation clearly had no effect on him. "And you're fat," he added just for good measure and left. Ouch. Equaliser - 1-1.

I still believed I had the moral victory and I knew I still had his chain, which in his desperate attempt to think up a witty retort; he had left in my possession. I only had to wait for 30 seconds or for him to walk back in – slightly, ever so slightly, embarrassed. "Can I have my chain back?" he sheepishly asked me.

"I've eaten it," I told him, and I rubbed my tummy. He just looked back at me with a confused expression. Eventually, I threw his piece of crap back at him just as it was presented to me. "Don't bother coming back again, pal," I told him as he hot-footed out of my shop. Score it 2-1 to me!

Following this encounter, Sabrina came up to me and said, "I thought you were brilliant. Do you want a coffee?" I answered affirmatively. That was unexpected.

(3.20 p.m.) It's the return of the Kowalskis. I had a feeling they'd be back and here they were and in greater numbers, and they introduced a new member – The widow Dowager Countess Chlamydia Kowalski dressed resplendently all in black. She even matched her outfit with black fingernails – and I ain't talking nail polish here.

Old Pa Kowalski, along with his elderly consort

and two of his sons – the battling ones – Kowalski the Monobrow and Kowalski the Younger came up to the counter and without hesitation, began arguing in their own inimitable way. I just stood and let them run out of steam before I greeted them warmly, to no effect. A good five minutes later, they called a nervous ceasefire and I tried again.

"She wants to give you for six months," the old man replied to my second greeting. The haggard woman then took off a stone set necklace and ever so delicately flung the bastard at me. I offered them a price, which was immediately and amazingly accepted without the usual arm-stretched requests for an increase.

"Shall I put it in Kowalski?" I asked.

And before he could answer, the crone yelled, "No. My name Kowalska!" (Kowalska being the female equivalent of Kowalski). I asked her if she'd been here before, which she confirmed and then offered me her first name. "It is Anna with four Ns," she shrieked. (No diary, I'm just kidding. Joking with my diary? What an unusual and pointless concept). I checked through the whole system for an 'A Kowalska', but without luck.

"Are you sure?" I dared to ask, to which promptly hit the old (but young compared to her) man, and started shouting in Polish.

"She's my mother. She's been here before," he timidly told me whilst rubbing his arm. I just couldn't find her anywhere and I was a little afraid to ask her for ID.

"Anna Kowalksa?" I asked in a questioning way.

"No, no, no. Not Kowalska!!" She hit the desk in from of them as the old man retreated a bit. "Him, Kowalski. Me, Krakowiak. Now Kowalski again!" Stupid me. I had wrongly assumed that his mother, who had already confirmed her name was Kowalska, had used the same name before. She had indeed pawned something before – 12 years ago. What an idiotic mistake to make. How could I not have remembered from all those years ago?

By now, the boys had become restless and began speaking loudly with arms gesticulating in a fashion which promised to escalate in a very short time. I completed the transaction and the angry old woman pushed the others out of her way and walked towards the door. As with my previous encounter with them, Pa Kowalski turned, quietly offering me a resigned "thank you, boss." They left, still talking very loudly indeed.

(5.25 p.m.) We left the shop at the normal time and as usual, Sabrina had her face in her phone. Is that possible? You can have your face in a book, so why not a phone? She shuffled off rather quickly almost falling over in her high heels. "Are you okay?" I hollered. Either she didn't hear me or she didn't want to stop because there was no acknowledgement of my concern. She carried on regardless, so it seemed like she was fine.

(5.45 p.m.) *Blockbuster* by the Sweet made its presence known to my fellow commuters through my open car window. I began to think that even though I often moan about my work, it really is the gift that keeps on giving. I couldn't hope for the Angelina Jolie-loving BBC to offer me the kind of entertainment I get from my customers. Certainly not this side of the Olympics, anyway.

Saturday 10th March 2012
Knees Up Mother Brown

(5.00 p.m.) Unusually, there were four of us in today. Kathy was in as well as Phil. A pleasant enough day was careering into what I knew would be a car crash of an evening, as we all had all been invited to one of our oldest (and I use the word advisedly) customers for an 'evening soiree'. For many, many years we'd serviced an old couple, who would regularly spend quite a lot of money with us, having bought a great deal of second-hand jewellery. In fact, back in the day, they were our best customers and they would often regale us with tales of old East London – many of which were mildly interesting. Their names are Bob and Mavis Davis. Yes, Mavis Davis. She must have rued the day Bob proposed to her.

Mavis was a kindly, generous woman and Bob was a crew-cutted, regimental, right-wing 'Conservative' (let me give him the benefit of the doubt here), with piercing blue eyes and a steely demeanour which would have made the Third Reich proud. (I realise that I've taken away any benefit of the doubt there). They were probably the most Cockney people you could ever meet who weren't Pearly Kings and Queens. They are very much 'jellied eels, pie and mash, Lord love a duck and *Doing the Lambeth Walk. Oy!!*'. Curiously, the thing that made Tom angrier than anything else was Chas & Dave. This had been going back years, and he still went on about his intense dislike of them. Let's face it; Chas Hodges and

Dave Peacock are the finest exponents of Cockney sing-a-long, plinky-plonk piano pub music there are, but Bob certainly didn't think so. His face would go red with rage at the very mention (which he would always bring up himself), of 'those bearded louts' as he called them. We never found out why though. I know he hated beards and Tottenham Hotspur-supporting Cockneys, but we never got to the real crux of his abject fury for Messrs Hodges and Peacock. Perhaps they tried it on with poor old Mavis whilst in the queue of his local whelk stall many years previously. I just don't know.

Several years ago, they began a tradition of inviting the staff to their flat for dinner. We had done well in putting it off for all this time, but when asked again recently, no one had the quickness of mind to think up an excuse; so we found ourselves having to finally accept their invitation. Although Mavis was now wheelchair-bound, she was apparently, a former catering manager for a big bank, so how bad could it be? Besides, it would be a giggle.

(7.30 p.m.) The evening of the gathering was upon us and as we stood on the doorstep of their high-rise flat, the four of us took one last collective deep breath; not knowing what delights would greet us on the other side. Bob answered the door with his usual strident military manner, making us feel ill at ease immediately. He really has a way with people. It became evident within moments that we were the only lambs to this particular slaughter as we were duly goose-stepped into the dining room and ordered to gaze at the feast spread out on the table for us. It was all under foil, so who knew what would be awaiting us. The excitement was palpable. All this before we'd even taken our coats off. In fact, it was a good 10 minutes before we were asked for out coats. We stood around talking to Bob, or rather agreeing with him about what a wonderful wife he had, "Ooh, don't embarrass me, Bob," came a joyful voice from the kitchen. Mavis wasn't yet ready to reveal herself to us.

Finally, Bob did take our coats and casually chucked them on the nearby 'rough to the touch', bottle-green, 1960s sofa, that felt as uncomfortable as it sounds. Mavis still hadn't even made her presence known when Bob instructed us to 'Sit!' Then our 'meal' was presented to us in a most splendid fashion.

Mein host marched over to the table before us and preceded to take off the aluminium foil from the tin platters to reveal corned beef sandwiches, irregular lumps of cheese, pieces of sausage roll, round fried 'globular things', brown pickled onions, a mixture of chip sticks and hula hoops, and I think, crushed Monster Munch. Incredibly, all the glasses were from different collections. The one that Sabrina got was plastic and I'm sure it was a child's Tommee Tippee one.

We seated ourselves and all of a sudden the sound of music filled the room – it was Trini Lopez!! Not literally. It was unlikely that Bob and Mavis would fork out to bring Mr Lopez across from the States for a 'One Night Only' show, and I'm not even sure if he's still alive and to be honest, but I can't even be bothered to check.

Tom turned around from the record player, resplendent in a sombrero and a worrying smile. Where did they come from??? It was a very peculiar, almost unnerving sight. There was nothing to put the food on, so no one touched a morsel.

"Won't be a minute," came the shrill call from the kitchen.

Mavis *still* wasn't ready. What was the hell she up to? I couldn't smell anything coming from the kitchen, so she wasn't waiting for something to come out of the oven. Perhaps Bob had just given her one over the kitchen table and she was struggling to adjust her wig. I was sure they told us to come round at 7.30, so they really should have been ready. We sat around talking or rather listening to Bob's stories of the army, which were terribly uninteresting. The nearest occasion he came to action was completing a 1,000-piece puzzle of the Bridge over the River Kwai.

Finally, in wheeled Mavis in. She was holding some plates. "Ooh, 'ello. I'm afraid I was one plate short. I didn't expect four of you," she announced and glanced firmly and disparagingly in Sabrina's direction. Mavis continued, "Not to worry, I've washed the dog's plate. I hope nobody minds." We knew we had to get out... and quick.

We needed for someone to cook up an emergency and quickly. As she bit into a sandwich, Kathy, with amazing forethought and timing, somehow 'cracked a crown' and she reeled back in terrible pain. "You alright love?" Bob enquired with a mouth full of corned beef.

"No, I'm in agony," spluttered Kathy. "I'm sorry Pete, but can you take me home? I need to cement it back in with that emergency stuff I've got" she blurted out. Her performance was so convincing (apart from the use of the word 'stuff'), that I wasn't immediately sure that she wasn't in genuine pain. Besides, I remembered her words from the car park incident a couple of weeks ago, so I knew she meant business.

"I'm afraid I'm going to have to take my wife home, Bob. It's been a lovely evening," I said with as much sincerity I could muster. It had only been about twenty minutes... "You can stay with Sabrina though, can't you Phil?" I cheekily questioned as I helped Kathy with her coat. Phil nodded in resignation and Sabrina smiled sweetly. I think she liked these old people and their ways and secretly I also think she liked that I got one over old Phil. Phil was not so pleased. For Kathy, it was a fine display of anguish which led to a speedy and very believable exit from the Twilight Zone.

Kathy kept up the ruse until we were safely in the sanctuary of my Mercedes, just in case Bob was spying on us from the window of his 5th floor flat. She was indeed faking it. Initially, I was impressed with her acting skills, but soon I began questioning other aspects of our married life, in particular, our nocturnal activities and wondered if she was as theatrical in those situations too.

My only regret about the evening was leaving poor Sabrina alone (well, with Phil) and not finding who Mavis had palmed off the dog's plate to. Mind you, now there were two fewer people to feed, perhaps there would be no need to use the canine's crockery after all.

Thursday 15th March 2012

Burning Love

(**11.15 a.m.**) Phil was in, so all my coffees today were made by yours truly. Phil doesn't drink coffee. He won't touch caffeine. He usually just drinks water or expensive fruit juices. Anyway, I had just made myself a cup when a very nice lady - Mrs Mullaly, who I have dealt with for many years, came in. She will often bring in some food for me. Her gifts of sustenance began with doughnuts and small cakes, but more recently the staple seems to be chicken. Chicken pasties, chicken pies, but mainly chicken sandwiches. Those sandwiches are sometimes chicken salad, sometimes Coronation chicken and sometimes (and this is the current favourite), char-grilled chicken with sun-dried tomatoes within a seeded wholemeal bap. These are not homemade affairs; they are always from local retailers and bought especially for me. I must say, at this point that I rarely take them because I don't really like chicken sandwiches. I do like chicken, but not chicken sandwiches. (My, that's a lot of 'chicken'). It's just a 'thing' I've developed over the years. However, on the last couple of occasions, my culinary admirer has outdone herself.

Beginning the theme, she brought in homemade roast chicken, roast potatoes, stuffing and a separate container with what I guessed was rhubarb crumble. I had to guess because it looked much the worse for wear following what I can only assume was a rather bumpy bus ride into town. "I bought it in for you because I like you so much," she told me. I actually ate this and I have to admit, it was quite tasty.

I told Mrs Mullaly, on her subsequent visit (which she came in empty-handed, I must report), that I enjoyed her sloppy leftovers – not the phrase I actually used, but she was delighted to hear it - so much so, that this time she presented me with an extremely large brown-coloured, mottled Tupperware box, which she proceeded to push through the drawer under the counter. It just about squeezed through. I quickly realised that it was not a brown-coloured box, but a clear box, full to the brim with some kind of curry. I reckoned... chicken. I lifted the container up and turned it round and inspected it, wide-eyed. The contents of this box could have easily fed four adults with plenty to spare. I told her I couldn't possibly accept this 'gift' but she insisted on me taking it. This was the sole purpose of her journey – just to feed me. It was very sweet of her but totally unnecessary. However, I was touched that she thought of me.

When she left the shop, I took the quite heavy container to show Phil in the hope that he would help me in disposing of the contents. I opened the lid quite gingerly, and the result was that it caused me and Phil to reel back in shock with burning eyes and tight throats. The concoction surely must have contained in no short measure, mace, Carolina Reaper chillies and perhaps a touch of napalm. I'm surprised it didn't melt through its plastic storage. Phil didn't have the resolve or the iron guts to chance a taste of this deadly mess, but I dared to dip the tip of my little finger in and place a very small dollop, very gingerly on my tongue. Ouch!! Out of the two of us, Phil was definitely the wiser one. It burnt on contact. It had to go. The only place to dispose of it was in the outside toilet – it's an old building and we are lucky enough to have one. I felt rather guilty because Mrs Mullaly had made the curry for me, but no one could have eaten it. No one.

The container may have to be burnt in our back yard to prevent injury to any poor animal that might come into contact with it. The usual garbage bags simply wouldn't suffice. I reckoned a small mushroom cloud would ascend into the atmosphere once it caught light. Still, it was a nice gesture by the old girl, though – I thought.

(12.30 p.m.) Phil had been on the phone for the majority of the morning, speaking to his new sea-faring pals. For a lad from Dagenham, he has done rather well for himself. Not having a wife and children, his life really is his own and he does what he likes, usually when he likes. The bastard. I know most of his money was inherited, as his family were big in scrap metal, but he's been keen to make his own way in life. I would never have believed he was from Dagenham, Essex. He had a very good public school education, speaks very well and has extensive knowledge of the art world. Not exactly what you'd imagine the offspring of Cyril 'Scrap Iron' Bryan. In fact, from the moment I met him at one of Melissa's college art exhibitions, and despite our different expectations in life, we hit it off. He was impressed with Melissa's work, even though he didn't buy anything. We began talking about my business, and with the understanding that I was looking for some monetary investment, he came on board. So Diary, now you know where Phil Bryan came from.

(3.45 p.m.) I had been hard at it all afternoon and was enjoying a brief period of respite. It was then when I noticed on the CCTV, a tall, rather dashing-looking, but materially dishevelled old fella, holding a Sainsbury's bag for life (which looked like it had reached the end of), and a broken umbrella. He waited patiently behind the person Phil was serving and when he was finished, Phil called out to me, "Here you go, Pete. This one's for you." I passed him to go into the pawn office, but couldn't help but notice a look of revulsion on his face.

I stood at the counter and asked, "How can I help you, Sir?" Immediately a waft of what I can only describe as burnt-out house (or burnt-out outhouse), and stale cat food invaded my nostrils. It literally knocked me back; such was the severity of the aroma.

"I want to take something out," said the man in a cut-glass Home Counties accent. The voice was as much at home with the vision and stench before me, as Brian Sewell would be as a porter at Billingsgate Fish Market. In fact, come to think of it, perhaps it was Mr Sewell on a particularly bad day. Anyway, he propped up his dying bag on the counter and took out a ball of mushed-up money and pawn contract and placed it in the drawer under the window in front of him. I just stared at it and then back at him. "It got wet," was the only explanation forthcoming. I looked at him, and he just raised his eyebrows and looked down on his piece of art. I drew a breath and reached under the window to gingerly pick up the cold, damp ball of expensive paper and plopped it down my side of the divide.

The first thing I did (with the aid of a couple of pens), was to retrieve the pawn contract and hope it was undamaged enough to read the contract number, so I could at least find out what the old stinker had in here and how much it was to get out. Fortuitously, this was relatively easy. The cost to take his item out, to my horror was just over £900. I knew my job of peeling £20 notes from the papier-mâché blob was going to be a long one. With the use of tweezers and pens, I started unravelling the notes and I carefully placed them on a table to begin the drying process. Phil leant, arms folded on the doorframe with a look of smugness, which had replaced the one of horror he displayed to me before.

After about 10 minutes, it became clear that he didn't have enough. He was about £100 short in fact. I informed the man, who incidentally hadn't even offered an apology for what he was putting me through, and he calmly said, "Oh, one minute." He then took out a smart rectangular leather wallet from the inside breast pocket of his rain-sodden Tweed jacket and proceeded to take out some brand new crisp notes. I looked on in astonishment. "I seem to be short" as he placed three £20 and one £10 carefully on the counter. "I'll have to come back with all the money later." He then pushed his

Sainsbury's bag under the window and asked me, politely to re-fill it with the money. It was like some kind of dirty, posh, bank robbery.

Of course, I offered to keep the money here until he came back with the extra £30, but he rejected my suggestion. I filled the bag back up and gave it back to him. I wasn't going through with that again and told him that the money would have to be dry and 'unmulched' when he came back. "Oh, that's okay. I'll just go to the bank and ask them to change it for me." Not a glimmer of guilt or irony. Unbelievable. Why he thought that I would be a better bet to handle his literally 'filthy lucre' I wasn't sure, but I was more than happy for some poor bank counter clerk to go through what I had to.

Anyway, he came back half an hour later to tell me that he had changed the money up and also to tell me he'd changed his mind about taking his jewellery out. Sometimes, I guess life and Brian Sewell look–a-likes just rock up and crap in your lap without a second thought.

(5.10 p.m.) Kathy called just before we packed up and informed me that she didn't feel much like cooking tonight. Quelle surprise. Tom, Melissa and the children were coming over, so I just said three words to Kathy "Chinese or Indian?"

"Chinese will do, but don't get it from that place up the road, again. Dawn tells me that they've had the health inspectors in twice this year already," she informed me.

"Well, if Dawn said so, then it must be true," I replied.

"Actually Pete, it is. You can learn a lot from her," I was told.

I could learn to be a total bloody neurotic, nosey cow, I suppose. Or perhaps how to spend all my time slagging off her 'friends' whilst playing bridge with the other 'friends' she'll be (covertly talking about), at her book club. Or maybe I could learn how to put all my tax money into tax avoidance schemes like she and her delightful whiter-than-white toothed husband, Frank (who keeps her in expensive clothes, gin and hairspray), does. Yes, I could learn a lot from her.

(12.45 a.m.) We had a very nice evening. The Chinese food was ordered from the new place in the High Street and it was pretty good. Even better, there was a fair amount left for lunch tomorrow – or breakfast if I feel that way inclined because that's how I roll. That's a phrase that Leanne often uses. I'm down with the kids, me. It's always nice when the kids and grandchildren come round. And, of course, Chloe and Charlie are absolutely delightful. It's lovely to have young grandchildren. I just hope they cause as much distress and irritation to Melissa as she did to us. Well, it's only right. If they're anything like their mother, I don't think it'll be long until she's pulling her long, blonde hair out.

And, so to bed...

Saturday 24th March 2012

A View to a Kill

(**10.15 a.m.**) It's been quieter than an abandoned graveyard here over the last week – at least, a graveyard that hasn't been overrun by drug addicts and booze-fuelled teenagers, anyway. I came back to work last Friday as I'd been ill. Man flu. I missed my appointment with Andy the Shrink on Wednesday and he can't reschedule, so I won't be able to see him until the 18th of next month. Sabrina has been particularly quiet, and I've been doing my best to ignore the nation's increasing, and media led fervour for the Olympics; but, after what seems like an aeon waiting, the entertainment returned – hooray!!!

A woman, I guess in her early 70s, came into pawn a piece of jewellery. I made her an offer, which she accepted and I asked her for her name and address as she wasn't sure if she'd pawned with us before. She told me her surname. "Kiss (pronounced 'quiche'). It's an unusual name," she said in broken English. I recognised the name and asked her if she was Hungarian. "Yes, yes," she excitedly responded, rummaging through her handbag, pulling out her passport (why she had her passport handy I do not know), and pressing it on the glass in front of me. "How you know I am Hungarian?" she enquired of me. I told her that I remembered a Hungarian footballer of the same name – Laszlo Kiss, who played in the 1982 World Cup finals. She stopped in her tracks and started shaking with her hands out in front of her. I thought she was having a stroke, so I immediately did nothing, and continued staring at her, anticipating some sort of collapse. "He's my son! He's my son! My son is Laszlo! He played footballs (yes 'footballs') for Hungary. He played in World Cup. My son! My son!" By now I realised that Laszlo Kiss was her son and he played footballs for Hungary… in the World Cup.

"Yes, I remembered he scored a hat-trick against El Salvador," I responded.

She then started another hands-out, shake-a-thon and kept repeating, "Yes, yes. He score a hat trick. My son, Laszlo score a hat trick."

"They won 10-1." I went on hitting her with facts.

"Yes, 10-1. 10-1," she went on. I think I 'facted' her into submission without even mentioning that he was the first, and I think, only substitute to achieve this feat at the World Cup. Anyway, we completed the transaction, whilst all the time she was mumbling something about her son playing football for Hungary or something. I couldn't quite make it out though… lol. Can I say 'lol' in a diary? Yes, I can.

Before she left, she told me that she would tell her son that I remembered him. I now felt like a close family friend and this became another one of my 'almost claim to fame' situations, along with the now un-PC late-night chance encounter with Jimmy Savile at a petrol station in Bournemouth, several years ago. In fact, it was a chance meeting where photographs were taken (of us, not any other sort, I hasten to add), and a few catchphrases cheerfully chuntered. It is an incident I don't actually talk about much anymore...

(1.10 p.m.) I left the shop in Phil's more than capable hands, because we needed some pens, and as Sabrina wasn't in today, I elected to go to and buy some. We run out of pens at an alarming rate here. About 40 percent are taken away by the punters, 40 percent end up in the breast pockets of mine and Phil's jackets which are taken home, never to return, and 20 percent never work in the first place. This is because they are normally bought from the pound shop and you get what you pay for. I decided to go 'upmarket' and walk up to WH Smith's at the top of the road; and as if to prove that not all my meetings with my pawn customers happen within the confines of the shop, I was met by one of them, a rather angry one at that, in Smith's.

I was perusing their wonderful selection of BIC pens. Incidentally, I've always thought it a little amusing when companies have two completely different and contrasting products in their retail range like BIC (pens and razors) and Wall's (ice cream and sausages). It's just an observation. And when I say amusing, it's obviously not laugh-out-loud amusing, but more of a comforting raised side of mouth/eyebrow combination. Anyway, I felt a tap on my shoulder.

"Hey, boss!!" No, it was not a Kowalski, but another semi-regular patron of mine. I couldn't remember exactly where he was from, but I guessed it was a former Soviet Socialist Republic. This man is huge. He had to be at least 8-foot tall and 30 stone and could crush a brick shithouse with just a flick of his wrist. Perhaps, I'm exaggerating slightly, but he was massive. The unusual thing about this guy was he has a constantly smiling face, coupled with an up and down cheery voice. Not a particularly bad combination, but this fella was utterly miserable and always told me of instances where a family member was desperately ill or he'd lost something or something had broken. When he first came into the shop, I thought he was just taking the piss, but I soon learnt he wasn't.

"You okay, boss?" he enquired. Without waiting for me to reply he continued 'Me... not so good. My car was stolen last week. I know who takes it. My brother-in-law. Police do nothing." His constant smile and raised eyebrows were almost 'laughing' as he relayed his story. "When I find him, I will kill him. He will die." I just nodded and tried to keep my facial expression as neutral as I could, because it is very difficult when someone looks so happy (even if they're not), to try not to smile with them.

As if to illustrate his point, he picked up a copy of The Daily Mirror and pointed to the cover and said, "You will see me in here soon. 'Man kills brother-in-law'." With a final cheeky grin and song in his voice, he informed me "I kill people. No problem." At this point, I was glad to be in a well-populated public place... just in case. I think the phrase 'smiling assassin' was made for him, and I dread to think what might happen if he ever saw him with a frown... if that was indeed possible. He walked out without buying the newspaper. I queued up to purchase my cheap (but not as cheap as the pound shop) pens before I returned to the shop.

(4.00 p.m.) The afternoon's business boomed and we'd served a lot of customers including one who almost defied belief. He was so confused that I was almost going to cancel his pawn contract because I wasn't sure that he was in control of all his senses.

Customer: I want to borrow some money. (Note: no 'please', so already he was at a disadvantage)

Me: I'll weigh it and see what I can do (I weighed chain). I can lend you £240.

Customer: I thought it would be worth £300.

Me: Look, I'll do you £250, but I really can't go more than that.

Customer: (begrudgingly) Oh no. Alright then.

Me: Right, £250 then. (I proceeded to type out all the details).

Customer: You definitely can't do more than that?

Me: No, that is the tops. If I could lend you more, I would. (I printed out the contract and presented it to the customer to sign).

Customer: Tell you what mate, can I just have £200? I don't really need anymore. (I took the contract back and tore it up very slowly, my lips pursed in mock disgust and maintaining eye contact).

Me: Are you sure now?

Customer: I was going to ask for £150 in the first place, but £200 is plenty.

Why can't people do things the easy way? I hope I'm not in any way like that, but maybe I am.

(7.45 p.m.) The notion that I may be a difficult person to deal with after all had been playing on my mind since that particularly trying customer, so I decided to ask Kathy. "Do you think I'm a difficult person to get on with?"

"Difficult, in what way?" she questioned. That query in itself suggested to me that I was, and in more ways than I dared imagine.

"Oh, just generally," I replied, without asking exactly what she meant by 'in what way?'.

"You're a kind and thoughtful person, but when you get a bee in your bonnet you become intent on pressing home your point long after it is valid. It's like your obsession with the Olympics. Most people think it's a terrific thing that they're coming to London," she quite delicately informed me.

I could see where she was coming from with regards to it being a great sporting event because I *will* concede it is great – apart from the sailing, synchronised

swimming and BMX cycling, that is. Oh and dressage –
Pfft. Dancing for horses. It's not a sport; it's a posh
person's freak show. I explained to Kathy once again,
that the whole thing is a smokescreen for an endless
stream of politicians and so-called Olympic ambassadors
to brainwash the public and make a lot of money. They
say it will create housing, jobs and opportunities for our
young and that's just a load of hyperbole and nonsense.
She sat in silence for a while before she piped up, "Yes,
but it's not just the Olympics with you, is it?"

"What do you mean?" I queried.

"Well, it's the way you…" just then as if completely
on schedule, the phone rang. Kathy jumped up to answer
it. We have had cordless phones for years and years, but
still, she insists on putting the handset back in its
charger after every phone call and she hates it when
anyone doesn't do similarly. She doesn't understand my
argument that it's called a cordless phone for a reason.

Anyway, it was Leanne on the phone. She, out of
all our children is the closest to her parents, and always
calls when she is away, even if it is from the other side of
the world, and even if it's *me* that is paying for the call.
She told us that she was coming home in just over three
weeks (on the 21st April), as she had 'things to sort out'.
That short phrase left me in a paranoid state. Perhaps
Leanne might have to come back home for a particular
reason. Things to sort out, eh? Like, have her three-
month scan perhaps? Oh dear. No, I mustn't get ahead of
myself. Not yet, anyway.

Saturday 31st March 2012

Hurry Up Harry

(8.50 a.m.) I met Sabrina outside the shop. It dawned upon me that she's almost always there waiting for me. Actually, thinking about it, I can't think of a single occasion when she arrived at work later than me. As I approached her, I noticed that for once her phone was not in her hand. She looked different too. I couldn't quite put my finger on it. Perhaps it was just that she didn't have the phone in her hand, I don't know.

We got inside; I opened the safes and turned the computers on whilst Sabrina put the kettle on. I fancied tea this morning for a change and told her so. She popped her head around the kitchen door and gave me a strange look, like I was asking for an early morning Moscow Mule or something, before going back to continue her chore. "Oh, and I deliberately mowed down three cyclists on the way to work this morning," I uttered. Nothing. It was clear to me that the fact that I wanted a cup of tea for a change was far more surprising that the notion that I callously killed several cyclists.

"Do you want some toast, Pete?" she asked a moment later.

"Yeah, go on, stick a couple of slices on for me," I answered.

"Marmite or peanut butter?"

"Marmite please."

"Okay."

I tried again. "I left them strewn all over the road. It was carnage." Again, nothing. I've heard of selective hearing, but this was something else.

(9.05 a.m.) We sat down together to have our breakfast as we usually do on a Saturday morning.

"So, why did you do it?" asked Sabrina.

"Why did I do what?" I enquired with a mouthful of toast.

"Why did you kill three cyclists and leave them strewn all over the road?"

"Oh..." I was a bit lost for words. She heard me after all. "I didn't really kill anyone," I said.

"Oh, that's good," she whispered, and with a worried look added, "You're not that sort of person and I'd hate to think you'd want to kill anyone, *even* if they were cyclists."

That made me laugh, but I didn't say anything else on the subject. A few questions emerged though. First of all, she must have heard me, so why didn't she answer at the time? Secondly, she surely didn't think I really did the deed, did she? And thirdly, if she did, she sounded genuinely relieved that I wasn't guilty of the crime. I concluded that:

she hears a lot more than she lets on;

of course, she knew I was kidding;

she obviously has a very dry wit that I was unaware of; and

she must think that I'm actually quite a nice person.

A wave of guilt washed over me as Sabrina picked up the dirty cups and plates and took them back to the kitchen for washing. Recently, I've seen something in this girl that I would never have imagined being there before. And she *did* look different. She was wearing lipstick. And is that eyeliner? Her eyes were certainly accentuated by the make-up. I can't remember if she wore much make-up before. Perhaps she did, but I was too oblivious to notice. She looked very nice actually. I didn't let on though.

(9.50 a.m.) It's always nice to welcome back a customer after many years away. One such individual returned and although I didn't recognise him immediately, he remembered me, and that was a little disconcerting.

"Don't you remember me?" he shouted in front of me.

"Vaguely," I lied, trying to buy me some time to think.

"I used to come here a lot. You were good to me... Well, not *you*, the other guy," he said. Nice. He placed a gent's platinum ring in the drawer under the counter for me to look at. "How much can I get for this? I want to sell it. I paid £800." Now, when people say how much they paid for something, this often means they expect to get a similar amount to sell or pawn it. In these cases, my answer always disappoints.

"I can give you £250 to sell or £220 to pawn," I informed him, fully expecting the backlash. "But I paid £800!" he screeched. I explained that one would normally get between a quarter and a third for pawning or selling a piece of jewellery because when you buy something new you are paying for manufacturing costs, import taxes and the very fact that it is brand new. Surprisingly, he immediately understood and accepted my offer to pawn it for him.

What he did next left me questioning the true reason for his visit. He took out his iPhone and scrolled through his pictures to show me something, "This guy is stalking me. Do you know him?" I looked and it was a picture of him with Harry Redknapp.

I told him who it was and he replied "Is it? I thought it was. He won't leave me alone. Look, here's a bit of film too." The film showed him sidling up to the former Spurs and Portsmouth manager on another occasion and Harry clearly saying, 'Oh, it's you again'. I think perhaps the stalkee is actually the stalker.

I did the pawn for him and as I was typing up the contract he asked me, "You know Jay Z?" "Not intimately," I replied.

"I got him too." He showed me some film of a DJ at work playing a track by Jay-Z. The half empty scout hut suggested to me that the DJ, who was also white, was not, in fact, the black, multi-millionaire international rap star. By this time, I was wondering if I should continue with the transaction as the guy I was dealing with was probably a bit delusional, to say the least. Then again, who am I to judge?

As he left, he did confide in me that he was a gangsta rapper. (There's the Jay-Z link). He turned at the door and warned me, "Don't tell anyone!" I showed him a 'my lips are sealed' mime and he left with an understanding nod and a very un-gangster-like Fonz thumbs up. Heyyyyyy!

(3.50 p.m.) This morning's fun was just the aperitif for this afternoon's main course. I sat at my desk listening to the football on the radio, which is my want on a Saturday afternoon, while Sabrina dealt with a customer. She called out "Pete, you might want to come in here for a moment. Could you serve this gentleman, please?"

This fella wanted to how much something would be to take out. Well, not actually take out, but just how much it would be *if* he took it out. Needless to say, he didn't have his contract. The conversation went something like this:

Customer: A'right bruv. I was telling the girl, but she didn't get me. How much is it to take my chain out?

Me: Okay. Do you have your contract with you?

Customer: Na mate. I'll tell you my name. (He tells me his name.)

Me: (Searching the computer database) No, I can't find it. Can you spell it for me? (He did, but I still couldn't find it.)

Customer: I know my name, bruv. (Knowing one's name is a good start, but I wasn't terribly surprised when I couldn't find it on my system.)

Me: What about your postcode? (He struggled a bit but eventually sounded confident enough with his reply. I searched without luck.)

Me: No, I still can't find you, I'm afraid. Did you use a different name?

Customer: What ya saying'? I don't know my name? Oh, hang on; it might be in my brother's name. (I searched under his brother's surname – yes, a different name, but to no avail. And then with his brother's postcode.)

Me: No, I still can't find you.

Customer: I don't believe it. Your teefin' my chain, bruv.

Me: No sir, no one is teefin' anything, but if you give me the right name and address I'd be able to find in no problem.

I like to be able to be helpful sometimes, so I

offered to search all the contracts on the day he bought it to see if we'd entered the details wrong or misspelt his name. He told me that he pawned it a couple of days before Christmas, so I had a clue where to look. However, still no luck. I relayed the bad news and he swore, called me a liar and left the shop – all pretty standard stuff for really. Less than two minutes later he burst back in.

Customer: 'Ere bruv. I used my friend's ID, didn't I?

He'd used someone else's ID which is a bit naughty, but at least I found his details. I told him how much it was and he sort of apologised and left the shop, reasonably happy. So, in conclusion, it was a different name, different address, it was actually a bracelet, not a chain, but at least it was before Christmas – not *just* before Christmas as stated, but before Christmas nevertheless – September 6th to be exact and his contract was now, way overdue to boot. Marvellous!

(5.20 p.m.) Sabrina and I left the shop together. I said "Goodnight. See you on Monday."

She paused before replying, "Goodnight Pete. Safe journey home, and don't be running anyone down... even if they are just cyclists. I'd hate for you to get in any trouble." She smiled and walked off before I could say anything.

Monday 2nd April 2012

Open Your Heart

(9.00 a.m.) I had been waiting for ten minutes for Sabrina this morning, which was a first. I soon noticed her 50 yards away, down the road. She was walking very briskly, almost jogging, which was very unusual because she is *always* waiting for me or Phil to arrive. A little out of breath, she informed me that the reason she was a little late (she wasn't late), was because she stayed at Daz's house the previous night and he was late waking up, therefore late dropping her off. I really don't like to think of her spending any time with that piece of work, but it's not my place to say anything. She deserves better.

(10.30 a.m.) Some customers genuinely believe they are always right, even when presented with irrefutable facts to the contrary. One such person that graced me with his presence this morning, was Giuseppe. He is not Italian (not in any obvious way anyway), and his first name according to his ID was Keith (?!) Still, he was a semi-regular punter who couldn't leave my shop without one drama or another. He would often bring up the latest big news story and wax lyrical with his take on it for several minutes and if my opinion differed from his, well, I'd be wrong. One thing that stands out in my mind was his insistence that he saw a third plane fly into the Twin Towers on that fateful day in 2001. As I say, he was never wrong. This morning's exchange went as follows:

Giuseppe: Hello, I've come to collect my chain. (He handed over his contract)

Me: Okay. (I look up the contract number on the computer.) That'll be £152.89 please, Giuseppe.

Giuseppe: What? I think you're wrong about that?

Me: No. That's what it is to collect.

Giuseppe: No way. That's like a million, billion percent interest. (He's not six years old, by the way).

Me: No, honestly Giuseppe, you borrowed £150 nine days ago. It's just £2.89 interest on top.

Giuseppe: How do you work that out? It's 300 quid interest.

Me: £152.89 on a £150 loan. How is that £300?

Giuseppe: You must think I'm stupid, mate.

Me: No, not at all. (Under my breath) A little confused perchance? (I said, affecting a patronising Basil Fawlty type manner.)

Giuseppe: (Looking resigned and a shake of his head) "I'm not coming back here again." (He then took out a wad of money and proceeded to give me a great deal more than he owed.)

Me: Hold on. You've given me too much. It's *one* hundred and...

Giuseppe: Oh, *one* hundred? I thought you'd said *four* hundred...

Me: No, no. How can it be that much? You only

took the loan out last week.

Giuseppe: Ahhhh, if you had said £250, I probably would have paid you it – no problem.

Me: I wish I had now. We'd both be happy.

Giuseppe: (laughing) Ay, you're alright, mate. You're The King. (He actually said that - 'The King'!!! Ha, ha. Brilliant!)

I gave him his chain back along with his change and on leaving he pronounced...

Giuseppe: You're the best, man. King Pawn... Pawn King. Yeah, you're the King of Pawn, but you did say *four* hundred.

He had to have the last word. He laughed and left the shop without giving his latest take on the big news story of the day, but he'll be back.

(1.10 p.m.) Sabrina asked if she could pop out to get some lunch and wondered if I wanted anything. "Where are you going?" I enquired.

"I thought I'd try Subway for a change," she answered. "I fancy a chicken teriyaki, but I know you don't like chicken in sandwiches, do you?" she continued.

She remembered. I didn't think that information would have even registered with her. "Yes, get me a..."

"Tuna and sweetcorn?" she interrupted.

"Yes, tuna and sweetcorn, please. Here's some money," I took a tenner out of my wallet and offered it to her with my outstretched hand.

"No, this is on me," she told me firmly. "You're always getting me lunch; so this time, I want to buy for you, okay?"

"Oh, that's very nice of you," I said. I was quite touched, really. That's the first time she's offered to buy me lunch. She doesn't earn *that* much and there was no need to offer. I don't *always* buy her lunch anyway – just occasionally when I'm in a generous mood. She left to walk the quarter mile or so to the sandwich shop and I just sat back in my leather swivel chair pondering the change in her. She's certainly developing into a proper three-dimensional person. I don't mean that to sound misogynistic, but considering that I just looked on her as nothing more than a shop fixture up until a few days ago, my view of her had changed considerably. Okay, patronising, but not misogynistic.

(1.30 p.m.) Sabrina returned and presented me not only with a foot long sub, which was twice as big as I was expected but also a large bag of cheese and onion. "Are you trying to fatten me up for privatisation?" I jokily asked her.

"I might be. You'd thrive in private hands," she saucily replied, as she unwrapped her teriyaki chicken sub. What did she mean? Am I reading something more into that answer that was intended? Am I not reading enough? I decided that to dwell on this young lady's musings would only serve to muddy the waters further. Besides, I was starving and my 12 inches weren't going to eat themselves. Ooh er, missus.

(4.55 p.m.) I was due to close up the shop a little early when I received a phone call from another regular of mine. Initially, it was just a fairly straightforward question. Now, when people start with a seemingly straightforward question and the answer is not what they are expecting it to be, they tend to ask it again, and again. Perhaps they want clarity or perhaps it's just the fact that they lie so much they subconsciously expect to be told lies in return.

The question was the standard, "My contract is a few days overdue, but will it be alright to come in for it next week?" Now, we always hold pledges for a few weeks after they are due because sometimes people genuinely forget, or sometimes they just need a little extra time. This particular customer is always very polite, always on time and usually, understands everything I say. Although I think he is of German extraction (certainly Northern European), his name is Paddy, which I wonder is his birth name. Bearing in mind that I had an East London barrow boy called Giuseppe in this morning and that a large section of my clientele has at one time or another changed their name for any number of questionable reasons, this in itself is not that unusual.

As soon as I told 'Paddy' that it was okay, and not to worry, his voice changed from a calm and collected timbre to a panicky one, "Are you sure? I'm never late, but are you completely sure I can come in next week?" I reassured him that everything was fine, but he insisted on telling me a tale of woe.

Sounding almost in tears, his confession went as follows:

"I have been out of work for three months and got myself into a bit of trouble with my monies. I began to gamble and the money situation got worse. I had big gambling debts and it was getting worse and worse. However, I had help from the Gambling Addiction Helpline and now I am in a better situation." (This sounded like a low-rent radio ad for the GAH – if it indeed it even exists.) "I know you don't need to hear this, but I need to confess." The phrase 'I need to confess' put me in mind that perhaps I should convert one of the enclosed pawn booths into a confession booth. I don't think that I'd make any money out of the venture, but the scope for more stories would be invaluable.

I told him not to worry at all and he assured me he'd be in by the end of the week. I wonder if he had a bet with someone that I wouldn't give him any more time to collect or renew his contract…?

(**5.25 p.m.**) We left the shop and I said goodbye to Sabrina. She's not in tomorrow.

(9.10 p.m.) Kathy had been on the phone to that overbearing know-it-all Dawn for ages. They certainly know how to talk – and bitch.

There was a big feature on the news about the Argentinean invasion of the Falkland Islands, which was 30 years ago today. I wasn't even 21 when that all kicked off. Not even 21, eh? Boy, now I feel old. Another thought hit me – Sabrina's 21. In fact, she must be 22 soon as I remember she had her 21st birthday last summer. It made me think. I wouldn't say I've had a bad life; not at all. I have three children and two lovely grandchildren and I'm not exactly past it yet, but I haven't done a great deal with it since I've been married. I wonder how Sabrina will look back on her life when she reaches the milestone of 50.

I seem to be thinking a hell of a lot about my young staff member at the moment. I'm beginning to genuinely care about her as a person. I have realised of late that she has a lot more to offer than I initially thought.

(9.45 p.m.) Kathy finally got off the blower. "So, how's Dawn?" I asked with all the fake interest and sincerity I could muster.

"She's fine. Frank's taking her away to Dubai for their wedding anniversary," she said in a 'hint, hint' kind of way.

"That's nice and expensive of him," I told her. "That's one way to spend the money he doesn't pay in taxes."

"You're so snippy when it comes to Dawn and Frank, aren't you?"

"Yep," I snapped and stood up to go to the fridge to get a drink. "They're ponces. Plain and simple," I expanded on my sweeping statement with my head in the fridge, searching in vain for a bottle of lager. "By the way, you know Sabrina actually bought *me* lunch today?"

 I have no idea why I even mentioned that.

"That makes a change. Perhaps you're paying her too much. Or perhaps *she's* not paying enough tax. Anyway, I'm going to bed." Her response filtered through to the kitchen with diminishing clarity. Kathy was almost on the upstairs landing before she'd finished what she was saying. She can be a bitter woman. That's probably why she gets on so well with Dawn.

(10.40 p.m.) Newsnight was on - 'The wasted millions of the London Olympics'. Hooray!! Get in there, Paxman.

Wednesday 4th April 2012

Pennies From Heaven

(7.45 a.m.) I had not been caught 'in the act' recently, so I was a little shocked to be subjected to the sustained glare I received this morning. I only sing in my car; not because I have a particularly bad voice, but I certainly don't think it's good enough for public consumption, unless one can call driving east on the North Circular Road on any given morning- 'public'.

It's amazing how I can sense someone's glaring, judging eyes on me when I'm looking in a totally different direction in my car, but I can't see a punter standing right in front of me, at work. The song I was warbling along to was, *I'm Gonna Make You A Star* by David Essex. I approached the same old pedestrian crossing that turns red as soon as it sees me. As my charge sheet lengthens for this particular kind of crime, I really can't imagine that this was my most heinous individual assault. In this day and age of hands-free communication, I really don't think that the image of people who appear to me talking or singing to themselves in a car is that odd anymore.

(8.55 a.m.) I walked around the corner and I noticed Sabrina, stationed next to the unnecessary tree outside the shop in familiar pose; head down, texting away with wild abandon. (Texting with wild abandon... yes, I like that). The continuity of life had been restored. Had she'd not been there before me for a second time this week, I would have been concerned.

(**10.45 a.m.**) A reasonably normal chain of customers was broken by a regular (and regularly drunk), female who came to pawn a 'gold' coin - except it was a bit... bronzy looking. It was a penny; a run-of-the-mill, albeit new issue, British 1p coin. You couldn't make this up. I reached into my pocket to get some change out because I had a feeling there might be an "Are you sure?" coming up, so I showed her an almost identical one, taken from a handful of loose change I had grabbed from my pocket. "You see; a penny," I showed her. When I pointed it out to her she kept apologising. "Oh, I'm sorry, babe. I feel so embarrassed. I've never seen one so shiny. I always come here, don't I, darling?" Etc. etc. Like that made a difference to me. It transpired that she even had a bet with her friend that it was a gold coin and now she owes her friend a drink.

She saw something else in my hand that caught her eye and asked, "Oh, what's that?"

"This one?" I replied picking it up with my other hand. Her barely-focused glaze tried to target the coin. "This is a special one. This is worth exactly 100 of what you've got..."

It took five seconds or so to register what it was before she spat out a laugh, which splattered the glass that separated the insane from the marginally sane. "Oh, it's a paaand coin. It's a new one, though. You're having a little joke with me, aren't you? I did wonder for a minute though. Ain't I silly?" she conceded as she laughed uncontrollably, expelling another cloud of spittle onto the glass.

I had the joy of cleaning up her mirth with a bottle of Mr Muscle window and glass (surely the same thing) cleaner and some cheap kitchen towel – the kind that disintegrates as soon as you look at it. Note to self: Ask Sabrina to get the pukka kitchen towel in future.

(12.30 p.m.) The day was bright and sunny, so I decided to step outside in the sun for a while and just view life in all its various forms. I was mighty glad I did as I saw something that you don't see every day. Whilst standing, admiring the beautiful people walking up and down this East London thoroughfare, my eyes began following a blind man and his Labrador guide dog as they approached the front of my shop. The man walked in a straight line at the last moment side-stepping, our advertising A-board that I usually forget to put out. He literally swerved, almost as if he sensed the obstacle in his path. His poor dog wasn't so observant though and it walked, head first into the metal object. Needless to say, the man (and dog) halted, and I went over to see if the dazed animal was okay. The man proceeded to inform me that even though he was registered blind, his eyesight 'wasn't as bad as it used to be' (whatever that meant for a blind man), and he didn't 'really *need* the dog', but the mutt was getting old and 'his sight wasn't what is used to be'. I couldn't help but think why he had a dog if this was the case. It seemed a little… wrong, but perhaps he was just saying that for effect.

The guy explained that he has to be careful where he walked now and especially where he crossed roads as the dog would often just walk out into traffic. The hound was also (apparently), a little incontinent, although the shock of bashing into a piece of temporary street furniture didn't provoke the poor pooch's bladder into action. So, all in all, he was a bit of a useless guide dog but, I'm sure, a wonderful companion.

This was indeed a heart-warming incident of an 'almost' blind man's friendship with a hard-of-seeing, incontinent, but devoted pet.

(**1.10 p.m.**) Lunch was a ready-made salad and some smoked mackerel. I managed to spill some balsamic vinegar down my navy shirt, "Oh, bugger it!" I exclaimed. Sabrina, who was sitting opposite me, chewing gum and quietly reading a magazine, jumped up and skipped to the kitchen. She quickly came back with a damp J-cloth and pulled her chair over to my side and started to dab the stain on my shirt. She did it very delicately, making sure she didn't spread it around. She was so close I could feel her warm, bubble gum infused breath on my face.

She carried on dabbing for a good while, long after the cloth's effectiveness had ceased. I just sat perfectly still and let her complete her task in silence, and just stared at her careful, almost mesmeric pressing motions on my shirt. She slowly backed off with our faces just a few inches apart. "There. It's not perfect but had you left it, it would probably never come out. After a spin in the washing machine it will stand up to scrutiny again," she explained. I unintentionally paused for a moment, still with my gaze fixed on her soft, unblemished features before thanking her succinctly for attending to me.

Without moving, she whispered, "That's okay. We couldn't have you walking around with a vinegar stain down your shirt, could we?" She slowly stood up and backed away. Once upright, she picked up her chair and returned it to where it was before, then sat back down and continued to peruse her magazine. I just sat in thoughtful serenity, trying to stop my mind from wandering to places I knew it shouldn't go. Fortunately, the quietude was ended by a customer who noisily made an entrance to the shop by tripping up theatrically. "I'll go," said Sabrina.

"No, it's alright. You just sit there and finish your reading. I'll go." I stood up and went over to the counter. I was happy someone came in actually, It broke the strange, but at the same time, rather pleasant silence.

(**5.35 p.m.**) Upon leaving the shop and saying goodnight to Sabrina, I realised that I have been in a quite pensive and reflective mood all afternoon. Sabrina's actions recently, although not really flirty, have certainly caused me look at her in a different light. Physically too, she appeared different. What was a meek and mild Plain Jane, had suddenly become a pretty, insightful and even playful young lady. I certainly don't look at her as just my assistant anymore. I now see in her a character that I find interesting and endearing. I wonder if there are any other feelings that might emerge?

(8.30 a.m.) I went down to the pub with my best friend, Clem. His name is actually Addison Clements, and quite understandably had been known as 'Clem' since childhood. What his parents were thinking of saddling him with that horrific moniker is a complete mystery. I've known Clem since secondary school, and apart from a six-year hiatus in the early 80s when he went to live in Belgium with a woman who was totally unsuitable for him, we've been very close friends. Naturally, Kathy isn't terribly fond of him as he's a 'bad influence' on me. (He might well have been 35 bloody years ago, but he's not now. I'm all grown up, you see). She's never actually suggested to me that we *shouldn't* be friends, as she knows she wouldn't have a chance of that happening, but she'd prefer it if we weren't.

As we don't live too close to each other anymore, I look forward to our nights out. It gives us a chance to put the world to rights. I'm glad he agrees with me, that the Olympics are going to be a disaster for the country as well. That's two of us at least.

(10.30 p.m.) I had been contemplating bringing up the subject of Sabrina all evening because once it's out there, it's out there. Mind you, it's not like anything has happened or is likely to. I mean, I don't feel anything for her... not in *that* way.

As the evening drew to a close, however, I did decide to eventually confide in Clem. He thinks I'm going through a midlife crisis. He reckoned she's looking for the father figure she clearly hasn't got in her life, and coupled with that, she has a useless excuse for a boyfriend too. I'm probably the only decent bloke she knows. I do know that Phil hasn't got any time for her. Having said that, neither did I only a short time ago. Clem offered to come down to the shop one day to 'cast his eye' over her and to 'advise accordingly', whatever *that* meant. I thanked him but told him I didn't think that would be necessary.

(11.30 p.m.) I got home and started preparing for bed. I closed the en suite bathroom door, being careful not to wake Kathy. As I brushed my teeth, I looked up into the mirror above the sink; and noticed my rapidly greying, bedraggled hair, eyes - bleary and slightly drawn, jowls - sagging further than I have seen them before and toothpaste dripping down my chin from the foamy mess around my mouth. "She cannot be interested in *that*," I murmured to my reflection, almost hoping that another voice (not Kathy's though), would say, "Oh don't put yourself down like that. Of course, she's interested in you. You're a real catch!" It dawned on me that there had rarely been a moment today when Sabrina has not been on my mind. The thing is though; I rather liked to think of her.

Friday 13th April 2012

Paperback Writer

(10.10 a.m.) Sabrina has been off this week on holiday. I don't think she's gone away, but she's not here and believe me, to be away from this place for any length of time *is* a holiday. Phil's been quite a laugh this week. He's been telling me about his youth as a boarder at a public school. It really is a different life. Some of the things he told me are exactly what you might think. He asked me to keep them to myself, so that is why I have not written them down on these pages. Suffice to say, the lad went through a lot... and a lot went through him. I say.

In a way, I'm glad it's just the pair of us two this week. It's given us an opportunity to bond a bit and it's allowed me to keep my mind off something (or someone) else. Nothing of any note has happened this week at all; nothing funny anyway... until this morning.

An Eastern European gentleman came into the shop and pledged a bracelet. As usual, I printed up the contract, signed it myself and put a cross in the space where the customer should sign. I gave him the contract and went into the back office to get his money. When I returned I noticed he hadn't signed the paper. I showed him where to sign again and pointed at the pen and imitated signing, as I so regularly have to do. "It's done," he said gruffly.

"No, you must sign there," I replied.

"No, the sign is done," he maintained. It definitely wasn't and I took back the contract and physically showed him again where to sign. I even tapped my pen several times in the place where he needed to sign as if to hammer home my point. He just tutted and pulled the contract towards him and shouted, "Look... signature is already there. I am not a writing book." Risking one of his great mauler's mitts being punched straight through the bullet proof glass on to my kisser, I requested him to sign again', to whit he placed another cross by mine. He put his mark down and slammed down the pen. On reflection he must have either assumed that I knew he couldn't write, thus signing for him, and then forgot what I had done, or perhaps, couldn't read - not even an 'X'.

He *could* count though, as he came back not half an hour later, fresh from a win at the bookies with a fair-size wad of £20 notes. Boy, he reeled off those readies like greased lightning. And with a gold-toothed grin, he collected his bracelet. He was no longer angry.

(2.00 p.m.) I watched on with delight as this time it was Phil who faced a similar difficult few minutes. This is not just a tale of an event, but more a study in human intelligence and interaction.

We have had enormous difficulty over the years in getting over the whole 'sign here' philosophy to many of my more troubled customers, just as I did earlier. I may be repeating myself here, but really, all someone has to do is sign their name in the box where it says 'signature' by the cross that we always place in the box, which is normally accompanied by a helpful tap or two on the box to reiterate the point. It really was a day for it.

I like the odd stat, so at the start of the year, I suggested that we started counting the number of people who (after all the above help), still managed to sign just one of the pages or sign in the wrong place or just simply fail to place a mark of any description on the contract. Up until now, the shop total is up to 78 incidences of non-signatory chirography.

I really try to make it as easy to understand, although with regular customers I might sometimes just hand over the three pages (all identical, one copy for the customer, one for us and one which stays in the packet with the jewellery), and disappear for a moment to get their money, expecting to find three signed contracts when I returned. A blank face and an "Oh, you want me to sign?" is sometimes all I get.

"Yes, just like the other 20 bloody times you've done it before you blithering tool!" I'd think/mouth/mumble/whisper/ scream, depending on how high the microphone is up or how deaf I assume the dumb punter was. Anyway, I digress.

This is what happened the today. A middle-aged Asian woman pawned some items and Phil started the whole 'please sign in the box on all three pages' game, and of course judging by her expression, I quickly assumed Phil would soon be adding another mark to our sheet of shame. There are two pens on the customer's side of the counter – one on a chain that hasn't worked in months and another 'free standing' one (often replaced) that *does* work. I like to see how many times they struggle with the inkus emptium one before trying the other pen. Sometimes they will persist and persist. They're the triers and normally the ones who will 'get' the whole contract signing process. The ones that attempt it once and just stare at the pen awaiting divine intervention are the ones who often have trouble understanding the whole palaver. They are my lab rats.

This woman today was slightly different. She understood the 'having to write something on the paper' bit and she even got through the wrong pen conundrum, but this was where her Krypton Factor audition went a bit belly up. It became clear that she didn't quite understand what to write on the contract. I crept up to the counter to observe this at close quarters. I watched Phil as he went through the signing procedure with her. I stood back in disbelief as she proceeded to copy his signature. She did one page and very carefully and diligently copied her original etching on the second and third pages.

He didn't stop her after the first page as he wanted to see firstly if I had to repeat the signing instructions to her, and secondly, to be certain of what she was doing. This was funny. To my amazement, she got the whole three-page thing but continued to facsimile Phil's signature. Naturally, he had to then explain that he didn't want her to copy *his* signature, he wanted hers and after trying to convey this a couple of times I thought she understood.

I was rather over-optimistic as she proceeded to pick up the other pen, looked at it when it didn't work and after Phil pointed to the other pen, she did indeed sign the reprinted first contract but had to be reminded to sign the second sheet, put and then reminded again to sign the third. She then gave us a look to suggest that *we* were the idiots.

I don't know, maybe we just expect too much. To me, such things are obvious, but that's only in *my* Universe. In their Universe, it is me who they write disparaging diary entries about.

We had a good laugh about this and even thought that the situation would make a funny comedy sketch.

(4.30 p.m.) As if to cement our belief that some of our punters are plain mad, I had a glorious example that confirmed it. I like to have a bit of fun with my customers on occasion. Sometimes, I do with their understanding and acceptance, but sometimes purely for my own entertainment.

A fine, moustachioed fellow came in, and before he even told me what he wanted to do, he requested that I check on my computer system to see if he had done business with me before. This in itself is not terribly unusual because some people like to stick with shops they'd done business with before – and it may have been years since their last visit. "The name's Billmore," he informed me quite enthusiastically, and with an incredibly high-pitched voice. I typed in the name, but couldn't find it on my system.

"Billmore?" I asked for confirmation.

"Yes, Billmore," came the squeaky reply. I typed it in again, this time audibly mouthing the individual letters. "B... I... L... L... M... O... R... E..."

"No! No! No!" shrieked my customer. "The name is Moore. My first name is William, but I'm known as Bill. Bill is short for William!" I was blatantly aware of this last fact but elected to just nod in agreement. "Moore is spelt M-O-O-R-E, not M-O-R-E," he informed me without a hint of sarcasm.

I saw this as an opportunity for a bit of fun and I asked him "Is the second 'O' before or after the other one?" I half expected a little chuckle or a sarcastic reply that he failed to produce a few moments earlier.

"Erm, I would say it was after the other one, but to be honest, I don't think it actually matters much anyway, do you?"

"I suppose not," I conceded.

Sarcasm and irony were evidently completely foreign to him. I then noticed he was wearing a bow tie. How could I have missed it before? That, along with the squeaky voice should have alerted me to someone with 'odd' status.

As it happened, Mr William 'Bill' Moore had indeed pawned with me before and as to the item he wanted to borrow money on... well, he had no intention to pawn anything. In his shrill voice that made Minnie

Mouse sound like Barry White with a heavy cold, the morning after a night on the brandy and Cuban cigars; he explained to me, "I just wanted to know if he was registered with me because... well, you never know, do you?"

"I certainly hope I've been helpful to you sir," I gleefully expressed.

His reply came with a voice that was now so high that I imagined that would have alerted the mutts in Battersea Dog's Home, "You have. Perhaps our paths will cross again."

Oooh, spooky!

(11.00 p.m.) Kathy made a most delicious fish pie for supper. Leanne called us from Australia, and she even paid for the call, this time. She'll be home soon. I can't wait to see my little girl again, regardless of her 'situation'. I mentioned in dispatches to Kathy of my suspicions that she might be pregnant. She dismissed them as paranoia. Moi, paranoid? However, if I am right, what can I do about it from here? Not a lot.

Kathy was in a particularly good mood. I wonder what or who's got into her. Haha, I spent most of the evening in front of the box, watching a particularly good thriller on ITV. Now, there's a thing. It was indeed a good day.

Wednesday 18th April 2012

Can't Buy Me Love

(**10.15 a.m.**) I was an unusually good mood today. I have realised over the last few days that my 'interest' in Sabrina is purely platonic, and I'm convinced that it's a two-way street. Perhaps I've got it a bit wrong about her boyfriend, Daz. Surely she wouldn't be with someone who has the 'notoriety' he's supposed to have. Most of my information about him has come from Phil and to be honest, I think he over-eggs the pudding a bit when it comes to tittle-tattle. Besides, apart from talking to her mother on a couple of occasions when she's come into the shop, I don't know how he's aware of Daz's actions anyway. I sincerely hope we're wrong about the lad.

(**4.40 p.m.**) The day had disappeared really quickly. A Romanian woman came in; one who regularly used us, sometimes to pawn, sometimes to sell some jewellery. On this occasion, she came in with another long-skirted woman, and asked in very broken English, how much I would pay to buy the handful of old gold she had. I offered her a price and she gratefully accepted. She smiled and said "I like you. You, nice man." That's always nice to hear, and I thought nothing of it, really. She continued, "My friend... she... you..." and pointed to me and her. I had no idea what she was trying to say. "My friend... You like her?" I politely answered in the affirmative. I didn't know her from Adam (or Eve), but I wasn't about to tell her "No, I don't like you at all. Be gone with you."

"She give you. How much?" she continued,

"I have to see it first. Show me what you have," I told her.

"No, not here," I was told quite assertively. I should have seen where this was going, but at the time, I didn't. I was still thinking 'gold'.

All the while this exchange was going on, the 'friend' just sat there, smiling at me now and again. "You go to her house," the vocal one told me.

"No, no, she must come here," I replied in no uncertain terms, gesturing my hands to press home the point. She looked around the pawn department and at the bank of large floor to ceiling windows looking out to the shop arcade and the street in bemused disbelief. I could tell she didn't completely understand me and perhaps, I thought, she couldn't hear me too well as the front door was open. I left my station and walked round to the front of the shop to speak to her face-to-face. I asked her how much her friend had to sell. "Forty," she replied.

I nodded and said "Okay." I thought 40 grams of 14 carat (as Eastern Europeans almost solely own). That would make a nice little profit for me if I could get it for a reasonable price. There was a fairly lengthy pause as I waited for her to tell me she was going to fetch the jewellery. "But, you nice man. She give you for 25." I finally twigged that she was not talking about selling *gold*, but pimping her friend out to me. I could now understand her obvious perplexity at the idea of performing in a shop window!

I wondered how exactly I was going to get out of the situation, bearing in mind that I had already apparently brokered the deal. I explained that I thought she was talking about selling gold. She just didn't understand what I was on about. "You give me gold," I tried to explain with accompanying hand gestures - hand gestures that had already got me into this mess.

"No, not me," she added firmly as she unbuttoned her long coat to reveal a sizable bump. "I have baby." Her friend looked a little non-plussed as it must now have looked like I was reneging on the deal and trying to book her pal for some night-time shop window shenanigans. This was getting me nowhere. I invited her to sit down and told her quite frankly, "I buy gold, not sex."

"But she is cheap," the now obviously heavily pregnant woman pleaded in a way that was trying to somehow impress upon me the fact that I should be grateful that I was getting her mate for a knockdown price. "She has many men," was her final gambit. I thought about advising her that being cheap and having many men wasn't the fantastic USP she clearly thought it was, but I had no prior experience in advising the local brass on their price structure and quality control, and it was not a good time to start. The two women entered into a short, heated conversation before standing up in unison, brushing past me and leaving the shop muttering something, probably very rude, about me, in

Romanian. I guessed they thought I was simply looking for a better deal and I was wasting their time.

I did, however, wonder what I might get for my £25, and if it included a premium for doing it in a shop window in front of an audience. I would never subject the local folk, even the real oddities that come out after dusk to that.

I slowly paced back into the office and slumped down in front of a giggling Sabrina, who observed the whole shebang. "Did you really not know what she was on about?'" she laughed.

"To be honest, I was just thinking about the gold. I was a bit blinkered, wasn't I?" I admitted.

"You were a bit," Sabrina agreed. I felt quite stupid and I continued with the crossword I was doing before being interrupted by the Whore of Babylon.

A minute went by before Sabrina piped up "Would you have, though? I mean, not with her and not a prostitute, but would you have slept with her if you found her attractive and she offered?"

Where the hell did this come from? I was stunned. What do I say? If I abruptly said 'no', that would make her feel silly and embarrassed. If I said 'no', and carefully explained my reasons, that would sound like I was simply lying. And if I said 'yes', well, that would open Pandora's Box right up.

I decided to deflect the question back to her. "If I did, what would you think of *me*?"

"It depends on who you said 'yes' to I suppose. I don't think you would do it with just anyone, but if you knew her, and she liked you, then maybe that would be okay." I wasn't feeling so naïve this time, and I would like to retract my thoughts about Sabrina from the start of the day. My mind was now working overtime and I was glad it was the end of the day. I changed the subject and announced that we were going home a bit early today. Sabrina stood up, smiled at me, and began to put the pledges away into the safe. Nothing more was said on the subject and we left the shop soon after. She is off for the next three days. I'm not sure if I'm happy about that or not. I'm glad it's shrink night tonight. I haven't been for two months and the subject of this evening's session seemed obvious.

(8.00 p.m.) I sat down bang on time, in the comfortable leather armchair in my counsellor's office on the ground floor of his house. The room is like the library I would love to have in my country pile. It's all dark wood and expensive-feeling leather chairs, with rows and rows of antique books that probably haven't been touched for a generation, almost covering two complete walls. Completing the scene was a couple of beautifully framed oil paintings on the non-book laden walls and a vintage grandfather clock. We really should have been smoking fat cigars and drinking vintage cognac in smoking jackets or perhaps we'd be playing a game of billiards in our shirt sleeves. A wager would naturally be made on the outcome - a princely sum of 100 guineas, I would suggest; such is the ambience of the room.

As the temperature was cold outside, so a fire was lit in the ornate fireplace. I would love to fall asleep in front of that fire with the just the gentle sounds of the crackling flames and the ticking grandfather clock with its heavy pendulum swinging to and fro, to aid my slumber. I'm sure each swing took five seconds; such is the relaxing, almost coma-inducing atmosphere. Time slooooows down dramatically in that beautiful room.

Andy 'The Shrink', or Dr Andrew P. Liddiatt, PhD. PsyD, to give him his full professional title, sat down, glasses perched delicately on the tip of his nose, ready to do his stuff. His stuff was mainly listening to me and offering the odd comment. I immediately bought up the subject of my new working relationship with Sabrina. As usual, as soon as I mentioned a female, he leant forward and took off his glasses. "Do you have any sexual feelings for her?" he asked almost hoping an affirmative answer.

"Not yet," I replied. Andy put his glasses down on the small three-legged table beside him.

"Not yet?" he repeated. "So you think something might develop?" he asked expectantly and with rather too much hope. He fidgeted excitedly in his chair.

"Well, no... yes... possibly," I answered with absolute conviction. "I'm not honestly sure what I want, and besides, perhaps I'm reading too much into our new burgeoning relationship," I continued.

"Relationship?" Andy butted in.

"Well, not a relationship in *that* way," I

backtracked.

"But the word and maybe even the desire for a relationship is on your mind, isn't it?" he reiterated. "It's not unusual for a man of your... our age to develop certain new feelings for younger women, even if we've known them for quite a while already." 'Our age?' We?' I think that Dr Andy may have had gone through a similar phase to me. Come to think of it, I've never thought about his marital status. There are no photos in the room at all. Perhaps he's been a naughty boy. That could explain why he was so interested as soon as I bought up the Sabrina 'situation'. I've certainly not seen him as interested in my life as much as I had done this evening.

I told him exactly what had transpired over the last few weeks and, he asked me if I wanted anything to happen between me and the girl. I suppose it was a perfectly legitimate question, but I really couldn't answer it without ambiguity. I skated around having to make a definitive answer, instead electing to ask a question back. "What do you think she's thinking?" I asked. I was kind of hoping he'd explain it away by saying she had to prominent male figure she can look up to in her life – she could hardly look up to the boyfriend, even if he wasn't as bad as the image Phil and I had given him. Andy didn't say anything of the sort. My psychotherapist, a man of letters (at least seven of them), as good as suggested that I 'suck it and see'. Without actually spelling it out, he suggested I act on my feelings, which were now clearly more than fatherly (if indeed they ever were. Should he really be saying this to me? I felt like I'd been given permission to have an affair. And if a doctor tells you to do something, then it can't be my fault, right?

(9.10 p.m.) As is my want, I sat in my car outside Andy the Shrink's house for a few minutes, just mulling over my session and the advice I was given. Whatever might happen next won't happen for a couple of days at any rate, because Sabrina is off. I don't think I'll tell Phil about it though. He'll either just laugh it off or make some blatant snide little joke the next time Sabrina's in work. No, things will remain just between me, my shrink and Clem – for now anyway.

Saturday 21st April 2012

The Power Of Positive Drinking

(8.00 a.m.) I met Phil, around the corner in the local Wetherspoon's, to enjoy one of our occasional Saturday morning breakfasts before work. They do a half decent bacon and egg wrap thing, and 'half decent' is normally good enough for me.

There's no escape from the oddities around here. At a table, nursing a pint of lager was another one of my regulars, who instantly recognised me, through his bloodshot, swimming eyes. We exchanged courteous nods and Phil ordered the wraps, a coffee and a decaffeinated tea from the bar. This particular punter is known (to me at least), to have somewhat of a drinking problem. A problem made even more obvious due to his morning location and breakfast beverage of choice.

The man, who I call Mr B, often stumbles around, whilst shaking quite a bit. Now, I'm not saying this was all due to his drinking habit, but I assumed it was. He looked quite agitated and offered me the explanation, "Me meds are playing me today." I nodded in acceptance, and he went back to staring out of the window and sipping at, what I guessed, wasn't his first pint of the day.

Our drinks were brought over while my partner and I were chatting about our expectations on the day ahead, and what strange happening were going to befall us. We needn't have wondered too much as one was developing just a couple of tables away.

Another man entered the pub, ordered his breakfast pint, and greeted Mr B excitedly. This bloke was not known to me, but I feel he was known to the Nintendo Corporation as he looked very much like Super Mario. Unfortunately, he wasn't wearing blue overalls and his cap was the wrong type, but the rest fitted wonderfully, including an unbelievably bushy upturned moustache. After a short exchange of mono-syllabic banter, Mr B gradually stood up and shuffled his way out of the pub to smoke a cigarette.

It was raining quite heavily outside and the covered area above the entrance was not big, so Mr B's face was virtually pressed against the glass door, fag in mouth staring, steely-eyed at the remainder of his pint *and* us. He was clearly very protective of his tipple and paranoid that someone would steal it.

Then Super Mario piped up and said, without any irony, "Don't touch his pint. He won't like it if you do." I just acknowledged his advice with a nod of the head. Mr B was still outside, red-faced, vigorously sucking on his roll up and taking a fair battering from the rain, which the wind was relentlessly lashing up. I thought it would be funny to stare at his pint for a few seconds and then back to him with a mischievous smile, just to see his reaction. He threw what was left of his cigarette to the ground and re-entered the pub in great haste. He was very wet from all the rain and water was dripping from his hair. He sat straight down and grabbed his glass. He was a little too eager to be reunited with his pint and with hands still wringing wet, it slipped out, spilling most of the remaining lager, bar a few drops, down him. Fortuitously, he caught the glass on his lap, before it fell to the floor. Super Mario burst out laughing and pointed at him as if he was directing us to the comedy. Mr B, with all the dignity he could muster, finished what was left in his glass and shuffled out of the pub, wet through from rain and lager; not a situation I would guess he was totally unused to, even at just gone 8 a.m. Super Mario, who shouted some kind words of barely decipherable ridicule, was still laughing as we prepared to leave.

This, although indicative of the sort of clientele I have is not a true classic; however, it so nearly could have been as Mr B narrowly missed falling down the open beer drop cellar doors, which had just opened by the drayman who was delivering. That would have been asking just too much though.

(5.25 p.m.) The early pre-work incident was the only one worthy of recording today; besides, I couldn't wait to get back home and wait for my Leanne's return. She promised to be home by 10 o'clock. She's insisted on getting a lift from her 'travel buddy'. I hoped that was a girl. I was quite prepared to drive down to Heathrow to collect her, but I wasn't needed. I wondered if her not wanting to be picked up was due to the 'condition'. She also wanted no fuss when she arrived home. In that respect, Leanne's very much like me. We like to get on with things with the minimum of fuss. Melissa and Simon, however, love a bit of pomp and circumstance and would expect plenty of bunting and an announcement in the local newspaper, if they were returning from an extended holiday in Thailand and Antipodes.

(8.30 p.m.) Kathy was in a good mood. We both were, in fact. She even gave me a hug when I came in from work. We ate homemade shepherd's pie for supper which was very good. She's awfully good at making potato-topped pies, whether they are of the fish, cottage or shepherd's varieties. We were hoping that the other two would be able to make it, but Simon is out of the country on 'business' – the business of coitus, I imagine and Melissa won't leave the kids at home with a babysitter at the moment because they have a cold… She would never forgive herself if anything happened to them whilst she and Tom were at ours. It's a bloody cold. Kids get them all the time. She did at any rate. She was in training bras before her nose stopped running. Oh well, I'm not interfering - it's their lives. So, it's just me and Kath.

(10.05 p.m.) A car pulled up outside, and out of the passenger seat stepped my little girl. She was wearing a heavy jacket, so I couldn't tell if she had a bump or not. Mind you, at only three months, it might not have been apparent. She hugged her buddy (a girl – good) and picked up her luggage as Kathy and I watched excitedly from the living room window. She trudged up the path, laden with her heavy backpack. We couldn't hold off any longer, so we rushed to open the front door to greet our youngest child's return.

Kathy was first and almost leapt on Leanne, crying and shrieking unintelligibly. Leanne dropped her stuff and embraced her mother. I waited my turn and eventually gave my daughter a big and long-overdue hug. We made it inside after Kathy decided to go in for seconds.

Leanne, still in her jacket, which impeded my view of what might or might not be an indication of a belly bulge, sat down on the sofa as Kathy rushed into the kitchen.

"Come on then, let me take your jacket. You *are* staying aren't you?" I jokily, yet impatiently asked her. She took it off. Great! No bulge. In fact, she looked svelter than she did before she went away. Leanne was always careful of her figure and rarely looked an ounce overweight. She definitely didn't take after me in that respect.

We were not out of the woods yet and I just had to ask, "So, what did you mean by you' had to get back to sort out some stuff'," I asked.

"Pete, for goodness sake. The poor girl's not been home for five minutes," Kathy chastised me from the kitchen door as she waited for the kettle to boil. I couldn't wait five minutes to ask her a most pertinent question, yet she couldn't wait two minutes before the kettle went on and the Battenberg came out. Yes, we still eat Battenberg. I'm really 85, you know...

"It's okay Mum, I can answer for myself," Leanne

interjected. That's my girl! "It's just that someone I met in Australia runs a travel company in South London, and she thought it would be right up my alley... pardon the phrase."

"Oh, thank God," I breathlessly articulated before slumping down into my armchair. I felt all warm and dizzy as the pent up worry evaporated away.

"What do you mean by that, Dad?" asked Leanne.

"Oh don't worry about your father. He's just being silly," Kathy butted in.

We spoke for a while about the job, and it did indeed sound like a great opportunity for her before Kathy disappeared back to the kitchen to make more tea. "So," asked Leanne, "How has everyone been?

"Oh you know," I replied. "Your sister's still a paranoid weirdo; your brother's probably screwing his way through Europe; your Mother's a bitch and I'm about to embark on a torrid affair with a girl considerably less than half my age. So, all in all, pretty good really." No, of course, I didn't. I just told her everything was 'fine'.

(11.10 p.m.) Leanne decided to turn in as it had been a very long couple of days for her, and she quite understandably needed her sleep. I had already taken her cases up to her room, so everything was ready for her. She kissed me and Kathy goodnight and I watched on as she started climbing the stairs. "Oh, by the way, Dad, I bet you're glad I'm not pregnant like you thought, eh?" Somewhat shocked, I just smiled in agreement and she continued her journey upstairs. I guess I'm not always as subtle as I think I am. Still, it's great to have my little girl back home.

Monday 30th April 2012

Pyjamarama

(9.30 a.m.) It is the last day before I go on holiday to Sweden and Norway (with Kathy). I love the Nordic countries and have been to them many times over the years. The people are very pleasant, and many who I have met, speak English better than wot I do (sic). I have deliberately, but not too obviously, kept a little bit of distance between myself and Sabrina for the last week or so. We have chatted and laughed a bit, but there has been nothing else. No flirtation and certainly no suggestions of any extramarital tomfoolery. And that's fine with me. It has been spectacularly normal at work, of late. I can't think of any weirdoes, drunkards, druggies or the hard of thinking that has been in, at all. That was until this morning.

As if to send me off on holiday in style, a customer possibly featuring aspects of all those categories stumbled in. Not to be confused with the angry lady who demands me to take her out for lunch, this one has a different, more subtle approach.

"When are we going out to lunch, Pete?" she cried from the front door as I sat doodling and counting down the minutes until my break. Well? When are we going out to lunch, Pete?" she asked again.

I usually fend her off with a "That's really nice, but we're short-staffed at the moment," because, I really don't want to go out for lunch with her. She's always nice to me, but then again, she's always at least slightly inebriated, sometimes rocking. Her long hair was exhibiting various stages of dye and peroxide and is that... yes, she was still in her pyjamas, I noticed under her silver puffa jacket. Quality. At least she was wearing trainers and not slippers. I asked (in jest), "Why so formal?"

"Oh, I came in my pyjamas, just for you," she said.

"I bet you did," I uttered.

"She then opened her coat and lifted her top up to show me her bare breasts. She smiled, blurted out "There you go," and then spat out a loud guffaw.

I wasn't quite sure what to say next, so I said something along the lines of "I see you've just come from home then."

"So, when are we going out to breakfast then, Pete?" she asked me. That's a new variation.

I remained calm, drew a large breath and told her. "That's really nice, but we're short-staffed at the moment."

She put her coat back on and said, "Okay, sweetheart, I'll see you soon," and with a blown kiss, and a brief tasteful flash of her posterior that she added as a late bonus feature, she turned, fell into the door and left. What a classy lady.

(2.30 p.m.) I had quite a bad headache, which had been developing all day. In fact, I often do before I leave the shop for any length of time. Strange really. Sabrina took charge and served most of the customers today. I feel quite relaxed about her capabilities now. I run quite an informal operation, but Phil can be a bit of a taskmaster at times, and will often have her running errands for him just because he could. I don't think she likes him very much, but he'll be the boss for the next fortnight, so she'll have to get on with it.

(3.45 p.m.) Good afternoon. What is about to unfold is a macabre tale worthy of the great Master of Suspense, Sir Alfred Hitchcock himself and in particular, his avian classic, *The Birds*.

I had been checking some monthly figures this afternoon (through the pain), when I happened to glance up and I noticed old Pa Kowalski outside, just standing there, smoking a cigarette. He was wearing his leather jacket and unfeasibly pointy, snow leopard print shoes, which he wears for special occasions like coming to my pawn shop. I glanced back down at my figures again and continued my task. When I looked up again, a few moments later, there were three of them outside my front door - Pa, Monobrow and an unidentified member of the Polish clan; the lesser-spotted Kowalski. They were just smoking and talking in what I assumed were normal speaking voices as I could not hear them, but their arms - they weren't a-flailing as they usually were. Again, I went back to what I was doing and thought nothing more about them. A couple of minutes later though, when I had finished, I happened to glance up again, and to my horror, yes horror, *The Birds* reference was becoming some kind of reality as there were no less than seven of them outside, smoking and conversing.

Now, at this point, I had to go to the bank to get some change, and as I didn't want to engage with any of them on my way out of the shop, I had to plan my exit with military precision. These people can talk and talk (and quite a lot of it, indecipherable), so not wanting to be ensnared in their talons (just keeping the ornithological reference), I planned to run out, get some change, and run back without being spotted by them.

I stealthily opened the front door of the shop and crept into the arcade, leaving the door to silently close behind me. Fortunately, the bank is in the opposite direction to where the Kowalskis had flocked. I sped up my walk and giving a single cursory glance to the ones I was leaving behind I was free and on my way. However, I hadn't taken into consideration the 'look out' man – Kowalski The Younger.

"Boss!!!" he squawked, which alerted the rest of his brood. And there, in an instant, I was besieged in Kowalskis just like Tippi Hedren did in the Hitchcock classic; but of course, it was Polish men and not seagulls.

From what I could gather from old Pa Kowalski (who was accompanied by the Dowager Lady Chlamydia Kowalski), he wanted me to know that everything was alright and he would soon be taking his/her jewellery out. He proceeded to tell me how bad things were and I think how bad his sons were. I nodded and sighed with raised eyebrows at the appropriate junctures during his tale of woe. As soon as I believed he was done with me, and that I could continue my journey to the bank, he produced his 'rabbit from the hat'.

"Here, look. This is my aunt." I thought he was referring to the angry old Duchess, but to my horror, yes horror, from nowhere an even older specimen of humanity appeared. This apparition had surely been raised up from the very pits of Hades. If the woman, I assumed was his mother was in her 80s, then this one must have been 110, if she was a day. He stood back as he presented her to me. I didn't know what to do. Bow, kiss her hand, lay prostrate on the ground so as to show my devotion to what may well have been the devil incarnate. She muttered something in Polish and she then was ushered away by a yet unlabelled Kowalski youngling. It was a very strange situation. Sometimes it's very difficult to separate reality from fantasy (and I use that word in a very disappointing way).

I told the Kowalski patriarch that I really had to go to the bank and wished him farewell. He just stood there in consternation as some of the peripheral family members disbanded. What else did he want? Had I dishonoured the family in some way?

"Come here," he whispered, ushering me back with his hands, and I walked back to the entrance of my shop where she followed. "My son – he cleans windows. He cleans your windows?" he sheepishly asked me.

"I'm sorry, but no. We already have a window cleaner. The same one for 25 years," I apologetically informed him. That is actually true. We've used the same company for over a quarter of a century. One of the window cleaners we have, I call the Window Cleaning Extra (although, I suppose, nowadays he should be called The Window Cleaning Supporting Actor). He's rarely been heard to speak. When I say "good morning," he'll often just nod and simply mouth his reply, just like an anonymous background character in a soap opera would do.

"Oh, boss, please," Kowalski pleaded as he mimed a window cleaning action; just in case I needed a visual aid. I repeated my previous statement. this time with the addition of my own, far superior, window cleaning arm movements, as I figured that as he knew how to communicate with the aid of hand and arm gestures, then it would resonate with him. It seemed to do the trick as he stood aside and then eased my passage (ooh err).

I hung around the bank a bit chatting to the staff, just in case the Kowalski's planned a second attack wave. I left the bank and they were no more. They'd flown the coop.

(5.30 p.m.) Before we left the shop, I parted some information to Sabrina that would hopefully put her in good stead for the next 14 days. "As you know, Phil likes his teas (as long as it's decaffeinated), but not coffees." Sabrina nodded in agreement. "And he likes three sugars." She nodded once more. I moved closer as if to offer a mock confession, "Just put one in... he'll give up asking in the end. That's what I did and now he makes his own when you're not in."

"That's good advice, Pete. I shall remember that," she whispered right in my ear, instantly making me feel tingly. She then gave me a gentle little kiss on my cheek and told me, "Have a good holiday. I'll miss you. You know that, don't you?"

I replied, "I do, and I'll miss you too." I shouldn't have said anything really, but she seemed like she wanted approval of what she'd just said. But, I will indeed miss her, a great deal.

(6.45 p.m.) I arrived home and found that Kathy, as usual, had everything in hand. I walked through the front door and was told immediately by my whirling dervish of a wife, "The cases had been mostly packed and I've hung up your travelling costume on your wardrobe door." Travelling costume? It's like I'm an 8-year-old Edwardian child about to embark on a trip to India in the days of the Raj. "Everything that had been left out of place down here by you has been put back into place by me," she said like Mary Poppins on speed. Kathy is a very organised woman, especially before we go away. That's when she goes into overdrive and becomes totally unbearable.

"We can go out or get a takeaway. I don't want to fill up the dishwasher again before we go away and if you think I'm going to start washing up tonight... forget it," she continued, whilst rigorously polishing the bannister.

"Hello dear. Had a nice day, dear? I haven't, dear. I've had a splitting headache all day and was just looking forward to having a nice quiet night in, with a nice quiet wife... dear!" I emoted.

"Okay, okay. What's got to you?" she stopped in her tracks.

"Nothing has 'got' to me. I just want to sit down and relax. We've got an early start in the morning and I would very like to spend the night here without any dramas or fuss," I continued.

She paused for a moment, raised her eyebrows and then scuttled off into the kitchen to fetch the takeaway menus.

"I don't want pizza and I'm not having Chinese again. Otherwise, it's up to you. Oh, and I don't fancy a kebab... or burgers... and I've gone off pasta at the moment," she instructed me, leaving me with little choice. I casually dropped each menu on my armchair as she struck off the options.

"Indian?" I sheepishly enquired as a last resort.

"I suppose so," she added. I know that she is having a difficult time of it at the moment, with her going through 'the change', and I am sympathetic (well sort of). That is one of the reasons why I'm taking her away and being in the company of two nations of folk for whom calmness is a hallmark, will hopefully reduce her stress levels. I sure hope it rubs off on her because she is becoming increasingly more difficult to live with.

"I'll leave it to you to order, but nothing too hot

and spicy. You know what I like. I've had enough hot flushes to last me a lifetime and the last thing I need is a chilli-induced one," Kathy announced as she slumped down, feet wide apart on the sofa. That was quite amusing for her. I picked up the phone from the sideboard and rang through our order.

Right on time, and completely predictable, because even though she told me to order for her, I knew she'd have to tell me *exactly* what she wanted... just in case I got it wrong, she announced "I'll have a chicken Korma and pilau rice... oh, and an Aloo Gobi please.... and get me a naan bread too... make sure it's a plain one (Okay, I *would* have got it wrong). And Pete..." she continued as I picked up the cordless phone to ring through our order through now gritted teeth, "You'll replace the phone on the charger when you're finished, won't you? Thank you. Oh, and the menus need to be put away back in the drawer."

I expected to find some paper plates and plastic cutlery waiting to be used on the dining room table, but no. Perhaps she hadn't thought this whole 'no more washing up before we go away' thing very carefully after all. 'Ha, ha... You didn't think of that, did you, love?' I thought to myself. Oh, unless I was expected to do it...

(8.30 p.m.) I was indeed expected to do it!

Tuesday 1st May 2012

The Lunatics (Have Taken Over The Asylum)

(7.30 a.m.) I hadn't intended to write this diary outside of work days, but there *is* a tie-in. We were due to catch an early morning flight to Gothenburg, so the terminal was pretty quiet. As we lined up at security, behind a handful of travellers, ready to present our tickets and passports, I heard a loud voice.

"Jeeeeeezus. I don't believe it." I didn't need to look around because I recognised both the male's voice and the familiar unforgiving timbre of his yap. It was my bad fortune to be lining up with probably my least favourite ever customer. He was known to all and sundry as Mouthy Dick, and it wasn't hard to see why. Loud, brash, unkempt… sure that can all be forgiven, but what an unbelievable bore. Already (as my pessimistic nature dictates), I imagined him sat down beside me on my flight to Sweden – and this is all before I even laid eyes on the creature.

So Diary, I'll give you a little background on this bloke. He was an occasional pawn customer who would always either:

Forget his contract and beg and plead to get his pledge out, knowing full well that he couldn't without the ticket; or

Belch, fart or swear behind other customers making them feel uncomfortable; or

135

Worst of all call me 'boy' or 'sonny'. He was *my* age. And no matter how rude I was or how much I treated him with obvious disdain, I could never get rid of him.

I unenthusiastically turned round muttered, "Alright?'

"A friend of yours, Pete?" Kathy sarcastically asked with a wide grin as I presented our documents. She was loosening up already. As soon as our passports and tickets had been checked, I grabbed Kathy's arm and ushered her through the entrance to the metal detector machine area (I think that's the official name for it), in a vain hope of losing him. How we were going to do that, I had no idea. But, of course, we didn't lose him, and he sidled up to me.

To cut a long story short, he continued to talk, with very little encouragement from me, until we arrived at the one open detector. He thought it hilarious to inform a security officer –"You'd better check his bag mate. I 'eard something tickin' in there." The security officer, thankfully, just shook his head and continued with his job. I offered a curt, 'see ya', before speeding off to look at some dolls in Scottish outfits and an enormous display of Walker's Scottish Shortbread in an adjacent hellish, tourist emporium. Kathy darted away to the perfume shop leaving me with the hand luggage. Why do they sell all this Scottish paraphernalia at Heathrow? Perhaps, they're constantly on display until some more-money-than-sense Yank buys one to take back to his massive extended family back in Virginia, therefore re-asserting the unbreakable link to his great-great-great-granddaddy, who was Scuddish... or perhaps, Irish. It wouldn't matter.

Anyhow, by this time, he was gone and I began to relax in my post security/pre-boarding haze. I didn't sleep too well last night and my headache was still with me.

When I saw that my gate was open I found Kathy, now holding three small bags, and we made our way towards it – which of course was the one furthest away, and just to make the journey even longer, the only travelators working were the ones moving in the wrong direction.

I was beginning to forget my unfortunate encounter with the loudmouth when I felt a nudge on my back and a loud "aye ayyyyyye" in my ear. The odious buffoon had returned and with it, my earlier premonition of a nightmare trip over the North Sea and beyond. He accompanied us, side-by-side to the departure gate. I couldn't believe my misfortune. He began prattling on about how the authorities cover up aeroplane malfunctions and how dangerous air travel was, but all I was thinking about was him coughing up his delightful plane breakfast all over me while, at the same time, laughing about some other uninteresting and tedious fact.

"So, you're flying out to Gothenburg then?" he said knowingly after clocking my luggage tag. "Done that," he followed up with a knowing wink before I was able to affirm his rhetorical question. "I'm off to Prague." The sudden realisation that I wasn't going to witness to him puking in his sleep in his aisle seat, and sandwiching me in between him and my ever-slumbering wife, who always has to have the window seat, lifted my heart.

"No, I've not done that yet," he chuckled.

Knowing full well what he meant. I offered "Oh, they'd better watch out for you then," or words to that effect. Why I even said that I don't know, but I was so relieved to finally be rid of him as we turned a sharp left to our preferred gate. He was gone, although my raging paranoia instructed me to nip back to the gate entrance and just watch him disappear to his own lounge. He did.

"Why did you even bother taking to him?" asked Kathy.

"I didn't think I did," I replied as we sat down to wait for our call. I began to tell her some stories of various encounters I have had with Mouthy Dick.

"Poor you," she said when I'd finished. She grabbed my arm compassionately and cuddled up to me. Yes, I do believe that Kathy was loosening up nicely. Long may it continue.

So, dear Diary, that is all for now. See you when I return to Blighty. Unless any of The Kowalski's are in an adjacent hotel room to us, then I'll be back scribbling away again. I can imagine the knock on the bedroom door to be confronted with "Please boss. You call reception for me. I need more pillow." Heaven forbid.

Thursday 15th May 2012

Don't Cha
(Wish Your Girlfriend Was Hot Like Me?)

(7.50 a.m.) Back to work, today. I've actually been back in the country since Sunday, but I fancied a few extra days off at home before returning to work. After all, I am my own boss and Phil is more than capable of running the business for a couple of weeks. We had a really good time in Sweden and Norway and I think it did us the power of good, especially Kathy, who seemed more relaxed and at ease than she has been for a long, long time. In fact, it was a delight to spend some time with her.

I sat in the car at 'my' pedestrian crossing and, I noticed no one around so I took the opportunity to belt out one of my favourite 70s songs '*Rat Trap*' by The Boomtown Rats, which was next on my playlist. I drove off on the flashing amber light without anyone viewing me. How about that? It was going to be a good day.

(8.45 a.m.) Sabrina didn't look so good this morning. In fact, she looked awful. Wait a minute, that's not Sabrina. That's Phil waiting for me outside the shop.

"Hello mate. Did you have a good time on your hols?" he asked as I approached him.

"Yes, it was great, thanks. I didn't expect you to be in today. Where's Sabrina?" I asked.

"I sent her home yesterday as she wasn't too well. Her mother called me when I got home and told me that she wouldn't be in for a couple of days... so, here I am. I didn't call you last night because it was your last day before coming back and I didn't want to disappoint you," he explained.

"What do you mean 'disappoint?' I asked.

"Well, I know that the two of you been getting on very well recently, and I suppose you were very much looking forward to seeing her again. I know she was longing to see you," Phil said cheekily.

'Disappointed'? 'You were very much looking forward to seeing her again'?? 'Longing'??? What had she been telling him?

I decided to say nothing too incriminating and just uttered "Oh, well," before pressing the button to raise the shutters to the shop. Clearly, she must have said something to him to make him suppose so much, but what? I knew I had to approach this subject very delicately.

(9.20 a.m.) Before I had the chance to challenge Phil regarding what he said earlier, my welcome back to work was complete. It's not uncommon for me to have to explain the simplest of notions to a customer over and over again. I'm sure by now, dear Diary, you are quite aware of that. Perhaps I'm unusual, as I tend to listen and absorb the knowledge that someone cares to impart to me. Many people do not.

A rather scatty woman, known for me for some years came in to release her pledge. "I want to take out my bracelet," she cheerily told me. Now, our contracts are white, whereas some of our competitors are pink or yellow, but some are white, too. Yes, she bought the wrong contract. The lady handed over a yellow contract and I told immediately that it was the wrong one.

"Ours are white," I cheerily informed her.

"Oh, okay. I'll go home and get the right one then. I only live around the corner," she happily replied.

A few minutes passed by and she came back and trotted up to the counter holding a contract in front of her – it was pink. "You have the wrong one again. Our contracts are white, not pink," I explained.

"White? I thought you said it was pink," she blurted. I assured her that our contracts were white and have always been white. "Okay. I'll go and get the right one," she repeated.

Ten minutes later, the confused woman reappeared to me waving a white agreement. Rather out of breath, she exclaimed "I just made it!!" as she slipped it through to me. It was the wrong one again.

"'This is still the wrong contract, dear," I told her.

"It can't be. It's white. You did say yours were white, didn't you?" she questioned defiantly.

"Ours are white, that's correct, but they also have our name on them and not another company's," I replied with just a hint of sarcasm. I don't think it unreasonable to expect a customer not only to be able to recognise colours, but to check that they had the correct shop name and address on the contract. She clearly thought it *was* unreasonable.

"You told me it was a white contract. I bought the white contract," she continued without a hint of pathos. I had to take a deep breath before I explained very carefully that it was not just the colour, it was the *correct* contract she needed to bring in. She sighed and gave me a look like it was me who was the idiot, then she took her white, (but not right) contract back, folded it up carefully and very deliberately before stuffing it unceremoniously in her oversized, tatty handbag. She then told me, "I shall be back with a white contract *with* your name on it." Maybe it was my fault. Maybe I should have told her earlier on that we can only accept agreements that we had issued. Whatever could I expect someone to do without this information?

Another ten minutes elapsed before she returned yet again, with a white contract that we had indeed issued her, but not for the right item. "This one is for a different item, madam," I proclaimed in a rather pompous manner. She looked at me; looked at the contract, which she pulled back from under the counter, and left without passing further judgment.

A further ten minutes passed, but she did not reappear – thankfully, as who knows what she would have bought in next?

To say that some people need to be spoon fed throughout their lives is to me, an understatement.

(1.00 p.m.) I thought it time to ask Phil about his cryptic comments to me earlier on. He had been busy most of the morning on the phone arranging another holiday and I wanted to wait for a natural lull in proceedings before I asked him what had been going on in my absence.

I sat at his desk and opened up with "So Phil, what is wrong with Sabrina? Did her mother say what it is?"

"No mate. Just that she was ill and needed a couple of days off. That's all, but she looked even paler than usual yesterday, and she was losing her voice," he candidly told me.

"So she missed me, eh?" I asked in a light way, trying to suggest no real interest.

"Oh yes," he replied in a very 'knowing' way. "I don't think she even realised herself how many times she said 'I really miss Pete' and 'I can't wait for Pete to get back'. I felt quite hurt," he continued, teasingly with a little sarcastic laugh. You've really made quite an impression on her, although exactly what sort of impression I'm yet to find out." I wasn't entirely sure if Phil was just having a laugh. I hoped he was.

"Yes, we have been getting on very well recently actually. She's a good kid. There's more to her that meets the eye," I said with all the 'genuine' innocence I could muster.

"More than meets the eye, eh?" Phil playfully asked, whilst sidling up to me and giving me a little nudge and a wink. "What have you 'eyed' then, you dirty old man?" He was clearly enjoying his line of questioning.

"No, it's nothing like that, and you know it," I protested.

"I knooooow. I'm just pulling your plonker, you idiot," Phil said. I was relieved to hear it. "She is very fond of you, though. I reckon she fancies you. She probably really likes the older... *much* older bloke. Besides, she's having problems with Daz again. You could be in there, my son," he said (betraying his public school education), but, I know you won't," he concluded, clearly playing with me.

"I'm sure she doesn't. She'll be back with him again soon."

"She's looking a lot prettier nowadays," Phil added. "It's probably all that slap she's put on her face.

"It's not slap," I countered. "She's just starting to wear a little makeup to bring out her features."

"Ooooooh, I think the lady doth protest too much," Phil retorted as he walked out of the office. *Was* I protesting too much?

"Ahh, don't be such a tit," I chastised him. I felt like I had given away too much and must learn to keep any feelings regarding Sabrina to myself, and perhaps I should tell her to do the same when Phil was around. This was beginning to feel a little clandestine.

(2.00 p.m.) After a period of self-imposed diffidence, the silence was broken with an episode I can only file under 'Lazy Bastard'. Of course, I know when people come to collect their items, they are not necessarily the same people who bring them in; and I know a wife can pick her husband's items up and vice versa or a father can collect his son's jewellery up, etc. As long as the person wanting to collect the goods is over 18, and they possess the original contract or a signed and stamped affidavit from a solicitor when the original has been lost or destroyed, then that is fine by me. I have no problem with that.

(Here I am again, describing the finer points of my job to a diary, again)

In all my years, I have never come across someone who has stolen a contract and then paid to collect someone else's valuables, but the law dictates we have to do this, much to the chagrin of our more careless patrons.

Occasionally, there are times when it is plainly obvious that the contract was not taken by the person doing the original pawning.

A young child came in the shop and as he walked gingerly to the counter, I looked up expecting to see a parent come through the front door behind him. The boy, who was no older than 10 years of age, had one of our contracts and as I waited for the door to open he tentatively pushed the paper under my window. "My mum wants to take this out," he informed me quietly.

"Where's your mum?" I asked.

"She's with her friend and my sister in the fish

and chip shop," was his rather timid reply. I told him he had to go and get his mum because he was too young to take it for her. The fish and chip restaurant is literally across the road from us. The boy left and crossed the road to the restaurant.

About five minutes later another child came into the shop, a girl aged about 13. I immediately assumed that she was the fish shop woman's other child and, of course, I was right. "Can I get my mum's chain back, please?" she politely enquired. I told her the same I told her brother, and she left to rejoin her mother.

Another five minutes went by and then entered Waynetta Slob, resplendent in her purple, stained towelling tracksuit, greasy hair pulled back in a Croydon facelift, and a face like off milk. She really was a spit for Kathy Burke's famous character.

"Why couldn't you give my stuff out to my daughter?" she asked, probably realising that her first bid of sending her primary school age son over was a tad ridiculous. "She had my permission," she added. There was a short exchange as I tried to explain my reasons and I think she understood. She passed me the money to collect her locket and chain and with the change instructed her daughter –

"Go back to the chippy and get three plaice and chips. That'll do for our tea."

I can only believe they feasted on curry rolls and chips for breakfast, too. Poor kids. As she left the shop and waited from my side of the road for her offspring to bring back the supper banquet, she perfectly took her fags out of her pocket and lit one up. The door was shut and I couldn't hear what she was saying to her young son, but I'm guessing it was something along the lines of 'I am 'aving a faaaag!!'

(6.15 p.m.) Whilst driving home, I couldn't get out of my mind, the exchange that Phil and I had this afternoon with regards to Sabrina. I think she's clearly got some feelings for me and to be honest, I have for her. The only thing I didn't understand was 'why?'. What could I really offer her? I'm married, far too old and no oil painting. I am rather flattered, though. And I *do* miss her. I hope she's not too ill and comes back to work soon. I had a good holiday and felt refreshed and replenished this morning, but now, I just don't know.

Wednesday 23th May 2012

Fools Gold

(8.50 a.m.) Who's this in my midst? It's Sabrina and she's finally back at work. I haven't felt much like updating my diary in her absence; not that anything much had happened recently. I even cancelled my appointment with Andy the Shrink last week (rescheduled for tonight). Sabrina has had a bad case of tonsillitis and was told to rest up as it was highly contagious. Her mother had kept us up-to-date with her progress by phone. Imagine if both she and I had tonsillitis at the same time? Phil would have a field day. It was good to see her again and she looked absolutely radiant. She beamed broadly when she saw me approach. I've never seen a bigger smile from her. Hmmm, nice teeth, too. "It's so good to see you again Pete," as she grabbed my arm. "I'm so sorry to have been off for so long," she said with such genuine sincerity.

"You weren't well. I wouldn't expect you to come to work in such discomfort," I explained to her.

Her hand still on my arm, she continued. "Oh, it was horrible and I was in agony, but I still smiled when I thought of you, and that helped me through. I needed to get back to work and see my Pete." She looked at me in 'that way' again. Evidently, her illness hasn't tempered any feelings she has for me.

Wait a minute... My Pete...? *My* Pete...? I felt excited by this, but a little apprehensive, too. I pulled the shop keys out of my trouser pocket and she finally released my arm. Whatever was happening between us wasn't going to disappear anytime soon. In fact, I'm sure the day of reckoning was almost upon us. 'My Pete', proved to me that Sabrina's interest in me was more than a mild flirtation.

(10.40 a.m.) It had been quite busy this morning, so there wasn't much of an opportunity to stop and chat. With the return of Sabrina, came the return of the lunatic fringe. I'm beginning to think the two are inextricably linked. In fact, I had two in a row. It was a dream double. The first one was a guy who came in to make a collection.

Me: That'll be £217.78, please.

Customer: £270... what?

Me: £217.78

Customer: Okay (Counts money). Will you take £260?

Me: I certainly would, but it only costs £217.78. (I punched the amount into a calculator and showed him.)

Customer: Ahhh, cheers pal. He counted out his money and said: I'm a bit short. Will you take £220?

Me: (Resigned) Yes, why not.

Customer: Oh, thanks mate. You're a life saver.

You can only give someone so many chances.

The second incident happened directly after.

I spent over 20 minutes of my time trying to explain the difference between precious metals and base metals, along with a little bit of elementary subtraction to a poor, simple soul. And believe me, I am being most kind with that description.

A young lady came in with a bag of 'gold' items with a view to borrowing some money – for that is my business. I weighed it all up and offered her £260, subject to testing. Most of it was hallmarked but there was one piece that needed to be tested. It was a bangle and found it to be a fake. I weighed it individually to see how much I needed to subtract from the amount I originally offered.

Me: The bangle is not gold, I'm afraid, so I will have to subtract £80 off my offer, so I can lend you £180 now.

Customer: Why can't you offer me £260 like you said?

Me: Because the bangle isn't real. It's not worth the £80 I factored in.

Customer: But it wasn't £80. It was £260.

Me: Yes, £260 in total if everything was 9 carat

gold. The bangle is not gold and therefore not worth anything. I have to take off what I would have loaned on it.

Customer: So why do you only want to lend me £160 now?

Me: It's £180!! Because I'm taking £80 off the £260 due to the bangle being absolutely worthless. It's probably not even made of copper.

Customer: So you want to lend me £180?

Me: (exasperated) Yes!

Customer: So, how much for the bangle if I did it separately?

Me: Nothing. It's not real.

Customer: It is. It's a real bangle. You said it was real copper.

Me: But it's not a real goooooold bangle.

Customer: The bloke I bought it from told me it was.

Me: It wasn't a bloke in a pub, was it?

Customer: No! (She paused) It was a bloke in a club.

Me: Can I ask you how much you paid for it?

Customer: £30

Me: You must surely have thought it was too cheap to be gold. (I knew she didn't because that's why she bought it.)

Customer: Nah. He told me it was real.

Me: And I'm telling you, in fact, I'm proving to you that it's not.

She then got on the phone and had a heated discussion with someone about the bangle's value and what she should do next. Judging by her questions to this other person, I assumed that he/she was on a similar intellectual and educational plain to my customer because as she finished the call, the first thing she said was...

Customer: You should give me £210.

Me: Why's that?

Customer: Because I only paid £30 for it.

Me: (I stared at her for a moment, convinced she was on the wind-up.) Look, I can offer you £180 for all the jewellery apart from the bangle.

Customer: Okay. Can I have the bangle back? I'll try and pawn it somewhere else.

Me: Good luck with that.

Customer: Awww, thanks. (She didn't get ironic sarcasm either.)

We then went through the 'please sign in the box on all three pages' routine as I probably go through with about a quarter of all my customers. I may be repeating myself here, but it's not unusual for them to sign in the wrong place, just the top sheet, leave one out, sign in the box *and* over my signature, sign in someone else's name, etc.

Finally, she left I noticed that the bangle had been left on the counter in front of me. I decided to leave it where it was as a gift for the next punter. I truly wonder how some people manage to put one foot in front of the other.

(1.00 p.m.) Andy the Shrink called me on my mobile to confirm that he was seeing me tomorrow night and not tonight. It was lucky he did, as I assumed we were back to Wednesdays following last month's change of days. He thought that I wanted to change to Thursdays indefinitely. I get the impression that he's not the most organised of people.

(1.45 p.m.) It was lunchtime and Sabrina once again went out to get me a tuna and sweetcorn sub from Subway. Just a six-inch one this time – six inches is enough for anyone... or am I kidding myself again? I paid for us both this time. Sabrina insisted on paying for hers, almost pushing the money into my hand. I didn't take it, but her hand remained in mine for a while longer.

"You really are so good to me, Pete," she said, just as I took my first bite of my roll... (or is it a sandwich?)

"Why? Isn't Phil good to you, too?" I enquired,

deflecting the statement somewhat.

"He's not *bad* to me. He likes to assert his authority though. You have time for me and you're interested in what I have to say and how I am. That's means a lot. Most of the men I know are just interested in themselves or what they can get. It's different with you. I feel very safe with you like you care for me," she confided.

"I *am* interested in you... interested in your well-being and your happiness here," I spluttered after putting my lunch down. "I like having you here. You're a very calming influence on the place."

Sabrina sat back in her chair and crossed her bare legs. She was wearing quite a short burgundy (but not mini), skirt and similar colour high-heel shoes – at least 3 inches, possibly more. A smart white blouse and black belt, and hair pulled loosely into a ponytail leaving a fringe falling down just past her well-shaped eyebrows completed the look. With her continued use of subtle makeup, she was looking good; very good. Just then, she received a text message on her phone and became all quiet and introverted again.

"What's up?" I asked as I watched her face drop.

"Oh, just stuff," she replied still looking at her phone. She didn't want to say any more for whatever reason and I left it at that. It seems that whenever our conversations get personal, something happens to curtail it. Perhaps it's that divine intervention again.

(9.00 p.m.) Leanne went out earlier. In fact, she's hardly had a night at home since her return from Australia. She's young and free. Lucky her. She's off for the interview at that travel company next week. I'm sure she'll get the job as she's a smart girl. She's not particularly academic, but she can think on her feet and she's a people person – a bit like me. Haha.

Kathy's gone to bed with 'one of her heads'. It didn't take long for her to her back to the old 'Kathy'. It's a shame, but not unexpected.

(1:20 a.m.) I fell asleep watching Newsnight, and as it was late I decided to kip downstairs on the sofa as I didn't want to wake Kathy up. I don't think my life would be worth living if I had.

Thursday 24th May 2012
Bloody Well Right

(**10.15 a.m.**) The sun made a very welcome return today, but I was not in the best of moods. Business has been slow and Kathy has instructed me to be home early as she is going out with her friends to see some crap at the cinema, (my words not hers). She's been in a particularly argumentative and sulky mood recently – still going through the change, and Phil has decided to bugger off for 10 days to the South of France to live it up with his new, moronic yachting friends. At least I have Sabrina. However, she's been particularly quiet since yesterday afternoon. I've even caught her crying just after we opened this morning. Perhaps she's finally worked out what a useless, philandering toe rag her boyfriend is. Yes, I have changed my opinion back, regarding him. My mood was not helped by a particularly insistent customer.

Occasionally, very occasionally, we have an issue here when someone disputes that the item they take out of pawn is the item they bought in. Sometimes, this is simply due to the fact that they may have several items of jewellery on several different contracts, and these issues are quickly resolved. Sometimes, however, they are just mistaken or even trying it on.

This guy wanted to collect his pledge, and I after I fetched the packet from the safe, He paid me what was owed and I took the piece out and placed it on the counter in front of him. He just stared at it for a few moments before grabbing it for closer perusal. I had given him a gold crucifix on a chain.

"Mine didn't have the little man on it," he told me quite definitively. Yes, he actually said 'little man'. I don't know how aware he was of Jesus and his death or how many gold crucifixes he had seen, but I'm guessing, not very aware at all. I assured him that this was the item he bought and he stood motionless. "No, this is definitely not mine. Why are you trying to give this to me?" he asked. I assured him again that this *was* his jewellery, but he wouldn't take my word for it. "I want *my* cross back, not this one."

I left him standing there, because the way I was feeling, I could have easily gone round to his side of the counter and lamped him one; such was my annoyance of his suggestion. I went to sit down in the back office in full view of my disgruntled customer. And as if by magic, he appeared to have had an epiphany and shouted, "The *other* cross on a chain, the one 'without the fella on it' was with my wife." He put the chain around his neck, winked at me and left. I would like to think he was pulling my leg with his remarks about 'the fella', but I can never take anything for granted in this place. Nothing surprises me anymore. Nothing.

(1.00 p.m.). Lunchtime, and I was about to pop over to the supermarket for another soul-destroying trek down the aisles of Hell to see what they haven't run out of, when Sabrina piped up, "Oh, I bought this in" and she peeled away the aluminium foil from a Pyrex dish to reveal half a particularly delicious- looking (albeit cold), baked pasta effort. I didn't even notice her carrying it this morning, such was my melancholy.

"That looks nice," I told her, genuinely meaning it.

"I made it myself, but there was too much for me and Mum to eat last night. I'll stick it in the microwave and we can eat it together if you like?" she expressed. Naturally, I was happy that I didn't have to across the road and I was eager to try something new, but it was the way she said that 'we can enjoy it together if you like'. I don't know, but that sounded kind of sad to me. It was like she was looking for some kind of acceptance. I nodded and off she went into the kitchen. Sabrina knows I can be a bit short with people and disillusioned with life in general at times, but she is never fazed by it. She is constant. I've misjudged her dull, sometimes lifeless appearance, and she's actually a very kind, thoughtful, if introverted soul. She dished up and we sat at my desk to eat. I felt the urge to find out a little more about my little Saturday-turned-everyday girl.

"I must say, Sabrina, this is exceptionally good," as I tucked into my tuna and sweetcorn pasta bake."

"I'm glad you like it. I know you like tuna... most of the time," she said in a slightly derisive way.

"I do. I never knew you could cook," I confessed.

"You don't know a lot of things about me," she replied cryptically. This was true. I didn't, and I really hadn't even tried to learn about little Sabrina Saunders at all.

"I know you like your phone and texting your boyfriend," I quipped, probably still with too much food in my mouth to be understood properly.

She giggled sweetly. "I rarely call or text him during the day, to be honest. He's normally busy... working." Now, she said that in such a way that told me exactly what kind of *work* Daz was doing. "I like to keep in regular contact with the children I visit."

"What children?" I enquired.

"The children at the hospice I go to," she said. I stopped in my tracks.

"You kept that quiet. I had no idea," I conceded.

"No, no one does apart from my mum. My dad's long gone, Daz doesn't particularly care what I do and I don't have too many friends – not close ones anyway. I've been doing voluntary work down there since before I started here." I really was stunned. "I can't go down there as often as I like as my Mum needs my help, too. She's got a mild form of MS, but sometimes things get very difficult for her." This girl, who I once believed was a bit of a dullard and a mug, was actually an angel. I think what saddened me more than her story was the fact that I hadn't even taken any time to think about her situation and the reasons for her casual, almost nonchalant manner and the regular faraway look on her face.

"I'd like to know more... if you want to tell be about it, that is," I calmly told her, as I put down the fork on my empty plate. Just then, and right on cue, a customer entered the shop.

"I'd like to tell you more, but another time. Another time," she conceded and picked put the dirty plates in the empty Pyrex dish and toddled off to the kitchen to wash up. I stood up to meet the customer and did the pledge, without really thinking what I was doing, because I couldn't get Sabrina's revelation out of my head. It's a pity I'm not in for the next few days because I really would be keen to know more.

(3.45 p.m.) It was business as usual. A customer just left me questioning the very basics of my primary school education and my capacity for working out simple sums without going bloody mad.

She presented me with her contract and to collect it came to £165.13. She gave me £180 in £20 notes. So far, so good, but then I provoked a suicidal fly to dive bomb into the dark black ointment of regret. "Do you have the odd 13p or even a 20p piece, so I don't have to give you back a lot of loose change?" I asked her, assuming I was doing her a kind service.

"One minute, I'll check, she told me as she rummaged through a rather old and battered tartan purse. "There you go, I've got this." She handed me a £5 note.

"No, I just need 13 pence so I can give you £15 back," I responded.

"But £5 is more than 13p, young man," was her unnecessarily patronising and bombastic reply, and she waved said fiver in front of her face.

"No madam, you've already given me enough money, it's just that I thought you'd prefer notes rather than the shrapnel," I told her, in the hope that it was just a simple misunderstanding from her side.

"Okay, so you want to give me how much change then?" she came back with.

"Tell you what, put the fiver away (for it was still being paraded in front of me), and I'll just get your change." I went away and returned with her pledge and the change - £14.87.

"What's this?'" my perplexed customer enquired.

"It's your change', I reliably informed her.

"But it should be 15 pounds something... You told me it would be." I tried to explain again the reason whilst cursing myself for even trying. She just couldn't get it. 'It should be £15.87. I can't believe that you are trying to con me out of one pound', she said vociferously.

"Madam, the total was £165.13. You gave me £180. The difference in change is £14.87." I even showed her the workings out on a calculator.

"You've fixed it, to try and rip me off. Don't think I don't know what's going on here. You said my change was £15 and now it's less," I was told in no uncertain terms. Apparently, I had re-programmed a cheap pocket calculator to give the answer *I* wanted, not the real one. I just wish that I had a brain so technologically advanced that it had the capacity to do that; in order syphon an extra few pence from all my gullible punters.

"Give me the calculator," she demanded. Normally, I'd resist as on two previous occasions a customer had left the shop with said arithmetic hardware. However, I was looking forward to her being hoist by her out petard and hoisted high. She did the simple sum, but clearly didn't like the result and tried again, the whole time with my steely gaze upon her bowed head. She then got her mobile phone out and tried the same simple sum on a contraption she was better acquainted to. "Oh, it says that's correct. But why did you want the extra fiver? Was that a tip for you, eh? Eh??"

I just stared at her with a 'poor misguided fool' look. Clearly, she wasn't going to back down in the face of a quite unequivocal fact. In a strange way, I admired her indefatigability in the face of such overwhelming evidence. She sniffed, turned 180 degrees and hot-footed it out of the shop. I doubt if I'll be seeing her again.

(7.30 p.m.) I had just finished my dinner - a pasta bake, would you believe? (I didn't want to say to Kathy that I'd already had one today, especially as Sabrina's was so much tastier). I attempted to interest Kathy in the revelation of my assistant. "You know Sabrina? She told me something that really surprised me today," I said loudly enough for Kathy to hear in the kitchen over the row she was making, trying to push in the dishwasher drawer as it kept jamming (for her, not for me).

"What did you say?" she shouted with audibly clenched teeth as she continued to wrestle with the dishwasher.

"You know, Sabrina, the girl that works with me (in case she'd forgotten that fact), told me something very surprising today," I repeated very slowly and emphatically.

"What? Has the silly cow finally discovered that her bloke is doing the dirty on her? You know these young girls are so stupid nowadays. She really needs a reality check. How can she go through life with her eyes shut like that? Boys are only interested in one thing. Besides, her parents should be looking out for her. I wouldn't trust her to be able to cross the road unattended, that one. Done it!" Evidently, the dishwasher was now closed.

Even for Kathy, that was extremely cruel. "Now you know why our children couldn't wait to leave home, darling. They have such a kind and caring mother to worry about them," I responded in a much quieter voice, knowing she wouldn't be able to hear me.

"What's that?"

"Oh nothing, dear."

"So, what about the girl?" she asked as she whisked back into the dining room to pick up the placemats from the table to give a wipe over before to putting back in the sideboard.

"Oh, you were right. She found out about the boyfriend. Terrible shame," I told her, realising it was a mistake to even bring it up in the first place.

"I told you. Silly girl. She was always going to find out one day. She'll still probably go back to him, anyway," Kathy cruelly summed up.

I don't know where this rhetoric had come from. I can't think that I even mentioned Sabrina and her situation before. I was very angry, but not wanting to start a row and realising I was running late for my appointment with my counsellor, I hurriedly said goodbye and left the house.

(7.55 p.m.) I sat outside Andy the Shrink's house, contemplating what to say tonight. What do I say to him? I decided it was probably best to tell him exactly what had been going on.

(8.05 p.m.) After a few pleasantries, we got down to business. I told him the latest situation - her time off; her apparent delight in seeing me and suddenly going quiet again after the text message, and the big revelation about her life, which has drawn me even closer to her. He explained that she was probably in some kind of emotional turmoil (you don't say), and her developing feelings for me are being played off her existing feelings for Daz, who she still loyal to. Heaven knows why though. I realised as well that I didn't pity her at all. Okay, I feel a little sorry for her situation, but I actually feel a tremendous deal of admiration for what she is doing.

I then continued to tell him about my wife's

negative, but very typical reaction and he said abruptly and succinctly "Jealous and bitter. They often get like that at her age and start going through 'the change'"". It wasn't at all what I expected to hear, but I found it impossible to disagree. He told me to take a step back and to be less confrontational because she is in a vulnerable state. He offered me similar advice with regards to Sabrina. I understood perfectly, but I feel like I've crossed the line already and it might be too late to turn back.

(9.10 p.m.) I sat outside my counsellor's house, in my car contemplating the session. Fifteen minutes must have passed before I turned the ignition and started my short drive home.

I arrived home and it dawned on me that Kathy had gone out. I was relieved as I'd had enough of her bile today. The cheerfulness and all round well-being from the holiday had evaporated. Besides, we are getting even closer to the summer spectacular of the London Olympics, and I'm sure there must be something in the news about it. No. No. No. I was not going to get all uppity and political this evening. It was a time for self-assessment and quiet contemplation. It's nice to have a little peace and quiet sometimes. I must suggest to Kathy that she should go out more often.

Saturday 26th May 2012

Tempted

(11.00 a.m.) Things have been fairly calm at home, but I feel like Mount Kathy could erupt at any moment. She'd been flitting around most of the day preparing for Leanne's ('not so' surprise), birthday party. It's not a surprise because I put my foot in it last week and let the cat out of the back – quite innocently. But nevertheless, the bag was now catless. Thinking about it, I think that could have been the catalyst of Kathy's huffiness since that moment. Too many cats.

She insisted that I stay out of her way while she prepared everything for the afternoon. It's only a small family gathering, as Leanne is having her proper party at a club in town later this evening. I'm sure she could have done without this little family caucus, but the wife knew best. Kathy wanted to arrange the party for the daytime, so her delightful parents could make it. Her dad doesn't drive in the dark and her mum doesn't like the night air. I think they're basically vampires in reverse. In fact, I shared that very thought with Kathy last week. Maybe that added to the build-up of impending ire. I really must try to keep my mouth shut sometimes.

(2.00 p.m.) I had been sitting on the sofa watching Sky Sports Soccer Saturday whilst Kathy nipped out to fetch some sponge fingers... yes, sponge fingers, for a 20-year-old girl's party. First, it was Battenberg cake and now sponge fingers. It's like Open Day at an old people's home. A while after she left, my mobile phone rang. It was Sabrina.

"Hi, Pete. I hope it's okay to call you," she said.

I was quite surprised but answered "Yes, of course," I stood up and went to the living room window, just to check that Kathy wasn't about to pull into the driveway. I don't know why I felt nervous as I hadn't done anything wrong. Mind you, perhaps it was the notion that I may do something wrong that made me feel guilty.

"As I haven't seen you since Thursday I just wanted to thank you for listening to me, and I'm sorry that we didn't have enough time to continue our conversation," she continued. "I really want to expand on what I told you. You deserve to know, and I will in person on Monday, yes?"

I replied in faux innocence and gave her a cheery "Oh, okay then." Whatever did she mean by 'other things'?

"I'll let you go now. It's your daughter's birthday today, isn't it?" she asked.

"It certainly is. We're expecting all the family around this afternoon," I told her. How did she know it was Leanne's birthday? I'm sure I didn't tell her; but, I suppose I must have. However else would she have known? So many questions, but so few answers.

"Okay then love, I'll see you on Monday," I

concluded within my normal personable manner.

"Okay then looooove," she playfully mimicked emphasising 'love'.

I put the phone down and went to replace it in its charger, but quickly realised that it was my mobile, but it's hard to go against my training. I planted myself down in front of Jeff Stelling again, and I wondered how I was going to get through the rest of the weekend without my imagination wandering all over the place.

(4.00 p.m.) The 'party' was in full swing – if a family gathering of three old people could. My father had not long arrived, late, as usual, and joined my in- laws, Leanne, Melissa and Tom and the kids (now over their colds, thank goodness), in the living room. Even 'Uncle' Clem made an appearance. Clem is one of the children's godfathers, but over time, we've forgotten which one. It's safe to say that the role doesn't hold much gravitas for anyone. Simon's expected no-show surprised nobody.

It dawned on me that I had no longer had any teenage children and I was now middle-aged, of that there is no doubt. Perhaps, I deserve a mid-life crisis. Maybe, it's my *duty* to have one. That sounded like a good defence of any possible infidelity.

(6.00 p.m.) With everyone gone, Leanne expressed to me how much she appreciated the party even though she knew that it was mainly for her mother's sake. It was like Kathy had to prove to her parents that she could still do it, however old her children were. We had a nice little chat for a few minutes while Kathy was in the kitchen. We spoke about all sorts of things, including the business. She even asked how Sabrina and her boyfriend were getting on. She went to school with Daz (or Darren as he was correctly called back then), and they had mutual friends. I told her that the whole on-off thing was a bit of a farce, and I didn't know why they were still seeing each other. She also couldn't understand why she was still with him. How good news travels, eh?

She ran upstairs to prepare herself to join her friends up in London for her 'real' party. Kathy had become whirling dervish, undoing everything she'd worked so diligently setting up some hours before. The half-eaten food had been disposed of in the correct wheelie bin outside – one of four different coloured receptacles. The uneaten food was packed up either in foil, Clingfilm or Tupperware boxes depending on its constitution, and the table was now clear of all non-edible objects. Yes, the plates and cutlery were in the dishwasher and after a short struggle to close the door, it had begun its cleaning cycle. All I had to do was reach up to the cornice and bring down the birthday banners that I had so expertly erected earlier on.

(7.30 p.m.) Kathy had now calmed down quite considerably and we actually had a nice little chat about the kids and how they've grown up so well. We had a laugh remembering the good times we'd had as a family before they all grew up and buggered off. Well, most of them did. It made me feel like I've done something worthwhile in my life. It's something I've not felt in a while; hence, my date with Andy the Shrink. My mood had improved and I wasn't even thinking about Miss Saunders from work.

"Let's go out for dinner!" Kathy exclaimed, quite out of the blue. "Your choice," she generously added. I waited for the usual conditions, but there were none.

"Chinese?" I suggested.

"Okay, but not..."

"...the one up the road on the corner," I interrupted. "Yes, yes. I know. We'll go to the new one on the High Street. We like that one."

"That sounds good," Kathy concluded.

(11.30 p.m.) We returned home and went up to bed together. Kathy was indeed in a good mood this evening because she even offered me the last spare rib at the restaurant. Of course, I gratefully accepted. She's not a bad girl, just prone to violent mood swings now and again. Just now, though, I wouldn't want to be anywhere else.

Monday 28th May 2012

Gimme Some Truth

(11.00 a.m.) We were very busy this morning, which gave Sabrina and me very few opportunities to chat. Besides, if we did start to converse, we would have only been interrupted. I had an idea. During a lull in the action, I suggested to the girl that we go out after work for a drink or (risking it), a meal, so we can talk without intrusion. Her eyes lit up.

"Going for a meal would be lovely," she said. I proposed The Rajdoot Indian, just off the High Road. I'd been there several times with Phil after work in the past. The food is good and ambience is conducive to a quiet chat. She was extremely excited by this prospect and duly agreed. Her demeanour appeared a little too enthusiastic actually; and, in retrospect perhaps, I should not have given her the option and just suggested the local pub. Anyway, it was done now. It wouldn't be busy on a Monday night, so we'd be able to hear each other.

I then realised that I have now basically asked her out on a date. Oops.

(1.00 p.m.) Lunch was light for both of us. Sabrina bought a packet of crackers and dutifully Marmited-up several of them for me. She had cheese spread on hers. The non-stop stream of customers of the morning substituted itself for the dearth of clients of the early afternoon. We sat in virtual silence eating our lunch. Sabrina flicked through one her celeb magazines, and I sat pawing away at an edition of Record Collector. It seemed to me that she didn't want to reveal anything else until this evening. Periodically, we'd both look up and our eyes would meet as if each of us was psychically alerted to the other's brief interlude in magazine reading. Each glance was coupled with the occasional sweet smile from her as if she was thanking me over and over for my dinner invitation.

(3.30 p.m.) There's a guy who comes in fairly regularly to see me. He's pretty jittery and will normally inform me of the date of his next visit, just to make sure we'd be open and that I'll be here. I suspect he has something like OCD, ADHD, HDMI, TTFN or RNLI. Today, as he reached the window, he slammed both hands down on the counter, looked slightly oddly at me and asked if I was in his brother-in-law's pop band. Instead of saying, 'No', straight away I asked what the name of the band was. His reply and, I'm guessing, nay hoping, I misheard it, was 'Rat Pants'. I told him that I wasn't.

He then asked, "What band *are* you in then?" I told him I wasn't in a band and I never was. "Are you sure?" he enquired. Now, is it just me or when someone responds definitively to a question regarding their life, I accept it as a fact. Why do some people still find that their assumption is more valid than the actual truth? Anyway, I told him I was sure, but he still continued with his belief that I was in 'Rat Pants'.

. "You played bass. I'm sure you did. It's *got* to be you. It was blue." 'It was blue'??? Ah, he got me... What a strange thing to say. It was like I was going to crumble at his relentless interrogation.

He eventually left, still disbelieving me. I mean, why would I lie? Now, the thing is this, there's old Fender Precision bass in the cellar from years ago when we used to take in musical instruments and, I believe it is blue too. I'm so tempted to just prop it up in his eyesight when he next comes in, just to play with his mind. He'll be convinced I've lied to him, and won't understand why. Or perhaps, I'll just sit on my chair and play it a bit and then look up, make eye contact, wink knowingly, and carefully put it aside with great satisfaction. Or am I just being cruel?

(5.30 p.m.) I had already called home to tell Kathy I was going to be late. I explained that I was staying behind to speak to Sabrina about a couple of issues. That's sort of the truth, isn't it? I didn't mention the restaurant bit, but I thought I might slip that into the conversation we might have when I got home. She didn't ask me why, which was good.

I closed up the shop and the two of us walked the short distance to the restaurant just chit-chatting about the day in general. When we arrived at the Rajdoot, we were seated by, what I assume was the owner. He's been there forever and I always see him when I've dined there before. He gave me a little grin as if to say 'Out with a young girl, eh? I bet the wife doesn't know,' before seating us opposite each other in the corner; immediately placing menus in front of us. We perused the options in silence for a few moments.

"I don't often eat this early," Sabrina said, breaking the quiet and continuing the small talk.

"Who does?" I rhetorically answered looking around the completely empty restaurant in an obvious and expansive way.

"You do make me laugh, Pete," Sabrina said. I like making her laugh.

The waiter came over and took our order. I looked at Sabrina and she went first. "I'll have a chicken biryani please," she said softly. Clearly, her latest foray into vegetarianism had ended.

"And a lamb pasanda, with plain rice for me," I requested. Naturally, as all waiters in curry houses ask, "Do you want any vegetable or bread with that?" Sabrina looked at me to take the lead.

"We'll have some poppadums and chutney please… oh, and a portion of onion bhajees too," I answered. Sabrina nodded approvingly. Before the waiter had a chance to ask about the drinks, I ordered half a lager for me and, without asking, a white wine for Sabrina. She looked at me approvingly. I had guessed right.

A couple of minutes later the waiter brought over the poppadums, mango chutney, sliced onions, the yoghurt sauce and that other dark brownish-green stuff that burns my eyes by just looking at it. I'd hate to know what it would do to my innards. Yuk. He also placed down one of those red, bobbly candle holders – another staple of Indian restaurants, which had been stuck in the 1970s, like this place. It is kind of comforting in a way. Everything changes so quickly nowadays and I like to know that there are some things that remain constant. He lit the candle within and after he disappeared, the ceiling lights were dimmed and the Indian music (which was probably on 8-track) was switched on. Even though it was bright and sunny outside, it was fairly dark and moody inside – a bit like me, really.

The flicker of the candle danced across the pale complexion of my dinner partner as she nibbled elegantly on a poppadum. She looked very attractive in the dim light and I have to say, my heart skipped a beat when she looked at me. Then again, perhaps it was the onions I had just eaten making a formal protest on their way to 'parts unknown'.

"I want to say how grateful I am again for taking the time to listen to me last week," she said. "I've not done very much in my life so far, and when the opportunity arose to become a part-time carer at the hospice, it was something I felt I needed to do. I didn't have an unhappy childhood, but I was unfulfilled. I'm an only child, and my father left us when I was a toddler, so it's been a real struggle for my mum. I realise I am very lucky though. I have my health, which is something we often take for granted, and somewhere to live. All these children and their parents have is the realisation that they will die soon," she added very sorrowfully. I told her

I thought it was a wonderful thing she was doing. Her face suggested she approved of my endorsement.

(6.15 p.m.) The main course was brought over and Sabrina expanded on her interest in helping at the hospice. She told me that Daz isn't even aware of what she does. Apparently, he would feel the whole thing was a waste of time. That information immediately took away any lingering benefit of the doubt I had given him, (and let's face it, there wasn't much of that). I felt it is an extremely noble thing she is doing and it made me feel guilty that I don't do any charity work to help the underprivileged. In fact, I really don't do much for anyone really.

We finished our curry and I announced "I'd like to come with you one day... to the hospice. Maybe I can help?"

"Really?" said Sabrina in a surprised, but excited manner. "I didn't tell you to make you feel guilty or anything."

"I know. You wouldn't do that. You have nothing about you that would be capable of such deceit. I *want* to do something. Yes, I do feel a little guilty, but that's me. I want to do something good for a change instead of just moaning about things like the Olympics and the terrible state of the road outside the shop." Sabrina's stifled a giggle, but it soon disappeared and a look of gratitude shimmered across her face.

"You're a lovely man, Pete. I would love you to visit

the home with me," she said joyfully. "And I know you genuinely want to, and that's what makes you so special. That's why I like you so much. I like you a lot. I think you know that."

I just nodded, not knowing quite what to say, and started to look at the dessert menu which had magically appeared in front of me. The waiter came over, but sensing this was a sensitive breakthrough moment, he backed off away from the table.

"I wish we could have more than a working relationship. I feel happy when I 'm around you," Sabrina quietly admitted.

I kind of knew this was coming, but it still felt like a surprise and caught me somewhat on the hop. I took her left hand in my right and pulled it slowly towards the middle of the table next to the candle.

"You clearly know I feel something for you too," I admitted. She nodded slowly. I put the menu down and took her hand in mine. "If situations were different, then maybe..."

"I know," Sabrina interjected in a barely audible whisper. She placed her other hand on mine and said. "If you weren't married and we were nearer the same age, then perhaps you're right."

"It's not an age thing, Sabrina," I corrected her, "but you're right about the marriage situation. It would create some problems, to say the least." She smiled. The waiter approached up again and our hands returned to their respective sides of the table.

We both chose to finish with a sorbet - orange for me and lemon for Sabrina. The conversation returned to the mundane subject of the shop for the remainder of the meal as if we were on a normal staff outing.

I was presented with the bill and Sabrina offered to pay her way, but of course, I declined. After all, it was my idea to go for a curry. I offered to take her home and she delightedly accepted. We made our way back up the High Road, talking and laughing about Phil and his lifestyle; past the shop and round the corner to my car. She doesn't live far away and, as her house is in a cul-de-sac, asked me to drop her off at the corner of the road.

"Thank you so much for this evening, Pete. It's really cheered me up, and the food was excellent. Oh, and we'll sort out a time and date when we can both go down to the hospice."

"The pleasure was all mine," I told her. She leant over and gave me a kiss on my cheek. I turned towards her and she took my face in between her hands and delicately planted a soft kiss on my lips. She drew away haltingly, and just looked into my eyes for what seemed like an age, but in truth could only have been a second or two. "I love... (she paused), how you make me feel, but I know the score. Don't worry. Business, as usual, tomorrow, eh?" She opened the door, left the car and walked the 30 yards or so to her house, looking around at me, twice. I waited until she went inside her house before I drove off and dared to think about what had just happened. She wanted to say 'I love you'. I felt a mixture of emotions - empowerment, joy, guilt and satisfaction, but in no particular order.

(9.00 p.m.) I parked up at home, and before I left the car, I had to remind myself that I was back in my 'normal' life. On entering the house, Kathy called out from the living room. "Is that you?" So naturally I replied, "No, it's him." What did she expect me to say?

"So, how did it go? I bet you had to crowbar information out of her," Kathy said in her normal, unforgiving manner. "Did she want a raise then?" she added in her usual, charming way.

"No Kathy, she's having a few difficulties at the moment and wanted a responsible, kind person to talk to.

"Responsible... you?"

"Yes, me. Who would have thought it, eh?"

"Oh, fine," she conceded, picking up on my displeasure with her line of questioning. I never can tell from one day to the next what sort of mood she'll be in; and to be frank, right now, I couldn't care less.

"I'm going to bed. Coming?" she asked, as she brushed past me as I stood at the door of the living room with my coat still on. I could tell she was hoping I'd answer in the negative and due to her current disposition, and the fact that it was not just gone nine o'clock, I passed on her kind and oh-so-warm offer. Besides, I had things on my mind - things I didn't particularly want to share with her.

Tuesday 29th May 2012

Chain Reaction

(9.30 a.m.) I was concerned that things would be a little difficult or awkward between us this morning, but Sabrina kept her word and it was indeed 'business as usual'. As a football manager might say, 'All credit to her. The girl did good'. I sent her out to get me a bacon roll for my breakfast. It's funny, but after having an Indian for dinner, I'm always famished the following morning. Of course, the same goes for Chinese, but following that, the hunger returns within an hour.

Sabrina had been on my mind ever since I dropped her off last night. I sat, on my own last night and tried to justify my feelings. I concluded that they were indeed justified and the belief that I'm due a midlife crisis rubber stamped it. Nothing of any note had been discussed about the previous night, particularly nothing about what was said between us as regards to the developing feelings we have for each other.

I ate my roll whilst opening the mail, and Sabrina went around cleaning and tidying up. She did brush past me once, although I'm not sure how deliberate it was. I wanted to say something to her, but I really didn't know how to start or even what exactly I wanted to say. I knew I had to place the whole notion of 'us' on the back burner or it will consume me and make our working relationship difficult, to say the least.

(1.45 p.m.) A had another phone call from Joy Ramsey; she's one of my dearest customers. She is always very courteous to the point of being overbearing, and everything is 'darling'. 'What time do you shut, darling?' 'What time do you open in the morning, darling?' 'I'll be in tomorrow/at the weekend/next week, darling'. When the current round of phone calls started, her contract wasn't even due – not even close, but she clearly wanted to reassure me that the redemption date was on her mind. Perhaps, she just thought I needed solace and the understanding that at least one of my customers was conscientious. However, she is *far* from conscientious.

Throughout this series of unnecessary calls,' later' soon became 'tomorrow'; 'tomorrow' became 'the weekend'; 'the weekend' became 'next week' and 'next week' became... Well, dear Diary, I'm still waiting, but at least she likes to keep in touch. Along with each jilted promise came a little excuse and I actually made a note of her reasons. To date, there have been seven of them all pertaining to the one £30 contract. They are:

My baby's ill.

I've lost my ATM card.

I'm ill.

I have to work.

My mother is ill.

I'm at the tube station and I'll be there in 10 minutes. (She wasn't).

I thought it was due next week.

However, the pièce de résistance came today when she called to say she was on her way to the shop to renew the contract, but she had forgotten it was at home. And that was because she was on her way to the hospital to visit her sister who is... ill, and it was her sister who was going to lend her the money to get the contract renewed... darling. Bang! Triple whammy. I had no option to congratulate her of this triumph of mega-bullshit, which I did so in a most sarcastic and unbelieving manner. She was totally oblivious to that fact, which I knew she would be.

(2.10 p.m.) Although I was pleased earlier that Sabrina had kept her promise to keep our relationship on a platonic basis, there was part of me that wished things had slightly... ever so slightly, escalated. I knew this might be disastrous, but it just felt a bit odd that she could just push aside her emotions and carry on regardless. I felt more like 15 years old than almost 51.

(4.20 p.m.) The curiously ordinary day took a turn for the bizarre. Quite a few of the incidents of late have involved people whose intelligence, manners and self-awareness were not high on their list of attributes. What happened here is a textbook example of this and featured a gentleman who failed desperately to grasp a scintilla of any one of those three qualities, and thus condemned him to nothing more than a complete idiot.

The man in question, I would say was about 20 years old. He had one of those small rucksack/backpack things on his back and had a general aura of vacant disbelief about him. It was a look that suggested that whatever I was about to tell him would be perceived as a lie or something totally alien to his comprehension.

Customer: How much would you give for this?

(He dropped a chain and bracelet into the drawer. Immediately, I realised he hadn't got the whole 'singular/plural' thing.)

Me: Do you want to pawn them or sell them?

Customer: What's the difference?

Me: If you pawn, you enter a contract to collect them. If you sell them, you'll get more, but that's it, you can't get them back.

Customer: I want to know how much it is to sell them.

Me: Okay.

Customer: But, what if I want to get it back? (still using the singular)

Me: You can't. Only if you pawn *them*, can you get *them* back.

Customer: Right. I'll probably pawn it then (persisting that there was just one item)... but I might not come back.

Me: You really want to sell them then? You'll get more money that way. Do you have any ID?

Customer: But, I do want to come back. ID, yes... but it's not mine. It's my brother's, but I've used it before.

This is nothing particularly out of the ordinary, so I took the ID, a medical card, and started to search for him on our system, to see if we'd had the item(s) before. I couldn't find him.)

Customer: Oh, I've not done it *here* before. It was somewhere else.

I was now pretty sure by the way this was going and that the ID probably wasn't even his brother's either.

Me: Do you have anything else at all?

Customer: Yeah, I've got a letter from the Social.

He fished the letter out of his rucksack and showed it to me. Naturally, this was a different name from his 'brothers,' but I couldn't even be bothered to challenge him. It's one thing someone having ID; it's another thing if it's theirs and it's something else, again, if they even understand why someone else's ID isn't *actually* ID. I offer him a price, which after much blank-faced deliberation, he accepted. I copied his details to my computer and printed up the contract. I spent a while going through the whole process with him.

Customer: Oh, I don't want to do it now.

Me: Pardon?

Customer: I just wanted to know how much it was worth if I pawned it.

Me: Then why didn't you tell me that before I asked for ID and printed up your contract?

Customer: (Not grasping anything that I had said.) You're pushing me into it. I reckon you just want to steal my chain.

Firstly, I had no idea what could have given him that impression and secondly, he was still under the assumption that he had given me just one item, so I probably could well have got away with nabbing the bracelet. It would have served him right.

Me: Tell you what, take your thingsssssssss back and we'll just leave it how it is. (I tried incredibly hard not to swear or insult this poor 'touched' soul).

Customer: I'm never coming back here again. You lot are just a bunch of thieves. (Not the first time I've been called a thief recently).

He snatched his jewellery back and looked at the gold in his hand and, I think, he finally noticed that there were two items.

This wasn't a particularly funny exchange, but it was indicative of what happens on a not too irregular basis and what probably has made me the commonly annoyed and curmudgeonly figure whom it was suggested to, to write a diary - just to show that things aren't that bad after all. Yeah, right.

(5.10 p.m.) I was about to start closing up, when Joy Ramsey, finally, and breathlessly burst through the front door. "I told you I'd be back. I must be one of your best customers, eh?" she happily asked with a wink. I fully expect that we will go through the same old dance when the new agreement is up in six months. Still, business is business.

(5.20 p.m.) I'm going to be off for a couple of days and I didn't want to leave the paperwork until I returned, so I let Sabrina go early. She looked at me for a moment as I raised the shutters to let her out, and I knew she wanted to say something. In fact, her mouth shaped as if about to speak, but she couldn't or wouldn't. I watched her walk across the road as the shutters slid back down again, thus obscuring the last image I would have of her today.

As the shutter finished its descent, I took a deep breath, walked back to my desk and picked half full empty can of Diet Coke that Sabrina had left. About to throw it away, I noticed the imprint her pale red lipstick had left behind on it. I put it down back on the desk and sat down in my chair. I leant back and found myself just staring at the can in front of me, in a trance, as if were the Holy Grail. I just couldn't throw it away. To chuck it away now would almost be like throwing away Sabrina and all the things she feels for me; but to keep it there would be like I was accepting that she truly has a grip on me – a tender, loving grip, but nevertheless a grip. It had now become abundantly clear to me that I was indeed regressing back into an angst-ridden teenager. I think I am walking head first into a whole lot of trouble - one way or another.

Saturday 2nd June 2012
Shine On You Crazy Diamond

(9.00 a.m.) It's a rare occurrence that all three of us are in on a Saturday, and it was the first time that I had been in both Phil's and Sabrina's company since Phil joked that we may have something going, on a couple of weeks ago. I knew I had to keep my thoughts to myself and not allow my face to deceive me. The expression 'I can read you like a book' was probably created for me. My phizog seems to tell anyone anything they want to know without even asking me.

Sabrina went out to get us all breakfast, which Phil had elected to pay for. In fact, he was very keen to pay and even said, "I'll get these" before I even finished asking who wanted breakfast.

(9.25 a.m.) Sabrina, who was wearing a new perfume, returned from the breakfast run and we sat devouring our food. I had my standard bacon roll, Sabrina, a sausage sandwich and Phil, a toasted bacon sandwich. There seemed to be a slight tension in the air and it was nothing to do with what might or might not be happening between me and the fragrant Miss Saunders. Phil appeared extremely jittery for some reason, which was most unlike him. He carelessly allowed a blob of tomato ketchup to drop from his sandwich, and down his front. Luckily for him, he was wearing a dark tie and that's exactly where it landed, thus avoiding his pristine lavender shirt.

"Oh, shiiiit," Phil exclaimed as he threw the sandwich down on his desk. He immediately jumped up and ran to the kitchen to try and remove the dripping condiment. I glanced over at Sabrina who was sitting opposite trying to stifle a giggle, whilst shielding her face with her (ketchup free) sandwich. She didn't rush to Phil's aid after his comestible catastrophe like she did for me, I might add. I was smiling widely and I winked at her and continued chewing on my roll. She gave me a huge smile back as Phil repeated his "Shiiiiiit" cry from the kitchen, this time with even more ferocity. He re-appeared to inform us "This is pure silk, you know," tugging on the end of his tie. He had made the stain ten times worse. We looked at his and said nothing. "It was a present from my ex-girlfriend. It's ruined!" he cried with rueful resignation.

"Then you must be pleased to have it out of your life too," I jokingly sympathised.

"Oh, shut up," he replied and retired back to the kitchen to have another go at salvaging what he had already confirmed, was a ruined tie. Phil was very proud of his appearance and rarely had anything out of place, but the way he reacted to this accident was unusually fierce. Sabrina looked at me again, and smacked her left hand as if to say, "You've been told off now." Something was clearly getting at my business partner. He eventually gave up the ghost and took off the tie before throwing it in the waste paper basket.

(11.30 a.m.) A farce worthy of the master, Ray Cooney, developed this morning. An old customer (aren't they all 'old'?), came by to cash a cheque. He's a scaffolder by trade and used to work at many of the UK film studios in particularly Leavesden, Shepperton, Pinewood and Elstree. (Are there any others?) Along with his stories of the studios (interesting), he would often go on about his son, (not interesting). One such story was about his semi-professional footballing son. One time, he'd be having a trial at Watford, the next time he was at Brighton, and the next time at Walsall. Anyway, the story went he had a second trial at Leyton Orient and his dad was again pleased as punch. So much so he even talked about buying season tickets, even though he was a big West Ham United fan. Now, I hadn't seen this guy for quite some time, about six months I suppose, and today he came in with another cheque. We made some general chitchat and I paid him out his money and then I remembered his son's trial.

"So, how did the trial go?" I asked.

"Not great, although it could have been worse," the guy responded quite sombrely. "Two years... they gave him two years."

"Oh, that's pretty good, isn't it?" I asked, not quite picking up on his downbeat manner. I guess my mind was still on Phil's unusual behaviour.

I really thought he would have bound into the shop to tell me his wonderful news; such was his excitement at previous trial invitations.

"Well, we're expecting three or four years, so two ain't too bad.

"I don't think two years is bad at all for someone of his age," I told him.

Stupid, stupid boy. I don't know how he got involved with that lot."

Even though it was only Leyton Orient and not his beloved West Ham, his attitude could have been a little more encouraging. It was a bit odd and I was beginning to wonder if we were at crossed purposes.

"We're not talking about his trial at The Orient, are we?"

"No, no, no," came the reply. "His trial was at Southwark Crown Court." Apparently, he'd been caught up in a counterfeit money scam and was now a few months into his prison sentence at Wandsworth Prison.

I chanced my arm a bit and being fully aware I was behind bullet-proof glass, I continued, "Still, it could have been worse. He could have got four years at Brisbane Road..."

It went silent for a rather tense moment before the fella came back with a very straight and succinct, "Yeah, I suppose you're right." And I think he meant it, too.

(2.00 p.m.) The phone rang and I picked it up. It was someone who wanted to speak to Mr Bryan. I handed the cordless phone (which I normally keep *out* of its charger).

I handed it to Phil. He disappeared out to back into the yard with it, shutting the door firmly behind him. He really was acting very peculiarly. A few minutes later, he returned and sat down at his desk, without revealing anything about the mysterious phone call.

(4.30 p.m.) It was a day of regular customers. Another one, a woman of my age, often pawns her very nice diamond jewellery with us. However, sometimes she'd just come in just to talk and tell me about recent events in her life. She was quite glamorous and outgoing, and I was never even sure why she came here to pawn, as a lot of her conversation would revolve around her going on exotic holidays and expensive items she'd recently bought. I'm not saying she was a show-off, but she was proud of her achievements and very much enjoyed informing me of what she'd been up to, who she'd been doing it with, and what she'd be doing next.

On several occasions recently, she told me about her pregnant daughter and when she was due. In fact, I knew so much about it I began to feel like I'd been somehow involved in the conception. Nothing bores me more than people who I really don't know; going on about their children, let alone unborn grandchildren. However, I must have given out signals that I was extremely interested because she was so excited at the prospect of bringing her daughter and the sprog in to see me.

Today, she kept her promise. A young woman entered my shop flanked by my friend, the glamorous diamond clad grandmother, and with them, half a dozen other fawning, baby-talking, jabbering extras. I went round to the front of the shop to grant them their audience. The grandmother ushered me through the crowd to see the baby, which her daughter had picked up and held in front of her out to show me. I felt like the Holy Papa. Was I expected to bless the child? Should I have anointed him with the sign of the cross? I mean, the way they were behaving, I imagined they must have been convinced he was the second coming.

Finally, he was put back into his manger... I mean buggy, and a few more minutes of pitiful baby gurgling and over the top face-pulling and 'peekabooing' ensued before the disciples left my premises and started the long journey back to Nazareth... or Stratford, as the case may have been.

And the people rejoiced for they knew they had seen Him and He did gurgle a bit. I turned and bade them farewell and good fortune, for I had much work to do.

(4.45 p.m.) Phil took me aside and finally revealed what the phone call was about. I had been waiting all day to find out what had got to him. He informed me that he was seriously thinking about selling his half of the business, and he had someone who would be interested in buying. This was a scenario I hadn't considered. I half expected him to tell me he was off gallivanting again, thus leaving me in the lurch, such was his puzzling behaviour today. I was left speechless at his revelation. He naturally gave me first option to buy his share, probably knowing full well that I probably couldn't afford it. I suppose he had to ask though; it was only right.

The phone call earlier was from the potential buyer; one of his boat/yacht/sailing friends. He treats the business as a bit of a part-time job really, bearing in mind how much time off he takes for his holidays. I suppose I knew that the time would come when he wanted 'out.' From day one, I realised knew he was never going to be as hands-on as I am, but he *was* trustworthy and house-trained – the ketchup episode apart.

Could I work with anyone else? Would I even want to, at my age? Should I just sell up? These were all questions I needed to think about and answer before I decided on my future here. And what about Sabrina? Not that I'm concerned that she won't find another job – not at all. How would I feel if I couldn't see her anymore? Curiously, at the moment, *that* is the question I may have the most difficulty in answering.

Friday 8th June 2012
Land of Confusion

(**7.50 a.m.**) It's been a week since Phil's revelation and nothing has really moved on. It's still a possibility he might sell up; and therefore, it's still a possibility that I might just jack the lot in. I haven't mentioned it to Sabrina or indeed Kathy, yet.

Whilst driving into work, I realised that I have been listening to the same 70s compilation for the best part of four months. Granted, it is a massive playlist, but even so… four months. It probably mirrors my desire for things to keep the status quo (who incidentally, do not appear on the playlist), and leave things as they are. I guess the idea of a change in my business and in my personal life, although sounding attractive at times, is something that may prove more difficult than I first imagined.

This morning's moment of pure embarrassment came, not from a fellow motorist; be they emergency service individuals or mere civilians, but from pedestrians, and a family of pedestrians at that. As I never know in what order my songs will play, I can never prepare for the particular level of humiliation I put myself in when singing along to them. The shame scale can go from the lowest level 1, which might be let's say, Gerry Rafferty's Baker Street (as long as one keeps one's mouth firmly shut without making any loud erroneous sounds during the sax solo, of course), The Jam's Eton Rifles or Oliver's Army by Elvis Costello, right up to,, a skin-crawling, teeth-clenching, bone-shuddering level 10 rated Wombling Merry Christmas or Loving You by Minnie Ripperton – not that either of those songs are on my playlist, dear Diary. Please believe me. I would suggest that this morning's moment of cringeworthiness (if that isn't a word, it damned well should be), was a level 5. A family of three, featuring a mother, her seven or eight-year-old daughter and toddler in a buggy, crossed the road at my hated pedestrian crossing, and they witnessed me warble along to *A Glass of Champagne* by Sailor. Thinking about it, it's more of a level 6 crime. Shame on me.

(9.45 a.m.) Sabrina told me that she'll be visiting a child in the hospice after work and wondered if I wanted to come along with her. I had nothing on, and Kathy was out tonight with the delightful Dawn, so I said I would. Besides, it meant I could spend more time out of the work environment with her.

(11.00 a.m.) A guy who hasn't been in for a while and, for some reason, always calls me Paul (which he did almost two dozen times in our brief conversation on this occasion), wanted to borrow some money as his brother had died at the weekend – yes, that's what he said. Interpreted on one level, that could be quite sad and depressing, but it was the way he justified it that made it sound humorous. Of course, it was a very unfortunate event, but the way he played it was in a very 'matter of fact' way. I decided to keep quiet during his opening salvo.

"Yeah, Paul. He just died, you know. You remember last time I came in, Paul? That was just after my sister killed herself, Paul. I was on crutches..." You *do* remember, don't you, Paul?"

I vaguely remembered something about that, but my expectations were already excited by what gem would be next. "Still, what ya gonna do, eh, Paul?" he continued, then laughed and shook his head tutting and sniggering away. I decided against correcting him with regards to my name today, which I regularly do. Think Trigger and Rodney from Only Fools and Horses.

Anyway, to cut a long story short, I lent him £60, and I thought he said: "that'll be enough for some weed."

"Oh, more than enough, I should think. You'll be out of your tree," I said continuing the eerily candid conversation.

"No, I'm not going to make it myself. I'll get it made up for the funeral."

I then realised he had said 'wreath', not 'weed'.

Some other confusing and slightly angry sounding words followed. There was something about chewing gum on pavements, and out-of-date sandwiches from Sainsbury's. I was confused to why he was far more upset about these trivial matters than the subject of his personal family tragedies. I failed to totally get the gist of all his disappointments, but neither did I care to. It would have taken far too long, and take up far too much time to question his diatribe.

On leaving, he offered me a cheery "Goodbye Paul" and as the conversation called for it I told him to 'be lucky' in my finest Cockney, just as he walked into the wall. Yes, for no reason apart from being a part of the most unlucky family, he just walked into the wall close to the door. One day I'll ask him why he calls me Paul... or maybe I won't. It's kind of nice to have a pawnbroker's nom de plume.

(1.30 p.m.) I had a microwave meal for one for lunch. It claimed to be a ham and mushroom tagliatelle, but I didn't believe a word of it. Yes, there was pasta in it, but as for the ham and mushroom, I would suggest reconstituted mulch and vulcanised elastic in a processed cheese and glue sauce. Mind you, I'm not sure that 'Mulch and Elastic Tagliatelle' displayed on the packaging would sell. Sabrina played it safe with a honey mustard chicken salad. I really should have taken her lead.

(5.00 p.m.) Not long before closing time, a woman of Arabic descent entered the shop to pick up a couple of pledges. The amount she owed was about a tenner more than she thought, so after a brief exchange of yes/no between us, her next course of action was to wave her hands around aggressively and swear at me in Arabic, or so I assumed. "Hey, that's enough of that," I chastised her in no uncertain terms.

"You speak Arabic?" she replied in amazement. I

just stood there staring at her knowingly with my eyebrows raised and lips pursed in what probably was in a very camp way. I don't speak any Arabic, but the suggestion was that I did. I waited in this strange, rather effeminate pose for quite a while until the woman offered. "I'm sorry, I'm sorry. It's not easy."

Is it not easy to apologise/be wrong/speak English/be polite/be mathematically astute? Who knows? There were so many choices. After I took her money, she pushed her £4 odd change back at me as what I assume was a kind of penance. I pushed it back in an act of great martyrdom. She quickly took the change back and bowed in remorse. She seemed so sorry and I wondered what she did say exactly. They say 'a little knowledge goes a long way', well, in this case, no knowledge at all went even further - a grovelling apology and an offer of monetary recompense. She could have been nice and paid the right amount in the first place, but chose to take the fool's route and it could have cost her – four whole pounds.

(6.00 p.m.) Sabrina and I arrived at the hospice. It wasn't at all how I imagined. In my mind, it was an old Victorian building with foreboding grey exterior and endless corridors, and mile-high ceilings, where a slight clearing of a throat would echo into a rumbling, booming, cacophony of sound. On reflection, I was probably imagining an 1800s lunatic asylum. In fact, the buildings were single-storied modern constructions. They consisted of bright, sunny walkways; pleasant, airy bedrooms instead of hospital wards; and a light, spacious dayroom. I really don't know why I was expecting to see a version of Bedlam, but I was certainly glad it wasn't.

We waited in the day room, sitting on one of the orange office reception area type sofas as one of the nurses; at least I thought she was a nurse. She wasn't wearing a traditional uniform or anything), pushed in a young boy in a wheelchair. He must have been about eight or nine years old, but it was difficult to be sure. He was very thin and his face was quite drawn. His eyes lit up when he saw Sabrina though. The nurse put the brakes on the chair, whispered something in the boy's ear and left him with us.

Sabrina introduced him to me, "This is Harry." I said, "Hello there. My name is Pete," and I stretched out to shake his hand. He slowly reached out his hand to mine. His grip was almost non-existent.

"He's got a bone-wasting disease and he's extremely weak," Sabrina whispered to me out of Harry's earshot. She didn't tell me specifically what it was and, to be honest, I didn't really want to know. "I've been visiting Harry for a couple of months now, haven't I, Harry?" she continued in a much louder voice and turning to the boy. He nodded slowly and very quietly mouthed 'Yes."

We had spent a good three-quarters of an hour with Harry in the dayroom before the nurse returned to take him back to his room. In that time, Sabrina read to him, told him about where she works and what a nice bloke I was... She drew a picture with him and did a puzzle on the table in front of him as he pointed out what pieces to place where. I helped where I could, but she was fantastic with him. She truly is wasted working for me in a shop. This should be her vocation in life. She's clearly natural with children.

Before we left, Sabrina gave him a hug and as he was being wheeled away, he waved and said "Goodbye" to me. It was a sobering moment.

"He likes you," Sabrina told me as Harry disappeared from view.

(6.50 p.m.) We walked back to my car and before we got in, I told Sabrina how great I thought she was with Harry, and that I would like to come back with her again to visit him.

"I'm not sure if there will be another visit with Harry," she forlornly told me.

"Oh, why's that?" I asked.

"The doctors don't expect him to live much longer. He's deteriorated so much since the last time I saw him. I was told before I arranged this visit that it might be the last one, but I didn't say anything to you because I didn't want you to appear sad or despondent in front of him. We can't do that. We have to keep our emotions to ourselves and not show the child. It's very hard to do." She stopped in her tracks and started to cry. "Coming here takes so much out of me." A single tear fell from her right eye and dropped down her cheek. As quickly as she wiped it away, one dropped from her left eye too. I just put my arms around her and held her, and she broke down. She held on tight as I tried to console her. I couldn't say 'Don't worry. It'll be okay' because it wouldn't be. I just hugged her and stroked her hair.

After a couple of minutes, I let her go. I was feeling pretty teary too but tried to keep it in. Sabrina had regained er composure a bit. "I bet you wish you never came with me, eh?"

"No, not at all. I'm glad I came with you this evening," I reassured her. I *was* glad. Firstly, I was glad that the children didn't live in the kind of institution I had imagined and I was glad to feel that we, well Sabrina mainly, had given a child a few moments of happiness, especially as he might not be with us for much longer. The one thing I did realise though was that Sabrina had immense strength. She knew exactly what poor Harry's situation was beforehand, but never showed it inside the hospice. I couldn't do that. I would be too upset because I don't have that inner strength.

We got in my car and I turned to her. "After what you told me, I don't think I can come here with you again," I confessed.

"That's understandable. I can tell it upset you, too. It took me ages to learn how not let it affect me when I'm sitting with a child who you know will die soon," she calmly explained, with a consoling hand on my arm. "In a way, I expected you to say that. I know you're a sensitive soul, even though you try not to show it," she continued, smiling through the tears. "I'm just glad you came down with me once. It means a lot to me."

(7.20 p.m.) I dropped Sabrina off at the corner of her road as I did last time. Her face was now dry from all the tears and she leant over to kiss me on the lips. I didn't want her to leave and there was a pause to suggest she didn't want to leave either. She knew she had to though, so she got out of the car and made her way to her house, turning once to smile and wave goodbye to me. I waited until she was out of sight like I did previously, before turning around to start my journey homeward. She is such a special, kind girl and I am so glad I went to the hospice with her to meet Harry. It was something I will never forget.

Wednesday 13th June 2012

I Remember You

(8.50 a.m.) Sabrina was outside the shop texting away, waiting for me as usual. Phil was on holiday (again), so I had her all to myself for the whole week. I say 'all to myself', but it was still business as usual. I'm sure I would get the odd smile or glance, but nothing had changed between us. It was like we're both waiting for the other one to make a move. I know I'm repeating myself, but it really is like being a teenager again.

Kathy has been very reasonable of late. No tantrums or snide comments, and that's led to a harmonious home life. Leanne is enjoying her new job, even though the commute to South London is long and laborious. She's out most nights still, even though she must be knackered. Thinking about it, I haven't really spoken to her a great deal with her recently, with all her extra-curricular activities, but I've never been one of those parents who says, 'while you're under my roof, you play by my rules' – firstly, because I hated to hear that crap when I was young from my parents, and secondly, because Leanne's never really given me any justification to go down that route. Melissa and Simon certainly have, but it was Kathy who would always come out with those tired old parenting clichés. "You treat this place like a hotel," and "If I spoke to my mother the way you speak to me..." etc. were her favourites.

(12.10 p.m.) The latest in a string of incidents featuring characters, to which reasoning and the ability to remember simple instructions were as alien to them as keeping a desk neat and tidy is to me, entered the shop. A middle-aged woman walked up and immediately started rummaging through her enormous, and probably bottomless, Mary Poppins-type carpet bag. She eventually pulled out a gold charm bracelet. I weighed it and offered her £300 to pawn it.

"Ooh nooo," she exclaimed in a mock posh accent. "Last time you gave me £500." I knew this was impossible and asked her for her name so I could look it up on our system. She had indeed pawned the bracelet before, about two years earlier, but for just £200. I explained this news to her, but she just stared at me, shaking her head vigorously, which covered up a burp (which was an unexpected bonus). Obviously, the shock had triggered some kind of gaseous reaction in her.

"No, it was definitely £500," she insisted. I assured her that it was £200, but she was having none of it. She then expelled a huge cough, although I assumed it was to cover up another burp, such was its ferocity.

She said the 'other guy' gave her £500 and was 'very nice' to her. I told her that it was, in fact, *me*, and I gave her *£200* last time and I was now offering her much more than that.

"Oh no. It wasn't you. The other man had a beard and was much younger than you," she continued. Well, I was younger then and I used to have a beard. "No, it wasn't you," she repeated. "The other guy was wearing a light blue shirt." (Two years earlier). What could I say? I'd been rumbled...

All of a sudden the realisation hit that she was in fact wrong. Probably everything she'd ever done or said was wrong too, but I'm presuming.

"You know, it wasn't you. I took it up the road and it was a different bracelet."

"So' I triumphalised (Is that a word? Well, it is now. I like making up words). "It wasn't me... it wasn't here... and it wasn't the bracelet? *This* is the bracelet you pawned here before," I said, holding it up in front of her face. She concurred in silence, without offering an apology. No surprise in that. I returned to script.

"So, I can lend you £300 on this bracelet." I told her with authority. Then came the coup de grace.

"No, she returned, 'I would still like £500? They did it up the road last time for me," she went on whilst letting out an unabashed belch. I tried to explain once more, doing extremely well not to lose my temper, but she eventually relented and accepted £300. I'd love to say she farted loudly on her exit, but that would have been just too perfect.

(**2.30 p.m.**) A young lady came in after lunch and was visibly panicking because she was overdue in collecting her pledge. Actually, she was almost in tears worrying that she'd lost her ring. In actual fact, it was slightly overdue, only by seven days, but as I always keep unredeemed contracts for a month or so and she hadn't even yet received her overdue letter, I explained that she still had a few weeks, and not to worry. She gave a huge sigh and told me that she was worried because she was going on holiday for a week from tomorrow. "Enjoy your holiday and come back at the end of the month if you want," I said. She reacted like she'd won The X-Factor. She was almost on her knees crying with relief. She stood up and continued to thank me, placing her outstretched hands on the glass, still crying. I felt like I was in prison and speaking my final words with my loved one before being carted off to the electric chair. "Oh thank you, thank you, thank you. You are a lovely man I could give you a kiss." I thought about nipping round to the front and to cash in on my promise when she blew me a kiss and left the shop.

I imagined that was the end of it, but five minutes later she was back (still wet-cheeked) with her mum. She approached me and, I thought she was going to ask what I'd done to her daughter. After all, a simple act of putting someone's mind at rest had exalted me to Messianic proportions and made her daughter into a gibbering wreck.

"You don't know how happy you've made my daughter *and* me," she said beaming. What could I say? I haven't made anyone's daughter happy in years - not even my mother-in-law's. "We'll all have a good holiday now - thanks to you. You're such a lovely man," she continued. Me? Lovely? The more I explained that it was really no big deal, the more thankful they were - blessing me an' all. I'm really not worthy of all this and what I should have said was 'I'm not the Messiah. I'm a very naughty (50-year-old) boy' - for I am.

I expect it'll be back to normal later with people wanting to 'punch my face off' - or just ignoring me. Parity, I was sure, would be restored.

(4.30 p.m.) I received a phone call from Leanne. She couldn't get hold of Kathy, but she told me she was staying at her friend's in South London until next week. It was her travel buddy – the one who suggested the job to her. I told her that it was fine, of course. She thanked me profusely. I really didn't know why as she's not a child anymore. I must admit, though, it was nice to be asked anyway. She is still a Daddy's girl at heart.

(11.30 p.m.) I went to the pub with Clem tonight. He told me that he's getting engaged to a woman 15 years younger than himself who he's just recently met. Over the years, apart from his two broken marriages, I reckon he must have been engaged at least half a dozen times; actually, it was probably nearer a dozen... A few months ago, I would have thought that he was crazy to get involved with someone so much younger than him, but that was a few months ago, and before I started considering getting busy with someone over 25 years my junior. Oh, the hypocrisy would almost be too much to fathom.

Wednesday 20th June 2012
Don't Let Me Be Misunderstood

(**9.30 a.m.**) It's quite amazing how things can all happen at once and then – nothing. I think I've had the dullest, most non-eventful week of my life. Kathy's been quiet; Sabrina's been quiet; work has been quiet and Phil has been quiet. It's been really... quiet. I haven't said anything to Phil yet, but I'm wondering if his pal who suggested he might buy his share of the business, has now gone cold on the whole idea. I'm going to wait until he tells me. I would have at least expected this mysterious buyer to have come down to the shop to have a look around and meet me, as I'm the bloke who makes everything work around here. Oh well, it's up to him. I'm reasonably comfortable in my state of relaxed nothingness at the moment.

(**10.30 a.m.**) As if news of my quiet satisfaction in life had reached the far corners of East London; in came a family to shake in up somewhat. It's the latest in the on-going saga that is my dealings with Poland's favourite family – The Kowalskis. This episode brings them off the street and back into the shop for some more cross-language shenanigans and physical abuse. It's all standard stock and makes a good yarn, but this one concludes with an ironic twist (or twit, as I originally wrote). Double irony.

The weather was miserable – wet and drizzly

(well, it is June in England, after all) when, from my desk in my office, I felt a gust of wind as the front door swung open and the booming, unforgiving voice of Pa Kowalski filled the empty void. I rose to meet him and indeed several of his flock who had followed him in. He was resplendent in his two- foot long, pointy Sideshow Bob shoes, black, MC Hammer pantaloons (I reckon his inside leg measurement must be around the 12-14 inch mark, such was the drop of said trouser), 1980s David Hasselhoff 'Berlin Wall-style leather jacket (without flashing lights unfortunately), a well-manicured Private Walker moustache and 1950s Brylcreemed grandad hair. To complete the look he had a chipped ciggie behind one ear. He was indeed the man about town – if the town was Krakow. I'm guessing even the fashionistas of Warsaw would have recognised his look as something left over from General Jaruzelski's time. He wouldn't have looked out of place holding up a Solidarity banner at the Gdansk shipyard.

Now, alongside him were his usual trusty lieutenants, Kowalski The Monobrow and Kowalski The Quiet (for he was exceptionally quiet). This simply turned out to be a reconnaissance mission to determine how much it would be to collect several items of jewellery, that he and other family members had recently left with us.

"I want to know how much to take out. Not now, maybe next week," he asked in a quiet, polite manner. Before I could even begin to look up his contracts, through the door marched Kowalski The Younger with a tirade of something I could only assume meant a very longwinded 'no'. There was much 'to me, to you', between the two main Kowalski protagonists as voices were raised higher and higher. Fists were soon being pounded on to the counter and I was truly at a loss as to why such a simple question could raise such ire with the lesser, Brylcreemed-bonce of the first in line to the Kowalski crown. Then it all became apparent. It was something I really was not expecting...

The youngster spoke unto me. "This" waving a contract at me is not unlike Neville Chamberlain's piece of paper after his meeting with Herr Hitler and confessed to me. "I take out now. My wife buys for me. If she doesn't see this on my neck... she kill me," before giving the old 'slit throat' mime. He had a very concerned look on his face.

The father, looking rather smug and amused then piped up. "She kill you...? *I* kill you." Oh, how he laughed. Monobrow joined in the jocularity before being jabbed in the guts by his younger, brawnier brother.

An aerated argument ensued amongst them all, which continued in increasing degrees of volume, as I just stood back, safe behind my bulletproof glass, and waited for an end to all the hoo-ing and indeed some might say a fair degree of haa-ing. I think they were actually arguing about who actually had the right to kill the boy. Was it his Kowalski The Younger's wife or his father's prerogative? Of course, there was only one way to find out – Fight!!!

They started what looked like some kind of shin-kicking dance, but without making much contact. I then wished I had another camera or two apart from the CCTV one filming all this. I can only wonder what goes on in their East London mansion. There must be a constant feeling of being on the brink of all-out war in there.

Then, all of a sudden, in came the old woman – not the *really* ancient sea hag who presented herself to me last time, but the original old harridan that I am pretty sure is Pa Kowalski's mother. The squabbling stopped in a trice and the ways parted for the woman in black (for she is always in black), approached the counter in a most regal manner. She glanced at me like I was the ringmaster in this circus of mild comical violence. She then spoke quite softly to her son something in Polish before sitting down on a nearby chair. Her job was done. The old man then told me, "She tells me to stop shouting and fighting." I told him not to worry. After all, I'm getting good value for all of this, aren't I, Diary? If they stopped all their nonsense, then what will I have to write about?

In an air of Entente Cordial, I retrieved the younger son's chain, and along with visible of relief, he put it on straight away.

And in order of importance, they left the building - firstly, the old woman, Pa, The Younger, and finally the runt of the litter, Monobrow. At the door, Pa turned round and said in an almost threatening voice, "We'll be back" (à la Terminator). I, for one, sincerely hope they do.

(1.00 p.m.) Sabrina, as is her want nowadays, popped out to Subway to get our lunch, for which we both individually paid for. When we sat eating it, she began telling me that she thinks that she may finally break up with Daz, as she was sure he was seeing someone else now. That's a lot of 'shes' there. I say 'began telling me', because right on queue a string of punters came in, so our conversation became quite truncated. Besides, I had the gist of it and I was happy for her. I hope she meant it this time. However, the bombshell was yet to detonate. It bought an explosive end to my seven days of nothingness.

(1.40 p.m.) When quiet was restored and the last customer had left the shop, Sabrina quietly asked me, "Are you pleased I'm finishing with Daz?"

"I am because I think you can do better. So much better. But, you know that don't you?" I questioned back.

"I know I can, and I know that *you* think I can," she replied. "Life is just too short," reassured the 22-year-old to the 50-year-old. "It's not just that I think he's with someone else; although that should be reason enough, it's the fact that I have feelings for you and those feelings are getting stronger." I was about to say something, but she cut me off. "Please, let me finish. This is something that has been playing on my mind for a while and I want to explain to you while I feel brave enough to do so. I know you're married, but I know you're not happy all the time," she added.

I think she actually wanted me to acknowledge this fact, but I was too stunned to react. She wants to run away with me, I imagined. What will I do? How would I break it to Kathy and the kids and my friends? What would I do with the shop? Do I even want this? All these thoughts occurred to me within a couple of second of her heartfelt speech.

"I know you won't leave your wife and I wouldn't expect you to, but I would love to spend some time with you... alone, for a couple of days, if at all possible," she continued in a much more conservative and less potentially destructive manner.

"I don't want you to decide anything yet. Think about it. It's a big step for you, but I think you would like to spend time with me too."

Still somewhat stunned, I said, "I would, very much, but as you said this is a big deal and perhaps I should think it over." I was flattered by her interest in me and at the same time amazed with her thoughtfulness and dare I say it... restraint, or am I getting a little too big-headed? Again, she was thinking about others over herself. She didn't want me to ruin my life for what was surely only going to be a fling at best. I am sure she doesn't want to run away with me. Or at least, I think I think that. This is precisely why I have to consider it. Act in haste, repent at leisure. That was another thing my mother would say a lot and I'm going to heed her warning.

Sabrina understood and tenderly cupped the right side of my face as she stood up to serve a customer who had just entered the shop. I sat observing her young, slim body dressed in a fitted white blouse and slim black skirt, thinking to myself what a lucky guy I am... or might be.

(3.50 a.m.) Nothing more had been said since lunch about our 'dirty weekend' as I knew there wouldn't be. There was a slight tension in the air, which was somewhat alleviated by my next visitor. Just when I think I've heard all the weirdest questions and off-the-wall comments there are, along comes someone with something so odd, so banal, that one has to assume he's either pulling one's leg or has to be slightly mentally unhinged.

An Asian gentleman came up to the counter with a very worried expression on his face.

"I have a problem," he explained to me. It's never usually a good way to start a conversation.

"I have some 22 carat gold from Singapore, but I need to sell it to someone who comes from Lithuania. Would it be more or less expensive if I bought it from India?" I was confused where or how to begin my answer. Assuming I must have misheard, I asked him to repeat his question. He did, and it was identical, but he did add, "I'm not from India myself. I'm from Bangladesh." Perhaps he thought this piece of salient information would clear everything up for me.

He confirmed to me that he *already* purchased gold in Singapore and I asked him why he would want to buy more, even if it was cheaper from somewhere else. He muddied the waters further with his response. "The Lithuanians don't mind if it's from Singapore, but if I sell to the Russians, they want it from India." I tried to explain that apart from anything else, gold is gold. Even though people often refer to 22 carat as 'Asian gold', it is invariably from Africa, just like most of the world's gold supply.

I conveyed to him that I think he was doing the right thing, although I hadn't a clue what he was on about.

.   "Oh, I knew you'd know. Thank you for your advice." He clapped a few times with a beaming smile and walked out happily. I had clearly made someone's day. It was a perplexing few minutes that finally wrestled me away from my constant thoughts of what I should do next. Oh, and there they were again.

(5.25 p.m.) As we left the shop, I assured Sabrina that I would give her proposal some serious thought. She understood and told me not to be hasty. I can't believe how mature and relaxed she is being about the whole situation. Certainly more mature than I could ever be if the roles were reversed. I think I would be in a constant panic until I got an answer.

(7.55 p.m.) I had been sitting outside Andy the Shrink's for almost 10 minutes, agonising whether to tell him about today's developments. I know everything that is said in there is strictly confidential, but I still didn't know if I could divulge to him what Sabrina asked me today. In a way, it would be like I'm betraying Sabrina's trust; after all, she is unaware that I see a counsellor. Besides, do I want anyone else to know about it? Then again, he *is* a professional. My concerns still unresolved, I left the car and walked up to his house.

Unusually, a lady answered the door. I had never seen her before. She was probably in her early 30s and quite pretty in a classical way. She explained to me that Andy was still in a session with another client. (I like the fact she said 'client' and not 'patient'). She showed me to another downstairs room to wait for him to finish. I wasn't sure if she was a secretary as I don't think he needed one. Was *this* the wife? Surely, she was too young. The girlfriend? A friend? Another 'client' who thinks she's his housekeeper'? I wondered.

(8.10 p.m.) Ten minutes later than advertised, the lady came to fetch me and led me to that lovely dark wood finished library/office that relaxes me so. Andy seemed a little distracted, and it was a while before we got 'down to business'. The weather and my obsession with the Olympics held precedence over my current state of mind and matters of the heart. Andy looked distracted and I wondered if his disposition was to do with the lady who answered the door. Perhaps his mind was somewhere else, too.

Eventually, we went through all the usual machinations regarding my general well-being and what else I was concerned about. I told him about Phil wanting to sell up and the usual difficulties I and having with Kathy. I was a bit vague and uninteresting and I hadn't yet managed to make him lean forward and take his glasses off.

"And how are things between you and the young lady at work... Sabrina, isn't it?" he asked with his right hand gripping the arm of his glasses, ready to whip them off as he was clearly expecting a more interesting insight into my life.

"Nothing much has happened on that front," I blatantly lied. "I think we've just accepted things are what they are and left it at that," I continued not really knowing what crap I was on about.

"Oh. I suppose that's a good thing. Yes, I'm sure it's a good thing," Andy concluded rather disappointed. He took his hand away from his spectacles, sat back and crossed his legs. "Things are on the up for me though. You've met Stacey?" he rhetorically asked me. "She's my new 'lady friend'." That confirmed my long-standing belief that he was at least separated from his wife... unless he had a particularly open marriage, of course. He's my age and his 'lady friend' was considerably younger than him. Perhaps I should have been more open and mentioned Sabrina after all, with him being a kind of kindred spirit. Then again, he appeared to be single and I assume Stacey was too. I am not at all single and although Sabrina is not currently single, it was hardly the same thing. I wonder if they'll be photos of Stacey in his office at my next appointment? I then thought of Clem and his new 'almost' fiancé. There was surely something in the air. All of these things were going through my mind as Andy continued his potted recent history.

My session continued in a largely unspecific and unsatisfying manner. To be honest, it was a bit of a waste of time.

(9.05 p.m.) As I sat in my car, there were three things that occurred to me. They were:

Andy seemed a lot keener to discuss *his* life than hearing about mine. Is my life (excluding the Sabrina thing) *that* boring?

I clearly wasn't comfortable in sharing a confidence with a professional counsellor. If I couldn't even do that, then surely I feel more guilt about the situation that I realise.

He didn't make up the 10 minutes that his previous 'patient' (I call us patients, even though the Staceys of this world might refer to us as 'clients') had stolen from me. I'm sure he'll still bill me for the full hour, though.

I concluded that any decision I will make regarding Sabrina will not be made in a hurry. She

already knew that and I was under no illusion that I will
have to think long and hard to make it. Long and hard...

Saturday 23th June 2012

One Moment in Time

(9.30 a.m.) I have to say I quite like Saturdays at work. Unlike most people who work in offices and would have a coronary if they were ever expected to work at the weekend, I always have been in retail in one form or another. So I'm used to it. I've always enjoyed a day off in the week and since I have my own business I can have time off whenever I like – or that's the theory. It's just unfortunate that I have a partner who thinks the same and often practices it whenever he pleases.

Sabrina is off next week and I'm still no closer in deciding what to do about her offer. It's a big decision for me. Either she is extremely patient or she's gone off the whole idea because she's been silent on the issue since Wednesday. I will give her an answer when she returns on Monday week.

(12.10 p.m.) I just had an unusual visit. A woman shuffled up to the counter and told me that she bought a ring in this shop in 1951 – many decades before I took over. She still had the receipt for it too and it cost £24 7s 6d. Okay so far, random, but okay. She then said she had lost the ring, and did I know what carat gold it was and what stones were in it. It was baffling on so many levels. I was feeling a little mischievous, so I told her I did. She sounded thrilled, but then I deliberately burst her balloon by telling her that I made an error and our pre-

1952 records went with the old King. She understood perfectly - which is more than I did. On reflection, that was a pretty cruel thing to do.

Note: tell Andy the Shrink that I've developed a nasty streak and see what he makes of that.

(12.30 p.m.) The previous customer was clearly just the starter to my crazy three-course oddball meal today. The main course was as follows:

A nice young lady came in. She walked up to the counter. She smiled. I smiled. She said "hello." I said "hello." She looked around and whispered, "I'm in the wrong place aren't I?"

I said, "I reckon you might be."

She smiled. I smiled. She said 'Goodbye'. I said 'Goodbye'. She left...

It was like a modern version of Brief Encounter, but without the trains, the tea and any other discernible references.

Is that a speck of dust in my eye?

(5.30 p.m.) I had to wait a while for my dessert, but it worth waiting for, as desserts usually are.

Upon leaving the shop, I stumbled (literally stumbled), across on old customer of mine who seemed rather lost and disorientated. We acknowledged each other politely with a half-hearted smile as the rather confused gentleman continued his journey up the road.

A few moments later, after I'd said goodbye to Sabrina, which was all too brief, I was walking to my car when there he was again, standing in front of me, just staring up at the facia of a bookmaker.

"I'm sure it was here," he said, eyes still fixed on the shop name. He then walked a few yards farther along and stopped outside the bank. "Or was it here?" All the time his eyes never made contact with me. He couldn't take them off the shop facias. The troubled fellow shuffled back to stand in front of the bookies. "No, I'm sure it was here." I thought I knew what he was on about, but I couldn't understand his heart-breaking disappointment.

"You're looking for Burger King, aren't you? It's been a bookmakers for over a year," I felt it my duty to tell him,

"I just can't believe it. Why? I don't want to have to go to *them*," he indicated by nodding his head in the direction of McDonald's down the street. It was like I just informed him that his family had been kidnapped by a band of fanatical 'Golden Arches' employees.

"I've come all the way from Canning Town. I walked, you know. It's a mile and a half away." And all for a Whopper? He finally looked down from the bookie's sign and shrugged his shoulders in acceptance of his plight. At last, he seemed to be at some kind of peace.

"I guess I'll have to find another one." He gave me a look of resignation and began to trundle up the road in the same direction I was walking, to continue his search. I waited a while on the corner, just watching this forlorn figure of a man.

The end credits theme of The Incredible Hulk came into my head as I watched him hopelessly make his way towards the next town, which may or may not have a Burger King. He was even wearing what looked like a khaki jacket that Bill Bixby wore in that sorrowful final scene of the 1970s TV show. I didn't have the heart to tell him that he'd be extremely lucky to find one up there either - just in case he got angry. I didn't think I'd like him if he'd got angry.

(7.30 p.m.) Dinner tonight was a double leftover surprise. Roast beef from last night and shepherd's pie from the night before. Let's face it, who doesn't love that particular fusion? I ate alone as Kathy wasn't hungry. She had far too much on her mind apparently. Why that has anything to do with eating dinner, I don't know. Perhaps I'll give her something else to think about soon enough…

When I was finished, I rinsed the plate and put it in the bottom drawer of the dishwasher, and then slid the drawer effortlessly back into the machine. Unfortunately, I felt I had to make public, my ease in succeeding in this operation, that Kathy continually makes such a pig's ear over.

"There. You always shut the first time for Daddy, don't you," I playfully, yet a little teasingly broadcast.

"You've always got to have a go, don't you?" sneered the voice behind me, as Kathy stood in the doorway with fists clenched.

"No, but I never have an issue with it."

"That's because you never bloody use it."

"Only because normally you won't let me near it in case I do it wrong. It's putting a plate into the sodding dishwasher, it's not brain surgery."

"And who washes all your clothes?" Kathy continued, going off at a tangent.

"You do. And you do it so well," I patronisingly told her.

Without picking up on the manner in which I answered her, she went on "Yes I do. I've had 30 odd years practice in washing and ironing your clothes, so you can just dribble gravy or coffee down them." This made little sense and it was like she was talking to one of the kids.

She went on, "Thirty bloody years loading and unloading that bloody dishwasher with your clothes and you just stand there mocking me."

Now, I had a choice here. I could either -

a) Apologise. That wasn't going to happen.

b) Leave the room and suffer an evening of the silent treatment or...

c) Pick up on the fact that she said 'dishwasher' when she meant 'washing machine' and that we hadn't had it for 30 years, thus causing her to flip her lid suffer an evening of the silent treatment.

As I was now a responsible adult and, after all, she was my wife, not an annoying customer… I went for the third option, thus being met with great wrath and anger before a long period of silence from the poor woman.

(8.45 p.m.) Things had just calmed down, and after Kathy had stormed up to bed, I sat down in quiet reverence. Normally, I would feel a bit guilty after we had a row, but this time I didn't. It would serve the old cow right if I ran off with a beautiful young woman who wanted to be with me. I bet Sabrina wouldn't complain if she had to wash my shirts. She'd probably love doing it, too. Hand-washing them with rocks by the river, even. Yeah, I can't imagine her behaving like a screaming banshee after a throwaway, yet hilarious comment about a dishwasher drawer.

(11.30 p.m.) As I got comfortable on the sofa, for that was my bed for the night, I became strangely troubled at my lack of guilt and concern over Kathy. Maybe I had just had enough of her moods and general bitterness. The more I thought about it, the more a weekend away would be just the tonic I needed. Maybe that's what Kathy needs, too. Clearly, she's had enough of me. It's just a shame that I have to wait over a week to tell Sabrina my decision. I know I can do it over the phone, but I think it's something that has to be said in person.

Saturday 30th June 2012

What A Fool Believes

(9.40 a.m.) I sat eating my breakfast, keeping a sideways eye on Phil, who since the ketchup incident a couple of weeks ago, has taken to wearing a napkin around his neck when eating. We were both on the bacon sandwiches this morning and jolly good there were too. After a while, I decided to ask him straight out about the bloke who was supposed to be interested in buying his half of the business. I got the impression from his rather vague reply that the bloke, now revealed as Ralph (pronounced 'Raif', of course), Fingleton-Butler had gone cold on the whole idea. I think that Ralph (really pronounced 'Ralf') was an exaggerating dreamer (pronounced 'lying ponce'). The thing is, I'm beginning to think seriously about selling up myself. Maybe it's time to try something new and this was the moment I should act. Decisions, decisions. I'll keep my powder dry for the time being and wait to see what Phil does next if anything. There's no hurry.

(11.15 a.m.) Just when I thought I have seen it all, the pawnbroking gods smiled upon me once more. This story starts the same way many others have in the past. The usual formula is as follows-

1. Guy brings in a chain.

2. Guy gets told the chain isn't real gold.

3. Guy maintains that it is.

4. Guy is told quite definitely that the chain isn't gold and therefore worthless.

5. Guy mutters/shouts/swears at pawnbroker and leaves the shop.

This guy stumbled at point number 4.

He had already placed a chain along with his driving licence in the drawer under the window. On inspection, almost *all* of the gold coloured plating had rubbed off, thus proving that the piece of jewellery had not just been bought off one of the local Gypsies on the High Street, but had been in his possession for some time. This evidence clearly suggested to me that this guy knew full well that his chain wasn't gold and he'd probably been it hawking around for a while.

We'd been through all the usual toing and froing to the validity of the piece and by this time, there was, in my mind, no ambiguity left on the subject. I told him in no uncertain terms that it was made of steel and was worthless. So, I placed the chain in the drawer in front of him.

"Okay, so if it's not real gold," he asked, "how much will you pay to buy it?" Evidently, I shouldn't have just said the word 'worthless' and instead replaced them with 'absolutely 100 percent totally worthless'. Perhaps that would have got through to his consciousness.

However, I didn't believe I was getting through to him with words alone, so I demonstrated by picking up a 5p piece from a dish of small change I have, and placed it on the tray under the window and pushed it deliberately towards him.

"That, in all honesty, my friend is infinitely more than it's worth," I explained to him. I was somewhat surprised to hear his response.

"Is that all, surely you could do a little but more, man." How much was he after? I was now conducting some kind of auction for this piece of faded metal crap.

I picked up another coin from the dish – a 10p piece and slid it through to my deluded customer, more to entertain me, to be honest as I wanted to engineer an amusing conclusion to this incident. He saw his moment and with lightning-fast dexterity, grabbed both coins and his chain, which had been lying in the drawer. Somewhat triumphantly, he put the 15p in his pocket and with a vitriolic guffaw; he swung his chain around as if to press home the notion that he had got one over me.

"See ya, pal! Thanks for the change," he shouted as he did a little victory jig. However, he left one thing behind.

Just as he'd finished his little dance, I raised my hand and revealed his driving license, which I was holding between two fingers. All I could do was to ruefully smile whilst shaking my head very slowly from side to side at the poor unfortunate fool. His grin soon disappeared. He had been well and truly shown up. What could he do? He could concede defeat, return to the counter and ask for his licence back with a heartfelt apology for starters. But, of course, he didn't, and he chose to about-turn and leave the shop. This was all for 15 lousy pence. Still, I'm sure he can put that towards the £20 it will cost him to get a new driving licence. What a prize mug.

(3.30 p.m.) It was a particularly quiet afternoon and there were two things on my mind. Firstly, there was Sabrina, naturally, as I was looking forward to telling her my answer on Monday, and secondly, the European Championship Final tomorrow night, which I'm also looking forward to. I'm fully expecting Kathy to be in her usual foul mood, so the football will be a welcoming distraction.

(6.45 p.m.) Surprise, surprise, Kathy was indeed in a bit of a mood, although I was expecting worse and it still may get worse. She'd been out shopping with Melissa and Leanne today, which had probably put her in the mood. The four of us had Turkish food tonight. I had a lamb shish kebab. I hadn't had a doner in yonks. In my mind, doner kebabs should only to be eaten on the streets between the hours of 10 p.m. and 3 a.m. by inebriated youngsters and those seeking a return to their youth. Hold on, maybe I should try one again soon then. Just a thought.

It was nice to have my girls around my dining table for a change. They were in a quite chatty mood, unlike their mother. Melissa told me that Chloe will be starting nursery in September, although not the local Montessori she wanted. She did seem a little disappointed that Tom's salary wouldn't stretch to paying their exorbitant fees. Leanne gave me a look that suggested 'spoilt cow'. I smiled. Tom is a bit of a pushover when it comes to his wife and Melissa is quite demanding. It's a marriage made in some people's idea of heaven.

We finished our supper and Melissa stood up and announced that she was leaving. I'm sure she doesn't trust Tom to look after the kids properly. He's a very capable person and fantastic father, but Melissa is always nervous when she has to leave her children with anyone, even her husband. She often plays and twiddles with her hair when something is on her mind, and today was no exception. In fact, her twiddling was so vigorous while she had her tea and baklava, she almost ended up with a French plait.

As soon as she had finished eating and twiddling, Melissa stood up to leave, giving Kathy the cue to gather up the dirty cups, saucers and plates. Without a word, my wife went into the kitchen and started to load the dishwasher. I raised my hand to request silence as I waited to hear the inevitable fight with the dishwasher drawer. I was not to be disappointed.

"Why won't this bloody thing ever work," she shouted, as she once again found herself wrestling with her nemesis. Leanne and I put our hands to our mouths in an attempt to stifle our mirth, but Melissa, who was not party to her mother's dishwasher foibles just looked puzzled and sat down again. Before I could explain what was so funny, the angry voice bellowed from the kitchen again.

"Oh, you lot think it's so funny, don't you? Why don't you just do your own bloody washing up in future? Oh, I forgot you don't ever raise a finger to help me. It's always left to me. Always me."

"But, I don't live here anymore, mum," said a confused Melissa. There was no reply from the kitchen.

Through the martyrdom, peeked through a truth, but this was no time for any generosity of spirit from me. I just can't be bothered with it anymore. Leanne, however, got up from the table and went to help her mother with the loading of the dishwasher. I didn't actually hear Kathy thank her, but there was no more shouting, so I assume she was happy for the help.

The drawer slid shut and the washing cycle began without further incident and Leanne came back into the dining room. I mouthed quietly to her, "Did the drawer close first time for you?"

"Yes, of course," she whispered back.

Melissa, never one to get involved much in family disputes, rose to her feet for the second time and announced she was going home. Kathy came out of the kitchen and kissed her goodbye before disappearing back from whence she came. I didn't know why, as the dishwasher was in 'full action mode' Perhaps she was just standing in front of it giving it 'evils' as the kids say nowadays.

(9.00 p.m.) We sat in the living room watching Midsomer Murders (boy, I am truly old now), but also thinking about the football. It seems amazing to me how sport can make people so happy or so miserable. I'm sure it's the number one important thing in the lives of many. I quite like football, but not that much, hence no mention of it in this diary, but it could never be all-consuming to me. In a way, I felt slightly envious of all the delirium I had fleetingly watched on my television over the last couple of weeks. I looked over at Kathy who sat, legs crossed on the couch, reading some crappy women's magazines, completely detached from everything else that was going on in the room; albeit it was just me and Leanne watching TV. I knew what would make *me* happy. Perhaps just a weekend away with Sabrina wouldn't be enough. Perhaps I would just take a leap of faith and go the whole hog and leave this place. The more I thought about it, the more tempting and enticing it seemed. I really don't think I would be missed very much at all.

Wednesday 4th July 2012

Too Many People

(9.05 a.m.) Nothing had changed much over the last few days at home, and I was still confident that what I was about to tell Sabrina was the right thing to do; for me anyway. I sat her down as soon as we got in the shop.

"Sabrina... in answer to your question – yes, I would very much like to spend some time alone with you," I told her. I was deliberately vague and quite formal as I didn't want to suggest it was a dirty weekend away or anything of that ilk – even though I've alluded to it as that, myself.

"Oh Pete, that's wonderful. I was sure you'd say 'no'," Sabrina replied almost relieved. It was like she was waiting for a marriage proposal. I didn't indicate at all that I had been thinking about a more permanent relationship. She stood up and made sure that no one was about to enter the shop, and gave me a lingering kiss. My heart fluttered. I still had to create a viable story to tell Kathy why I was going away for a few days. Perhaps, I would tell her it's something to do with Phil's yacht pals and they've invited me down to Weymouth for the weekend. Mind you, I will have to shut the shop though... and what would I tell Phil? Clearly, there was much to think about and plan. I was rather excited by the prospect though.

(10.30 a.m.) A distraction to my train of thought came in the guise of a familiar group of people. It's been a couple of weeks, but The Kowalskis are back - and they're back with a bang and in greater numbers!

I heard a small kerfuffle outside and it got louder as it got closer. It became apparent that it centred on East London's first family of disharmony. As they began to permeate my shop (I say that, as it was a gradual progression – in a bit, out a bit, in a bit, etc.), voices and tempers rose, and the cacophony became almost ear-splitting. I leant over my microphone and coughed loudly to get their attention. They stopped immediately. It was nice to feel in control of the heaving mass of humanity, which now numbered a very impressive, but wholly unnecessary nine members and featured new, previously unseen Kowalskis.

Along with the stalwarts, Pa, Monobrow, The Quiet and The Younger (The Fab Four), they brought along '80s' Kowalski; a younger member of the troupe who, along with a highlighted mullet wore a fairly garish 'shades of brown' jumper with a huge leather and suede eagle design on it, grey stonewash jeans, and what I'm sure were Diadora, yes, Diadora trainers. 'Surprised' Kowalski, who like Monobrow Kowalski, had a singular eyebrow, but it went up in the middle to give its donor a constantly concerned or startled air, (think Michael LeVell – Coronation Street's Kevin Webster). Next on the production line was 'Mini Pa', a smaller, more compact, travel-sized version of the Kowalski patriarch. Then we had The Dark Lord of The Kowalskis – 'Darth' Kowalski; who wore a full-length Matrix-style black leather coat, black mock-snakeskin boots, a black cap, black sunglasses and a black hair/eyebrow combination to finish off the look. And to complete today's Kowalski collection was 'Coco The Clown' Kowalski; a female clan member in her mid-30s, who possessed the most garish blue and purple makeup and deep red lipstick (that looked like it was applied with a grouting pump). It was a sight rarely seen outside the Big Top of Billy Smart's circus. If only she had a big red nose instead of the mere pink Karl Malden special she already possessed. Her three-foot long faded copper earrings completed an unusual, and dare I say, a quite breath-taking image of womanhood.

So, the nine of them now were now quiet and seemingly unsure of what do with the cessation of hostilities. Through the throng (say that after a few Jägerbombs), bowled Pa Kowalski, for he knew how to assert his authority.

"All my contracts are lost," he told me in a quiet, sheepish manner.

"All *yours* or all *Kowalski* contracts," I asked him with trepidation, as I would imagine numbers reaching into the 40s were missing if he meant *all* contracts.

"No, just mine. He (pointing at Monobrow), lost them all." It then kicked off again. Monobrow beat his clenched fist on the counter and stamped his metre long pointy leopard print shoes on the wooden floor. Pa thrust out his chest in a show of 'head of the pride authority' and prodded his opponent first in the chest and then in the face. All the Kowalskis started stamping and squawking, except the frightening spectre of Darth Kowalski, who simply turned his head slightly to observe the pandemonium all around him. It seemed that everyone else joined in, just for the sake of it. I really thought it was going to kick off properly, so I did the only thing I could and ran off to get my phone in order to film the ensuing chaos. Sabrina was looking on in sheer wonderment. Just then, Monobrow was unceremoniously ushered out of the building by the remaining males with Darth bringing up the rear. This left old Pa and Coco, who didn't really get involved. I guess she didn't want to smudge her makeup any further than it was already strewn across her 'Streets of San Francisco' mooey.

I looked for all Pa Kowalski's contracts up on the computer and luckily there were only three in his name. I was most relieved at this as I started to print out the replacement affidavit forms for him to take to a solicitor. He knew the procedure and it was no surprise to him what he had to do next. He gave them to Coco for safekeeping, and she put them in her enormous oversize patchwork trousers – no, just kidding. She simply folded them up very small and stuffed them down her bra. They left without another word being spoken in anger or otherwise.

With all these characters, the Kowalskis kind of remind me of a furious, dysfunctional Eastern European Wombles. They all have different, but varying angered personalities. Great Uncle Poland overseeing the daily chaotic episodes that flare up in every waking hour.

Underground, overground, *Kowalskiing* free. The

Kowalskis of Silvertown; common are we. Nah, that doesn't quite work.

(4.00 p.m.) Sabrina popped out to buy some biscuits to have with our coffee. Like a good girl, she came back with a packet of Maryland cookies – not Sainsbury's own brand, but proper ones, *and* a packet of Fox's Viennese. She knows her biscuits that one, or at least she knows what I like. We sat chomping away at them and discussing where we might go for our weekend. The Lake District looked favourite, although I wouldn't care if it was a Premier Inn in Watford. I did tell her, however, that I couldn't yet give her a date as I still had to create a reason for disappearing for a few days. She understood perfectly. I think the very realisation that we were actually going to do this thing was enough for us all to be getting on with. I could have finished all the biscuits as I hadn't had any lunch today, but as it was only tea-time and I'd be eating dinner by 7, I thought better of it.

(7.30 p.m.) I wasn't eating by 7; in fact, what had happened had left me without an appetite at all. When I got home, I was confronted at the front door by Leanne, who directed me to the living room where Kathy was already seated. I sat down next to her as she nervously started to say something that neither of us expected to come from the lips of our youngest child.

"You know that I've been going out a lot and staying over in South London a lot recently," she began. We both nodded as she continued. "The reason for this isn't because I didn't want to be at home... well, it was partly as you've been on at each other a lot all the time lately." I looked at Kathy, not having a clue what Leanne was on about. "That's beside the point though. The fact is that I've done something I'm not too proud of and I felt guilty and too embarrassed to tell you, so I thought it best to stay away whenever I could."

"What is it, Leanne? You're worrying us," Kathy sympathetically asked her.

Leanne clearly in great anguish drew a deep breath and said. "I got myself pregnant... or at least I thought I did."

Kathy and I were stunned into silence. "This was when you were in Australia?" I concluded, thus proving my original suspicions correct, or so I imagined.

"No, Dad, it was after. On the night of my birthday," Leanne went on. Before we could ask anything else she added. "I thought I was pregnant up until yesterday."

"What do you mean, Leanne?" Kathy asked rather less sympathetically.

"I missed my period last month and I don't know why... well, I assumed it was because... you know," Leanne tried to explain. "The thing is I was too scared to take a pregnancy test because I was sure I was. I'm not, though."

I didn't know whether to be relieved or angry or what. It was a bolt out of the blue.

I asked Leanne. "Were you taken advantage of?"

afraid to hear the answer.

"No, Dad, I knew what I was doing. I had a bit to drink, but I was quite aware what was going on," she answered. I suppose I should be grateful for that.

"So, who was the boy?" I blurted out.

"Don't ask her that. She won't want you to know," Kathy answered for Leanne.

"It's Okay Mum, I want to get it out in the open. No more secrets," she paused, took another deep breath and said "You remember Darren from school? I think he was seeing your girl from work, Dad," she said calmly.

My heart sank. This was a double blow. So many things entered my mind as the rage built up. How should I react to this? My daughter had sex with that piece of crap; thank goodness she wasn't pregnant though. I didn't feel angry with her, but hugely disappointed. Should I mention it to Sabrina? That would make her feel really stupid as she's still with the toe rag. What would it do to her? I quickly realised, however, that my concerns over Sabrina were very much secondary to my daughter's right now. Whatever Leanne did, she was brave enough to tell us.

Kathy stood up and hugged her, saying. "You stupid girl. You stupid girl," in a wavering voice as she tried in vain to fight back the tears. I then hugged her too and told her I was glad she told us. Well, what more could I say right now? The thing that *did* cross my mind was that if I did have 'extra-marital' relations with Sabrina, then surely I would be no better than Daz.

Then rather unexpectedly, Kathy turned to me and hugged me. "I've been quite awful to you recently, haven't I?" she asked, her face still wet with tears. This was another bolt out of the blue. I could have agreed, but in a moment of clarity, I realised that it wasn't just her. I was fully aware that changes were happening to her and it was never going to be easy. I really hadn't done enough to help her through it. Instead, I had just been thinking about myself and what *I* wanted and that was quite unacceptable. I held her in my arms and conveyed my thoughts to her in the best way I could.

"I need to go away for a few days, Pete. I need to recharge," Kathy announced. I've been thinking about it for a while and I arranged it a couple of days ago. I don't know why, but because I didn't want what I was feeling to defeat me, I'd put it off time and time again, and that's made me angrier. I realise that there's not much I can do about the physics my situation, but I don't want to be on edge the whole time and I don't want *you* to feel like you don't want to be here because you have, haven't you?" I nodded. The irony wasn't lost on me. Had I'd been aware of her impending trip a few hours earlier, I could have arranged mine and Sabrina's weekend away with impunity. However, that moment had passed. I told Kathy that it was an excellent idea. Leanne, who was sat down on the armchair, began to cry too, before standing up and hugging us both.

I felt that this was a pivotal moment in our marriage. I comprehended in that short time that I didn't want to go anywhere anymore. I had my family and I love them – all of them.

Those 10 minutes or so of my life had changed everything. All of a sudden, Sabrina was the last thing on my mind even though I had to address both my feelings for her, the whole 'going away' thing and now I had to decide whether to tell her about Daz. These matters will be addressed soon; but for now, my thoughts are with Leanne and Kathy and Leanne and Kathy alone.

(10.45 p.m.) Kathy made a pasta bake for supper, which was lovely and for the last few hours, all three of us had been talking about the past and indeed the future. Kathy showed us the brochure of the retreat she picked. She's going next Monday for a week. It'll do her the power of good, I'm sure. Wednesday 4th July is a watershed moment in my family's life. There will be tough times ahead, but we'll face them as a couple and as a family.

Monday 9th July 2012

You Better You Bet

(9.30 a.m.) I called Phil on Saturday night to ask if he would go in this morning for me, as I wanted to take Kathy to the train station. Luckily, he wasn't away, so it was no problem. My wife wisely elected to take the train down to the retreat in Bournemouth. It's never a good idea to begin a stress-free, relaxing week away sitting in the Monday morning rush-hour traffic with the inevitable hold-ups our wonderful motorway system provide.

As I carried her case (rather a small one for Kathy, it has to be said), she reiterated to me what she conveyed at the weekend.

"I can't promise you that I will come back a changed woman and I don't expect you to be a changed man, but I hope we can be a little 'different' from what we are now," Kathy told me. "I just really need to escape my everyday life at the moment; and besides, I wouldn't want you to change... too much. If you did, I'd wonder if you were seeing someone else," she jokingly added. I stopped in my tracks and offered her an almost chaste look.

"You just take it easy and relax down there," I said changing the subject subtly, or as subtly as is possible for me. After the 'you know where the washing powder tablets are' and the 'you know the dustmen come on a Tuesday now?' routine, I kissed Kathy goodbye by the

251

automatic ticket machine. She purchased her ticket and walked through the barrier towards the platform, but she turned around to give me an almost 'worried' smile as if she was thinking to herself 'I bet he'll forget to put the bins out tonight'. I wouldn't bet against that myself.

(11.20 a.m.) I parked up quite near to the shop and I just sat for a few moments thinking about how I was going to break the news to Sabrina. I realise that I do a hell of a lot of thinking in my car.

(11.25 a.m.) I walked into the shop and Phil was serving. I went straight to the kitchen to make myself a coffee. Sabrina followed me in and took over my task for me. I thanked her, and let her do it without protest and made my way to my desk. A few moments later the coffee mug appeared from over my shoulder and landed with a bare female arm attached to it.

"You okay, Pete?" Sabrina asked with a concerned accent.

"Yes, okay thanks. Kathy went away for a week this morning. She's been under a lot of stress recently so she's having a few days away from home," I told her candidly.

"So, you're all alone then?" responded Sabrina teasingly.

"Not quite. I still have Leanne at home with me," I answered honestly, without a hint of the suggestiveness that Sabrina's last comment possessed.

"Is everything alright?" she asked, clearly picking up on my downbeat demeanour. I didn't want to reveal my U-turn to her just yet.

"Yes. I'm just a bit tired as I didn't sleep that well last night." Sabrina sat down at Phil's desk. I don't think for a moment she believed me that nothing was wrong, and I really wanted to explain myself there and then, but I had to hold fire.

(12.15 p.m.) Phil had left and it seemed as his departure was the trigger for today's brush with lunacy. A very excited, middle-aged man approached the counter with the news that today was his lucky day. It was so lucky, in fact, that he had to pawn his ex-wife's wedding ring to make it lucky. I would say he was pretty lucky to have the ring, (perhaps he cut it off her still warm hand after ending her life and ending their marriage in one fell swoop – or am I getting ahead of myself here?). Anyway, before I did the paperwork for his loan, the fellow pulled out a small bundle of approximately a dozen betting slips from an inside pocket and joyously told me in no uncertain terms, "One of these has to win."

Far from being large wagers, all this guy's bets were small; just £1 or £2 per slip, ensuring that even if he did win he probably wouldn't even break even, let alone be up on the deal. He was vehemently telling me that apart from the Grand National, and The Derby, he only gambled on one other day of the year, and this was it. "It's my mother's birthday and I like to remember her by having a few bets on the nags. I mean, I used to have a little bit of a problem with gambling, but it's all under control now," he protested. I have no idea why he felt like he had to confess this to me, but this was probably the most 'normal' thing he said to me. Apart from anything else, by purely by admitting that he *used* to have a problem, it suggested to me that he probably *still* had a huge problem. Years of working with and listening to the general public have left me quite cynical.

I completed the contract for him, gave him his money, and it was then that the conversation took the rather odd turn. From another inside pocket, he produced a scratch card – a winning scratch card mind – he had won £5.

"Will you buy this off me for £5?" he asked.

"No thanks. Why don't you just take it back to where you bought it and claim your prize?"

"No! I'm not going back there," he answered, flustered, Before I could even ask him why, he followed up with an even more bizarre request, "If I gave you £10 will you go up the road to the betting shop, and put some more bets on for me?" I assumed that he may have disgraced himself in some way in the bookmakers and had been barred.

"Why, what have you done?" I cautiously probed.

"Nothing. I promised myself a long time ago that I wouldn't go into a bookies again." I was flummoxed as it was in direct contradiction to what he'd said previously.

Even though I knew there would be an equally nonsensical and peculiar come back to my next question, I asked it anyway.

"But you've already been in one today. Why don't you just go back?"

The increasingly odd bloke stood back, straightened up, and in a triumphant and almost bombastic manner extolled to me, "I have failed myself once today, and I can assure you I am not proud of that, but I will *not* let myself down again."

I reckoned that this was some kind of mantra he learned at Gamblers Anonymous. Of course, I was sorely tempted to explain to him that even though he wasn't physically entering the bookmakers and placing the bet himself, it was still his money and he was still gambling, but I think this revelation may have sent him over the edge again.

I politely explained that I couldn't leave the shop, and he left in the same happy manner in which he entered, but my curiosity had gotten the better of me. I wondered if he was going to return to the scene of the crime. I told Sabrina I was just going to pop out, and I made my way up to Ladbroke's where the bloke's betting slips were from. I entered the shop and who did I see arguing with an old man over a polystyrene cup of coffee? It was my now, not so happy-go-lucky, ex-gambling pawn customer, who was then in a heated debate with a dishevelled old bag lady, seemingly over the ownership of the hot beverage. He didn't notice me, and I slipped back out of the shop and returned to work.

Sometimes you follow trouble and sometimes trouble follows you, but it's usually best to leave trouble well alone, especially if there's the prospect of being drenched by a cup of cheap, lukewarm coffee.

(2.15 p.m.) I approached Sabrina who was stuffing envelopes with overdue notices. I wasn't going to wait any longer.

"Sabrina. It's about our... well, it's about... you know... us going away," I stuttered. I wasn't going to sugar-coat it, but I wasn't quite brave enough to speak with any sort of conviction.

"You've changed your mind, haven't you?" she guessed without a hint from me...

"It's not that I didn't want to, it's just that situations have changed, and I am very concerned what might happen if it didn't just remain a one-off," I explained. Although that wasn't the whole truth, it wasn't exactly a lie either.

"I know Pete. To be honest, I hadn't really given much thought to what might happen afterwards. It was a nice idea, and I know it would have been a lot of fun," Sabrina replied with a wisdom and humility beyond her years. I didn't expect her to fall to the ground in front of me, hands clenched together, bawling and wailing, "Whyyyy?," but I did expect a little less understanding. It's just what I'm used to, I suppose.

This wasn't the end of it, though. I still had the 'duty' to tell her about Daz. Even though their relationship was, by no means, a strong one; and I'm sure she knew he wasn't at all right for her, I just couldn't stand back and let her carry on with him knowing what I know. I wasn't about to tell her today. Even though she took my rejection well, I didn't feel it right to lay this on her now. I will let her know and soon. I just have to find the right moment.

(6.15 p.m.) Kathy called me on the house phone, not long after I got in. It was like she sensed that I'd just got home. She told me that she'd settled in nicely and was already feeling somewhat rested. I wished her a good evening and told her to make the most of her break. The funny thing was, she didn't mention bins, washing, cleaning or even the dishwasher, which is a good sign. I even placed the phone back in its charger without being reminded.

Leanne was out again – behaving herself, I hoped; so I invited Clem round for a bite to eat. I didn't cook, of course, but my favourite Chinese up the road, on the corner did and were all too happy to deliver their delights right to my doorstep. The alleged visit from the health inspectors hadn't resulted in its closure, so as long as the food tasted good, which it certainly did, and I didn't get ill from it, which I normally don't, then that's fine by me.

It must be a day of broken relationships between old men and young women today because the latest in a very long line of engagements for Clem had just ended. It was the girl, Janey, who ended it. She felt that she was not ready for commitment. It seemed she knew Clem well and knew what was bound to happen, better than he thought. He was not at all heartbroken or crestfallen though, such is his devil-may-care attitude to women and relationships. I was very tempted to tell him my news, but I thought it best to keep it to myself. It's best to let sleeping dogs lie, and all that.

(8.30 p.m.) We knocked back a few beers and watched a Panorama programme about... The Olympics. It's funny, but I'd really not given it much thought over the last couple of weeks. Clem was trying to convince me to view it as a sporting spectacle and not as the expected financial disaster I knew it would be. Perhaps, I was looking at it through my increasingly bleary eyes, but it was just about possible that I'm wrong and the majority of people are right - unlikely, but possible.

I have to say, I kind of missed Kathy, today. Over our many years of marriage, we had not spent too many nights apart and although I was enjoying my evening with my old buddy, but there was a figure missing from my living room.

(11.20 p.m.) We'd had a good night and after Clem had gone, I chucked out all the empty foil containers in the kitchen bin and stacked all the half full containers (or is it half empty? I must consult Andy the Shrink), in the fridge ready for either breakfast/lunch/dinner tomorrow. I'd brushed my teeth and got into bed. I heard the front door open and close. It was Leanne. She ran upstairs and put her head around the door to wish me 'goodnight'. I couldn't have rested easy knowing she was still out.

It was odd to be in our bed alone. It wasn't necessarily odd to sleep alone as I had done my time sleeping on the couch downstairs. The night was temperate and the duvet was crisp and cool. I laid my head down very content and relaxed until... "Shit! The bins!" My calm and relaxed state was rudely interrupted by the realisation that I was irresponsible idiot after all. I sprung up, put on my dressing gown, and hurriedly rushed downstairs. I don't know why I was in such a hurry as the dustmen (I know they're not called that anymore), wouldn't be down my road for another eight hours at least, but I could just imagine Kathy coming back all relaxed, walking up the garden path, unable to resist peeking into the wheelie bin and seeing a week's worth of Chinese and Indian foil food containers and microwave meal boxes. Put it this way, I would be very surprised if she'd just laugh it off.

(11.30 p.m.) Job done. I slipped back under the duvet with heavy eyes. It had been a busy few days, one way or another. I still had one more task to address regarding Sabrina, and I don't know how or when to broach it, but everything else right now was just mighty fine.

Saturday 14th July 2012

Here Comes The Rain Again

(8.00 a.m.) I have leapt into the 1980s with my musical tastes today. My 1970s playlist has served me well, or badly depending on one's standpoint. I knew it was time to change when *Come Up and See Me (Make me Smile)* by Steve Harley and Cockney Rebel came round for the third time in as many journeys. I began with my 80s MP3 collection this morning, and as if to welcome me to a new decade, the entire North Circular must have decided to present red lights to me at every single opportunity. This provided other motorists or pedestrians with the chance to catch me singing along to such horrors as *It Feels Like I'm in Love* by Kelly Marie and *Japanese Boy* by Aneka. Fortunately, those two songs haven't raised their 'One hit wonder-ful' heads yet. Just missing out on *My Camera Never Lies* by Bucks Fizz, the song that I was observed butchering was *Geno* by Dexy's Midnight Runners.

As I glanced over to my left, whilst paused at a pedestrian crossing in Barking, I saw a very old man in a very old car – I think it was a Morris Ital. He sat with both hands on the steering wheel, wearing what I initially thought was string back driving gloves, but he might have just been extremely wrinkly. His glazed, watery eyes were fixed firmly on me like I was the epitome of the kind of people he despaired at. His despondent stare suggested to me, 'I fought in the war for *this*?' Or maybe his cataracts were playing him up.

Anyway, it didn't bother me, and as the lights changed, I winked at him and left him for dust.

(9.20 a.m.) I've been back on the old bacon rolls this week. Sabrina offered to go out and get them this morning, so of course, I couldn't stand in her way. I have been living on takeaways and readymade meals... and bacon rolls since Kathy's been away. It's not like I can't cook or even dislike cooking, it's more of the fact that I like takeaways and that I'm a lazy bastard. I don't know why I'm writing that in my diary. It's not like I'm going to read it back and be shocked by it.

As we sat opposite each other devouring our breakfast, I saw *it* and almost choked on my roll. On the fourth finger of Sabrina's left hand was what looked suspiciously like an engagement ring.

"An engagement ring?" I spluttered.

"Daz asked me to marry him last night and I said yes," she replied in a rather sombre way.

I couldn't give her my congratulations and instead offered a simple 'Why?'

"Well, he asked me and... I accepted. That is about it really," she timidly responded. It was like the old, scared 'wouldn't say boo to a goose' Sabrina was back. I instantly regretted not being brave enough to tell her my information. I'd had days to inform her what Daz had been up to, but I just wanted to keep the week ticking along without incident. I had been very selfish. I now knew that I had to tell her and tell her quickly. If she still wanted to marry him, well that was her decision. She would go down in my estimation, but I can't run her life for her. I just hope she'll change her mind.

(9.25 a.m.) As luck would have it before I had the chance to reveal Daz's true side to Sabrina, in came the customers. First up today was someone for whom the simplest instruction seemed like a challenge of epic proportions. She presented me with a couple of chains and a ring, and an amount to borrow was quickly agreed upon. The problem started with me saying. "Sign on all three pages in the box" – I showed her exactly where to sign as I often do. So far, there is nothing at all unusual about this episode. However, I have longed for the day when someone is honest enough to admit, "Sorry, I'm an idiot and I don't know what the hell I'm doing." Well, that day arrived and the admission was almost voiced verbatim.

So many times I have informed a customer where he/she has to sign and they have just failed to grasp what I said. I tell them to sign, show them where to sign by putting a cross in a box next to where it says 'signature', and sometimes even tap the pen loudly where I need them to make their mark. They might sign over my signature, on only one copy or just simply look at the paper with wide-eyed bewilderment awaiting further instruction. Have I described all this before, or am I experiencing déjà vu?

The excuses they give are usually on the lines of –

"Oh, I've left my glasses at home."

"I'm all over the place today."

"I thought I only had to sign the top page"

Or the blatant lie, "You told me only to sign one page."

So, when this woman admitted to me that she was an idiot, I immediately felt vindicated. At last, some real honesty. However, that feeling didn't last long, as she looked rather forlorn, and I felt a surge of guilt.

"Oh, don't worry about it," I told her, "It's an easy mistake to make." Easy mistake? Easy mistake? Why did I say that? It should be almost impossible to make that mistake following all that coaching. I had disappointed myself and now I might have to wait another 20 years for a similar admission of fatuity.

(9.35 a.m.) This is a shortie (or is it shorty?). It was raining outside as it had been since I arrived. A bloke had not been in before and was confused by the process of pawning - what ID was, what a pen was and what way up its supposed to write, etc.

I gave this bloke all the usual clues where to sign (as listed above), but to no avail. I tried again and luckily a drop of what I assumed (and hoped), was rainwater dripped from his nose, landing exactly where he needed to sign. Divine intervention once more perhaps?

"Just sign where your nose dripped," I said exasperated and went to get his money. I came back to see that he'd signed halfway up the contract under his address. I hadn't noticed the other drip. Oh, how we laughed when I told him that he signed in the wrong place. Well, he did anyway.

(10.20 a.m.) Finally, the tide of punters had gone out, and it was just Sabrina and me. I locked the front door and lowered the shutters.

"What's going on Pete?" Sabrina enquired.

"I wanted to talk to you about something and I don't want us to be disturbed," I told her.

"You've never done this before."

"This is important and once I start I don't want any interruptions," I explained. She looked rather nervous as she sat down opposite me in our 'breakfast' positions.

"Is this about us?" Sabrina questioned.

"Not exactly," I responded. "It's more about you." Her face told me that I'd only muddied the waters somewhat. "A few weeks ago my daughter Leanne went out for her birthday with friends." Sabrina listened in silence. "Anyway, the long and short of it was, she met Darren... er, Daz that night, too. They'd been to school together." This proved to be more difficult than I thought. "Last Sunday she admitted to me and her mum that she'd slept with Daz and she thought she was pregnant, and it was him. He told her he was single," I explained. Sabrina sank back into her chair.

"You've known this since Sunday? Why didn't you tell me before now?" she asked me with a slight tinge of hostility in her voice that I'd never heard before.

"I only told you on Monday about me changing my mind about us and... well, I didn't want to tell you even more bad news. I never expected you to get engaged to him. I was going to tell you soon, but then you came in with a ring on your finger."

"I don't know what to think. Is she sure it was *my* Daz?" I nodded forlornly.

"What are you going to do?" I asked.

"Well, he can have his fucking ring back for starters," she angrily replied as took off his ring and slammed in on the desk. I'd never heard her utter a 'bloody' before and now a 'fucking'?

"I'm so sorry to have had to tell you that, Sabrina. I know it was hard to take in."

"No, I'm glad you did. I've been a real idiot. It's not like I didn't know his reputation," she admitted. "You know I've always had feelings of low esteem. I didn't think I could do better, that's the thing. Then when you showed interest in me and we became friends... we *are* friends, aren't we?" she interrupted herself.

I nodded vigorously and said, "Of course, we are."

"I felt attractive and like I was something."

"You *are* something, Sabrina. You are a wonderful, caring and pretty young lady," I reassured her and I grabbed her hand. I stood up, still holding her and she rose with me. "What you need is self-confidence. I have to be honest; I didn't spare much thought for you until a couple of months ago, which I deeply regret now. You changed your image slightly, didn't you? A little makeup and different clothes?" Sabrina nodded. "Now, that might make me a bit shallow, but it showed me a different 'you'. I became interested in you and your thoughts on various matters. I found out all about your life, and your work in the hospice and I became genuinely attracted to you, but not just your looks. I do have feelings for you... genuine feelings, but our circumstances dictate our actions, unfortunately. I like to think you've made me think differently, too. I was trudging along, moaning about stuff that I could do nothing about and you gave me something else to think about. I will never forget our visit to the hospice. Not just because what I saw there, but what I saw in you. You made me want to be a better person." Sabrina began crying and pulled me towards her and hugged me.

With her head still on my shoulder, she said. "I'm so glad I met you Pete, and I know we would have had good times together, but you are so right about everything."

"Oh, I don't know about that, and anyway, why are you so bloody understanding?" She didn't answer, but I felt her laugh silently as she held me tighter.

"We have to re-open, sweetheart," I said, even though I didn't want our cuddle to end. She stood back and wiped her eyes. "Look, I'm always here for you to talk to about anything you like. You know that, don't you?" I said.

"I know and thank you," she replied. She walked into the kitchen. "Coffee?" she asked, as she filled the kettle."

"Yeah, go on." As if I was going to say no. I unlocked the door and raised the shutters expecting to see hordes of people waiting impatiently to get into the shop. There was no one waiting, but the rain had stopped and the sun made a welcome appearance.

(5.20 p.m.) The rest of the day went quite quickly and we were very busy in patches, but no more nutters or the hard of thinking. It was time to go home. At the front door, I noticed that Sabrina had put her ring back on and she saw that I noticed it. "I want to take it off in a dramatic fashion and throw it in the bastard's face," she exclaimed.

"Good girl," I said. "If you want to talk, I'm around. Kathy's not back until Monday, so I shouldn't have any interruptions if you want to chat."

"She kissed me on the cheek as the shutters rose (and that isn't a euphemism). I watched as she strode off down the road. I do hope she'll be okay.

(7.00 p.m.) I entered my empty house and made my way to the drawer in the kitchen that housed all my takeaway menus. I cast a disinterested eye over them and I thought how glad I'd be when Kathy gets back and cooks for me again. At least they'll be no leftovers to heat up; not for the first night anyway. Being on one's own certainly has its benefits, but I do miss the old girl.

Monday 16th July 2012

Cigarettes & Alcohol

(9.00 a.m.) First things first - I asked Sabrina how everything went when she confronted Daz last night. Before she opened her mouth, I noticed that her wedding finger was missing the ring, so that was a good sign.

"I went over to his house as he was home from 'work' early. I stood just inside his front door, and just came out with it, accusing him of sleeping with your daughter," she said in a no-nonsense fashion. "He thought about lying, but I just stared him put and he soon floundered. He knew that I knew and just confessed there and then. It was fairly simple really, and I just walked out."

"Well done you," I beamed. "And the ring... Did you throw it in his face as promised?

"No. I calmly placed it down on the table by the door, smiled and walked away. I had considered throwing it at him, believe me, but there was something quite satisfying in the way I did it. Anyway, he didn't or couldn't say anything, and that was that."

I was very happy for her, although she did seem a little, if not heartbroken, then certainly disappointed. Well, who wouldn't be in her position?

(9.45 a.m.) I had to go to the bank this morning to get some change. I stood in the queue for the business till which can be quite a laborious and dull occupation, but today, it certainly gave me cause to smile.

I had just got to the front of the queue when I felt a tap on my shoulder.

"Hello, mate. You alright?" It was a very old punter of mine called Gillian, who let's say was no stranger to the grape or hop. I politely replied in the affirmative and asked how she was and how her weekend went. "Oh, you know. Pretty good... I think," she told me in her distinctive loud and expansive way. "To be honest, I had so much to drink that I really don't know what I did or who I did it with.

I remembered that on her last visit to my shop, she told me she was going to Ibiza for a week as she'd never last a fortnight.

"I thought you were going on holiday today, Gillian," I asked the middle-aged peroxide mirth maker. She stopped in her tracks as I stepped forward to be served.

"Oh my God!!" she screamed. "Today?" She stood for a few more seconds in disbelief before she ran out the bank as far as her four-inch heels could carry her.

I approached the teller and she looked at me in disbelief, I just shrugged my shoulders. Within 30 seconds, Gillian was back. She sashayed back down the line to resume her place in the queue and as I caught her eye, she happily reported. "No, silly. It's next week. What am I like?" A few people in the queue started laughing. She took a deep, relieved breath as the next cashier became available, and she walked up to the counter before she stopped in her tracks. "Oh, I forgot what I came in for," she cheerfully informed the whole bank. Cue more laughter from the line. "Ah yes. I have to pay a bill," she gleefully told her audience.

A couple of minutes later, I finished my business and so had she. We left the bank together and parted company when we reached my shop only about 100 yards down the road.

"You know, love, sometimes I really don't know what I'm doing, or where I am," she admitted.

Bearing in mind that she wasn't (visibly) drunk at this point, I found it rather difficult to offer her any succour, except to say, "Just make sure you get to the airport on time, next week." She stared at me and the realisation hit her.

"Of course, travel money!! While I'm up here I should get some, I suppose. Tata love," she shouted as I watched her totter back up the road to the bank.

"Goodbye, Gill!! I shouted after her and she raised her hand to acknowledge me." I half expected her to come into to borrow some money on her jewellery as no doubt she'd left her money at home... which was exactly what happened not 10 minutes after.

(10.40 a.m.) Not long after Gillian left, my second slightly batty customer of the day made his way in. I have had everything from marriage proposals to death threats and most things in between during my tenure here, but this was one of the most unusual incidents and involved a middle-aged Liverpudlian man by the name of Mr Buckie, who was no stranger to an alcoholic beverage or five. He came in demanding the return of an article that was about a year overdue. It was no longer here.

After trying and failing to take me out with an ill-aimed right cross (yes with the thick bulletproof glass between us), he left me with this wonderfully crafted threat. "I'm going to take you outside, take all your clothes off and make you cry." I still can't work out what he was he was trying to say because I'm sure he didn't fancy me. I hate to think how he was going to make me cry though.

He stumbled out and sat on the ground against the shop window. I left him there for a while before popping outside to see what he was up to. He was up to nothing apart from sleeping in a puddle of his own making. I couldn't be sure if it was urine or the cider he had been drinking, and I really didn't want to get close enough to confirm its constitution. As I stood over him, and clearly not recognising me, he coughed/slurred, "Aright mate, I'm goin'... I'm goin'." He staggered to his feet and made his way down the road, violently veering from side to side. He left me his calling card on the ground - an empty can of Strongbow peeking sheepishly from its brown paper bag dwelling, and a couple of dog ends. I went inside to get a bucket of water, which I used to wash away the alcohol/urine solution.

(**1.10 p.m.**) Luncheon was delayed by my third oddity of

the day. A regular Monday afternoon punter came in to pawn her boxing glove pendant. We call her Mrs Craggy – for that is what she looks like, although her name is actually Mrs Sharp (which thinking about it, she is too - Sharp of tongue, not sharp of mind).

"How are you, Peter?"

Before I was even able to reply, she was off, telling me about her latest ills; both physical and family centred. She's had a chest infection for over 18 months and boy, do I know about it. So do her doctors, but 'they don't know what the bloody hell they're doing' according to her. Still, as she told me, it's nothing to do with her smoking two packets of ciggies a day.

I know that Mrs Craggy at least once a week frequents the 'amusement arcade/gambling pit' just two doors away from me. The big news last year was that they started opening 24 hours a day, and they'll provide their patrons with free coffee and biscuits – although I doubt very much if the coffee is filtered, and the biscuits are anywhere near those German Bahlsen Choco Leibniz biscuits - the ones that are more chocolate than a biscuit. (Note to self: The next time Sabrina is out on the biscuit run – Bahlsen!)

Anyway, Mrs Craggy will spend most of Monday afternoon/evening gambling away her pension on her favourite machine, and woe betides anyone who dares to have a go on it while she's outside, having a fag and coughing her lungs up. She often complains that she machine is fixed and today was no exception. I tried to advise her either to stop or go elsewhere, but she wouldn't have any of it.

"It's all I've got, Peter," she told me reticently. Anyway, this was not the kernel of the story.

Whilst signing her contract, she brazenly asked me. "Peter, do you need any Viagra, because, I've got loads." I looked at her in surprise and replied in the negative, but she continued, "or do you know anyone who would want them?" I didn't have my list at hand, so I once again declined. Unperturbed, she gave me the contracts back and proceeded to take a handful of double-packed pills out of her handbag. "One of my sons works for a pharmacy," she continued. I wondered if he perhaps worked part-time with very strange and short night-time hours at the chemist over the road because they recently had someone 'working' for them for just one night; and he had a hell of a lot of perks - maybe including a draw full these diamond-shaped, blue pills. I'm just surmising, of course.

"Normally they're £21 each, but we, (The Mother & Son Drug Pedalling Co.), are selling them for a fiver the pair. They'll keep you up like a bleedin' tent pole," she continued. I was a little nonplussed by the whole operation, to be honest. Once again, I declined again and wished her a good day.

She put her contract, money and knocked off pills back in her bag and gave me a final glorious, rasping cough before she headed out of the shop and to brave the elements for the ten yards to her next stop. "Good luck," I shouted.

"I'll fucking need it," was her breathless, curt response, no doubt referring to the gambling *and* her new drug-pushing venture. There's nothing like a little bit of optimism to get you really excited!!

(4.15 p.m.) Lunch was a distant memory, as I hoped Daz was to Sabrina. I do hope she's true to her word and doesn't let that little scumbag sweet talk his way back into her life. I don't want to see or hear his name again myself, although I still have the compunction to lay him out, so if he should turn up here one day... I looked up from my desk because I heard raised voices outside. I marched out of the shop to see what was going on. In the warm sun, began the biggest non-contact fight I've ever seen. I don't know how it started, but a group of about a dozen 16-25-year-old males had gathered in two equal packs just outside my shop. There was a fair bit of shouting and arm-waving going on, but due to the language barrier (I think it was Romanian), I had no idea what the dispute was about. One angry, Adidas track-suit-clad young man kept pointing at his shoe - Adidas, naturally. Perhaps they were nicked from the other mob or maybe he exchanged them for a girlfriend or something, and he wanted his prize back. I was only guessing.

Every so often, one of them would make a little foray into the no man's land between the two warring factions and offer his best Victorian pugilist's stance — you know the one. If only they were in white long johns and heavy black boots, well-slicked back hair with a central choirboy parting and handlebar moustache. It would have been a nice change from the black and gold Adidas affairs.

As the voices rose and the insults escalated, the two sides parted. I witnessed a McDonald's cup, complete with top and straw, thrown at an opponent by one of the younger, less vocal foot soldiers. I suppose it was like a very low-rent Molotov cocktail. It avoided his intended target by some way and exploded on the ground.

That drew a collective 'Ooooh', from the gathered audience. There were some very small pieces of ice and tiny puddles of carbonated soft drink everywhere. Oh, the carnage! It could have really kicked off then, but no one was going to take the risk of getting a leftover remnant of hamburger, with its deadly slice of pickle core, in their face; and as quick as it began, it was over.

And so, with a few pantomime laughs and a selection of singular and plural finger gestures, the two sides declared an uneasy truce and went their separate ways. Peace was restored and the street returned to a lifeless, depressing thoroughfare as if nothing had ever happened.

(5.10 p.m.) The fifth and last incident of what had become one of my most memorable days here occurred just before closing time. By then I was feeling a little mischievous and the final punter of the day was just crying out for me to vent my mischief on.

The woman, who had just collected her pawn,

asked me. "Have you got the right time, please?"

I looked at her, looked at my watch and feeling quite facetious, I replied "Yes." She nodded and made her way to the exit, before stopping dead in her tracks and turning around adding "Oh, what is it then?" she asked

"What is what?"

"What is the time?"

I told her. "Time is relative, and its importance can only be defined by the individual's acceptance of its rules of uniformity." Of course, I had no idea what I was on about but gambled safely that neither did she. I thought it sounded quite good though.

Nevertheless, I was pleased with my answer and the expression it left on her face before she uttered without an inkling of comprehension. "No, you don't understand. I want to know what the time is." I guessed at 5.11 p.m.; I couldn't even be bothered to check. She scuttled out of the shop and I was doubly satisfied with my performance and (as I checked my timepiece), my unerring time-telling accuracy. Yes, I really was in that kind of mood.

(5.20 p.m.) Just before I set the alarm, Sabrina got a call on her mobile. I watched her as she dropped on to her chair ashen-faced. Her face literally went pale. She listened intently to who she was talking to open interspersing with the occasional "Yes" and "I understand." When she finished the call, she started crying.

"What's up, love," I asked in deep concern.

"You remember Harry, the boy we visited?"

"Of course."

"He died this afternoon. Apparently, he asked the nurse, not long before, when I was going to visit him again.

She burst into tears. I walked over to her, knelt in front of her and put my arms around her. She was inconsolable as she began shaking.

"I was going to visit last night, but instead chose to confront Daz," she managed to convey.

"You weren't to know. It could have happened at any time."

"I knew he was dying, and I could have seen him one last time yesterday, but I let him down," she continued.

"Just wait a minute," I said assertively and I grabbed her hands, "You went out of your way to spend time with that little boy and he appreciated that. If you hadn't have visited him, who else, apart from his parents would have?" Sabrina didn't reply, but she knew the answer. "You gave him something to look forward to and you were someone he trusted and let into his life. You did a wonderful thing and meant a lot to him. Please don't feel guilty."

I took a tissue from a box on my desk and wiped her eyes.

"I guess you're right. You're a good man Peter Dawson. Thank you. Thank you for everything," she said as she looked at me through her red, tear-stained eyes.

"Ooh, that sounds kind of 'final'. Are you giving me the elbow, then?" I said trying to inject a little jocosity into the proceedings.

She just smiled and said, "I'll be okay. Let's go home." I felt awful for her. It's been a terrible couple of weeks for her. I think I'll take her for a drink next week after work.

(6.15p.m.) I drove home in rare silence. I couldn't get Sabrina and Harry out of my mind. Although I knew there would never be anything romantic between the girl and me, I still care a great deal for her. I knew the news about Harry would upset her for quite a while and I would do whatever I could to ease the pain, but I still felt pretty useless in the scheme of things. She's a resilient girl, but this has knocked her for six.

Saturday 21st July 2012
Making Your Mind Up

(9.00 a.m.) It's my birthday! And I'm at work! Yay! Kathy and Leanne were still in bed when I left this morning. We don't really make a fuss with birthdays much anymore. That included last year – my 50th when Kathy had her vomiting illness, so our planned trip to Venice was cancelled. We do cards and presents in the evening when I get home if I am working, and today will be no exception.

I don't know why, but Phil had turned up at the same time as me this morning.

"Did you think I was off today, Phil?" I asked as he opened the shutters.

"Nope. I just wanted to come in. I wanted to see you," he replied. I assumed he had some news for me about his future here. Sabrina, who had been quiet all week, wished me a happy birthday as we waited to enter the shop.

Phil overheard her and as he unlocked the front door offered me a 'heartfelt' "Oh, of course, it's your birthday. Happy birthday, mate. Damn keys!! You would think I'd know which one unlocked the front door my now." Sabrina looked at me as Phil struggled to find the right key and forced a smile. She's still very much affected by Harry's passing.

(9.30 a.m.) Sabrina was serving and this gave Phil the opportunity to take me aside for a chat.

"I'm not selling," he announced without fanfare.

"Quick and to the point, as usual, Phil," I said.

"Well, the old sod was leading me on. Wasting my time.

"You don't say."

"Why do you say that?

"Look, I don't know exactly what Tarquin Twistleton-Farquarharson-Campbell-Smythe and you were talking about...

"Ralph Fingleton-Butler," he interrupted clearly not picking up on my hilarious re-working of the toff's name.

"Whatever. You hardly mentioned anything about him to me and *he* never once offered to come down to the shop to meet me and look around. Didn't this seem a little odd to you?" I concluded.

"I suppose so. I thought it was a bit strange in the first place, to be honest. Why would an old sailor want a piece of an East London pawnbroker?"

"Precisely," I told him, "and go and make me a coffee. He forced a laugh and walked into the kitchen. I sat down at my desk and just watched Sabrina finish with her customer. She *does* have a lovely figure.

(1.20 p.m.) I had a customer years ago by the name of

Rose West. I had always hoped that she would be the first of a whole 'same name as murderers' subsection of my client list, but no one has ever added to this list – until this morning! I was so excited to see the ID with the name Mr P. Sutcliffe. I was thinking, 'Please be Peter. Please be Peter'. So, when I asked him his first name, and he confirmed it was Peter, I let out an audible "Yes." The guy must have thought I liked the name Peter very much or I perhaps I he thought he was the real Yorkshire Ripper who had somehow escaped Broadmoor, de-aged about 35 years (for he was about 30 years old), and then needed to pawn his mum's old brooch. And what did I need to catch this vile killer? I just simply to ask him for a recent utility bill (which he also wouldn't have had if he were the real PS). The thought occurred to me that he was probably born after 1981; therefore, his parents knew full well who they were naming him after. The callous swines.

Anyway, that's two killers in my midst. When he left, I started to go through our computer records to check for any Dennis Neilsons, Ted Bundys, Harold Shipmans or John Wayne Gacys. I do have a Charles Hanson. So close, but no cigar. But for now, at least I have *two* murderers on my books - The owl-faced crone of Cromwell Street, Rose West, and the Happy Hammer(er), Peter Sutcliffe.

(1.20 p.m.) To celebrate my birthday, Phil bought us all lunch. McDonald's all round. Hooray! Well, at least it was something. I shouldn't be ungrateful. As soon as we sat down to eat, someone came in and Phil jumped up to serve. As he did, Sabrina reached into her handbag, and pulled out a card and handed it to me.

"Here, I don't want you to open it now. Open it when you're on your own with no one else close by," she added with a giggle.

"Okay, I'll open it later this evening. How are you feeling now?"

"I'm feeling a bit more philosophical about things and I'm trying not to blame myself, but it's still hard to take in," she said. She paused for a moment and continued, "In fact, Pete I've been doing a lot of thinking recently and I have reached a decision."

"That sounds ominous."

"I wasn't going to tell you face to face, but I've just realised that would be a fairly callous thing to do to you."

"Ah, the card," I said, tapping my breast pocket. She nodded.

You've been so good to me and I've really enjoyed working here, but it's time for me to move on. A while ago, I applied for a job within the NHS, to work within a hospice. I trained to be a nurse after I left school but foolishly didn't complete my course. A few days ago, I was offered a position. I have to work for a qualification, but there is a lot of hands-on training and much of it is practical. It's something that I want to do, Pete," she continued.

"Wow, you kept all of that quiet. I never knew you

trained to be a nurse. Is this decision anything to do with... us?" I whispered, making sure that Phil was still preoccupied.

"Partly," Sabrina said, "but due to the whole Daz thing and Harry, I think the time is right for me to move on. I'm so grateful to you for everything, and you know how I feel about you. However, you must feel like it's a bit 'difficult' for us sometimes. I know I do."

"I do feel it, yes. If I was in your position, I would probably do the same. You're a young girl and your future isn't here. It would be a terrible waste of your talents," I reassured her. I knew everything she said was correct and I could never ask her to reconsider, but the news still felt like a lightning bolt. How can I imagine coming into work and not see her pretty face again? It'll take some getting used to.

Just then, Phil came back into the office. "What's up? Don't tell me you're upset that I'm staying," he said chirpily.

"What do you mean?" Sabrina asked.

"Oh, Phil thought he had a buyer for his share of the business. It's a long story... actually, it's not. It's a very short story. Someone said he was interested, but it turned out, they weren't. End of," I explained.

"Yep, that's it in a nutshell," added Phil.

"Oh, I see," Sabrina mumbled in a surprised manner.

After a moment's pause, I piped up. "Sabrina's

leaving us, Phil. She has a great job opportunity, and I've given her my blessing." I don't know why I said that. I mean she's not my daughter, and she's not getting married, but Phil accepted the sentiment."

We'll miss you," he said, with not a scintilla of surprise. I'm not sure if he was very genuine with the comment either, but Sabrina thanked him anyway.

(3.00 p.m.) Continuing my recent theme of Eastern European women who either don't know their name or where they live, a middle-aged woman presented me with her ring (stop tittering, diary), and I asked her name.

"Petroska, but the name last time was different." This story sounded familiar. I waited for a moment for her to tell me her name the last time she came in, but I think she must have assumed I was psychic because she just stared blankly at me.

"So what was it last time?" And if to continue my series of stories by my favourite Polish family, she informed me 'Kowalski'.

"Okay, so that was your name before you married?" I asked in hope.

"No."

"Is it your married name?"

"No." This was hard work.

"Your first name?" (knowing full well that wasn't).

"No."

"Your sister, mother, grandmother, next door neighbour, pet gerbil?"

"No." This was now becoming a quest, I said, exasperated. I asked: "Who is Kowalski?" (That sounds like an instantly forgettable late 1960's American police drama. *Who Is Kowalski...?* A Quinn Martin Production'.

"I don't know. I found the ID and showed you last time." Found. Not to cast aspersions, but I wondered if she found it in the street or about someone's person or belongings.

I just smiled and stared at her and she looked back like she had just said something completely normal and understandable.

"Right then, do you have some ID that I can see now with your correct name?" I asked. She took out a Polish ID card from her bag and I would love to tell you that it was yet another name and even a picture of someone else, but alas and alack, it was a true image of the woman now confirmed as Petroska.

"See, I told you. Petroska. I'm not a liar," she protested.

Not a liar. An idiot perhaps, but not a liar.

(4.10 p.m.) Phil popped out and I continued my abridged chat with Sabrina.

We sat in our usual places; I at my desk and she at Phil's, and I asked her, "When are you thinking about leaving?"

"As soon as is convenient, but I don't want to leave you short- handed. I'll stay as long as you want me too," she generously offered. "To be honest, I was going to leave today and you'll read why later."

"Oh, I'm not going to stop you if you really want to go today, but I would appreciate it if you could stick around for a few days until we can sort something out," I asked her.

"Of course I will. I was being selfish."

I smiled broadly and she returned the compliment. Phil soon reappeared.

"I return bearing good news. I have found someone to replace Sabrina. My niece will step into the fray; for a while anyway," he breathlessly announced as Sabrina stood up to allow him to take his place behind his desk. "She'll start Monday week, but I asked her to pop in next Friday to meet you." he continued.

"Bloody hell, *that* was quick," I spluttered.

I was a little taken aback at the speed, efficiency and indeed lack of subtlety of Phil's action, although Sabrina didn't look like she was offended, but then again, she wouldn't. I thought it was a little thoughtless as Sabrina was just sitting there listening to it all.

"Well, if you want to leave today, then..." I said.

She paused before shrugging her shoulders and conceded, "I suppose it would make sense. Thank you."

"Don't worry, we'll pay you until the end of the

month," Phil added at the same time the called his niece to confirm the position. At times Phil can be so undiplomatic.

(4.15 p.m.) Two women made their way in and one of them asked. "Do you change US dollars?" I assumed she wanted to change into Pounds Sterling. I explained, or at least tried to, that we were not a money exchange. Sometimes, when people ask a similar question because they do quite regularly, I tell them 'Yes, I can exchange it for gold', and direct them to our retail department. It amazes me how few understand sarcasm.

I wasn't in the mood for fun, so I told them there are many money exchange shops right across the road. There are too many to be truthful. The line of shops goes like this –

Newsagent (with money exchange)

Money exchange shop

Money exchange shop

Clothes shop

Mobile phone shop (with money exchange)

Money exchange and cheap crappy toys shop

She nodded and they went across the road to change their dollars. Guess what shop on that list they went into first? It beggars belief. It truly does.

(5.25p.m.) The end of an era. Phil left a few minutes

early and that left me to say goodbye to Sabrina on my own. I gave her a cuddle and £200 as a farewell gift. She began to cry.

"I'll miss you, Pete. I'll miss you a lot," she said in a soft, almost anodyne way. "You've got your birthday card, haven't you? As I said, some of what I wrote won't be a surprise to you anymore, because I didn't expect things to move on so quickly, today. I patted the left breast pocket area of my jacket again. "I will try to come back to see you from time to time," she added.

"I know you will." I was not at all convinced she would. I sensed she wanted a clean break, and coming back here would only ignite memories, both good and bad.

Outside the shop, with the shutters down, I once again embraced Sabrina and gave her one last kiss on her cheek, and then... she was gone. No more Sabrina. I walked around the corner barely believing that this was probably the last time I'd ever see my lovely assistant. It's a sad, sad moment.

(6.50 p.m.) I returned home, and to my astonishment, the family had arranged a surprise party for me - a very early evening surprise party. I entered the house and everyone yelled 'Surprise!' as is traditional with such occasions.

Kathy explained to me, "As you missed out on your 50th last year, I couldn't let your birthday go without doing something for you. I knew I couldn't get rid of you for a few hours so that's why it's early," she explained as she removed my jacket for me and placed it on the coat hook in the hall. It was indeed a lovely thing to do. Melissa, Tom and the kids were there as was Leanne, Kathy's parents, Clem, Phil (so, that was why he left work early!), Andy the Shrink, which really surprised me and left me relieved that I didn't tell him the extent of my relationship with Sabrina; and even Dawn and Frank were there, although I don't know why they were invited.

Andy approached me and said, "Kathy thought it would help you realise that you are a good person and people care about you a great deal."

I shook his hand and although I understood what he said, I still didn't understand why he was there. And, he didn't come with Stacey.

Before I even had a chance to greet anyone else, there was a ring at the front door. Kathy skipped by me to answer it. Who was standing at the door? Why, it was Simon.

"Hi, Dad. I thought I'd make an appearance," he joyfully declared. I cantered over to hug him, and as I did, I noticed a woman; a heavily pregnant woman standing behind him. As I released him, Simon ushered this woman in front of him and entered the house and candidly announced. "Oh, Mum, Dad, everyone, this is Magda. She's my wife." Magda nodded and said hello to everyone in broken English. Can you actually break *one* word? "Magda is from Hungary, or at least she was. She's from Rickmansworth now... as will I be, very soon," Simon continued with gusto. After a moment's hesitation, we all made our ways into the living room and people started to eat. It was one shock after another, today. I must say, my head was reeling somewhat.

Leanne took Magda aside and tried to engage her in conversation, although I'm not sure how much my new daughter-in-law would understand.

I cornered Simon, and before I could ask him anything, said, "Yes, *she* is and yes *it* is." He knew exactly what my line of questioning would be. That boy is a total mystery to me.

Simon ushered Magda over and she said, "Simon is a very nice man. He makes me happy." Now, why did I think she'd been primed to say that?

(8.15 p.m.) This was certainly one of my more eventful days in recent times. Everyone was so nice to me. Those vultures, Dawn and Frank, left after they'd picked the carcass of my buffet clean. I'm sure the only reason they turned up was the prospect of a free meal. Kathy laid on a nice spread – plenty of crudités and dips, chicken legs, sausage rolls mini samosas, falafels, etc. None of it home cooked, of course, but it was nice. Thanks, Mr Waitrose. I'm glad I didn't see any Battenberg cake or sponge fingers though. However, there were some party rings, but they were for the grandchildren.

Phil put his arm around me and whispered "We'll talk on Monday," and he made his way to the door, thanked Kathy and kissed her, for far too long in my opinion. Andy was next to leave after saying to me quietly. "I look forward to our next session," and he winked and said goodbye to the others. Clem took his cue and playfully slapped my face and left as well.

I was left with the family and a small pile of presents and cards in the corner of the living room. Just as we were about to interrogate Simon in the usual Dawson family way, he stood up too and announced that he and Magda were off. "I'll swing by next weekend and tell you guys all about it, but we really have to get back home now. Magda's mum is due to call at 9.30."

Magda smiled and came over to shake my hand. "That's not the way we do things in this family, Magda," I said as I embraced her and kissed her on both cheeks. Everyone else followed suit. I gave Simon a hug and said. "Just make sure you come over next weekend. Maybe just call ahead, eh? Oh," I added whispering into his ear, "I'll tell your Mum." He nodded, patted me on the back, and exited the house with his pregnant wife.

(8.45 p.m.) We'd had a family discussion and Leanne, who had a brief discussion with Magda, informed us was financially sound and had qualifications in economics and high finance, which was a relief to me, but then again Simon is no fool. The baby, my grandson is due in less than six months. That was about it, but I'm sure we'll find out more next week.

I had just remembered Sabrina's card, so I offered to take the three full black sacks of rubbish, which were parked by the kitchen door, out to the bins. I left the house with the three sacks and dumped them in the brown wheelie bin at the end of the drive. I then walked a few paces up the road in order to obscure myself behind a large bush. I opened the card and a folded up note fell to the ground. I picked it up, unfolded it tentatively and began to read it. This is what Sabrina wrote:

My Dear Pete,

By now you are aware that I am leaving the shop. It was a hard decision, because you mean so much to me and I loved working with you. I have tried to suppress my emotions of late, but the thing is, I have feelings that won't go away. I love you Pete, and I am not satisfied just to make general conversation at work, knowing you are going to go home to Kathy afterwards. Nothing would have made me happier than to 'run away' with you, and I know I would have made you happy too. I could never express the extent of my true feelings as I knew it would compromise you, and put you in an impossible position. It killed me not being able to tell you, but it wouldn't have been fair to anyone.

You might have guessed by now that I have already told Phil that I'm leaving. I couldn't go back to work after I had told you how deep my feelings run. I didn't want to deceive you like this, but it was the best way to do it. He doesn't know anything. I just told him last week that I'd be too upset to tell you in person.

Everything else I told you is true though. I have been offered a position within the NHS, but not necessarily at the hospice, we visited. Besides, what Daz did to me (and Leanne), is still pretty raw and this whole area brings painful memories for me. I think I'm doing the right thing.

I'm not sure if I'll see you again as my placement might be far away, but you'll always be in my thoughts.

Happy birthday, my darling Pete, and be happy. I will never forget you, and what you mean to me.

With love always,

Sabrina xxx

I stood still in stunned silence. I honestly had no idea how much she felt for me. Even though things fell into place for her today, she didn't know it when she wrote the note. Most of all, I feel sadness. Not so much for me, but for Sabrina. I'm 51, and although I gave it some serious thought at one point, I know where my place is. She's so young with her whole life ahead of her. She'll find someone who'll treat her like the wonderful person she is.

I looked at the card which simply said, '*Dear Pete. Happy birthday. Love Sabrina*'. That can go on the mantelpiece. The note, however, will have to find a secure and private home as I can't bear to throw it away.

I drew a deep breath and suddenly realised why Phil was so unsurprised at Sabrina's announcement. He knew all along and had already arranged her replacement. I made my way back into the house, where I found Kathy and Leanne sitting over Melissa, who was crying and in a right old state. They were combing out blobs of pink marshmallow from her hair. It seemed that Chloe and Charlie have had their sticky confectionary laden hands all over Mummy's blonde bonce. I looked at Tom and the children who were sitting quietly on the sofa. I glanced at Tom who trying to suppress his laughter. I then carefully placed Sabrina's card above the fireplace and retreated to a safe distance. Could I *really* swap this life for another one?

Friday 27th July 2012
Merry Xmas Everybody

(7.50 a.m.) Just for old time's sake, I switched back to the 1970s compilation in my car, and of course, that blasted pedestrian crossing stopped me in my tracks. It was like it was giving me a huge, red middle finger. Just for a change though, when another car drew up in the adjacent lane, I was not singing. I hadn't sung at all this morning, in fact. One track had just finished, and for old time's sake, and as a tribute to my former colleague Sabrina, who would laugh whenever I told her about my early morning driving shenanigans, I decided that whatever song came on next I would sing along to it at the top of my voice. A few nervous seconds passed before my choice was revealed. It was *I Want You to Want Me* by Cheap Trick. Normally, I wouldn't entertain the idea of singing a song like this, as it is definitely nearer a level 10 than a level one in my Cringeworthy Scale, but a deal's a deal. I sang I was viewed, I sang louder. The words were quite poignant considering the way Sabrina felt about me and it seemed kind of fitting that the mp3 player randomly chose this song.

(9.00 a.m.) Well, this is the day when it all begins. The whole London Olympic bandwagon has pitched up in Stratford, just a few miles from the shop, and it seemingly has everyone aboard. All the great and the good will be there tonight; Seb, Boris, David Cameron, The Queen, Tessa Jowell, Dame Kelly Holmes, Chris

Martin of Coldplay, Bob Carolgees and Spit the Dog...
and I really don't think there's much chance of me being
able to ignore it.

It's been just me and Phil all week, and although
it's been alright, I really do miss Sabrina; even more
knowing the extent of her feelings for me. I had thought
about phoning her but quickly realised that could
complicate matters. It's odd, but she's not been
mentioned at all. It's almost like she never existed. I
cancelled my appointment with Andy the Shrink on
Wednesday as I couldn't face just talking about my
everyday life and Simon's 'homecoming. The fact that
Kathy invited him to my party I thought was a quite
odd. Now though, he's a little too close to home – in fact,
he was *in* my home, so I now don't think I can ever tell
him about what has happened or indeed what didn't
happen. I think I will end my sessions with him very
soon.

(10.50 a.m.) A mother and daughter came in, and as I
was already serving someone else, they waited patiently
to be seen as Phil was in the little boy's room. Now, I
assumed the following conversation wasn't supposed to
be for public consumption, but I have microphones
behind my bulletproof glass and MDF panelled pawn
booth. (Armed robbers take note - you can't shoot me in
the face, but you'll make your point by easily blowing my
legs off), and I heard everything. The gist of their
conversation seemed to be about the relationship
between the daughter and her boyfriend. From what I

could understand, he was no good for her and she should get rid.

"I don't know why you're still with him," the mother enquired, "especially after *that* incident," and then she gave what can only be described as an 'incy wincy spider' hand gesture. Ha! More like incy wincy crab. Still, it's nice she reminded her daughter of that happy time. The daughter nodded in resignation and tutted. It was probably just another day down at the STD clinic for her.

"Well, that won't happen again," she responded firmly.

Now, I couldn't be sure if that meant she was giving him the old heave-ho or that incy wincy and his mates had no natural habitat down there anymore.

The mother continued, "You can still let him see the kid though."

The 'kid'? What a nice way to talk about your grandchild - who incidentally was not present, (unless she left him in the buggy chained to a lamppost outside the shop). And then came a piece of motherly advice that was so touching, so heart-warming that it almost drew a tear from my eye, "Don't worry about him, Chantelle, you'll get another one." Now I assume she didn't mean another 'kid', and she actually meant another unfussy male to cavort with, but when daughter put her arm around mother and said, "Oh fanks, Muuuum..." well, even the hardest men would well up.

Anyway, by this point, I had finished my dealings

with the customer in front of them and now it was Chantelle's mother's turn to be served. She asked to borrow £50 on a pendant and chain, which I agreed to, and as soon as I passed her the money, she handed over a tenner to her daughter for some cigarettes. Once again, Chantelle thanked her mum and she delicately placed a kiss her on her age-ravaged, sallow-skinned cheek.

There's nothing like the love of a mother for her errant daughter. Her advice, no doubt passed down from generation to generation of this traditional East End family, I hoped would be heeded. And, the love of a daughter for her mother, who just pawned her 'No.1 Mum' pendant, so she could keep her daughter in Sterling Superkings for a few more hours, was quite touching.

(1.45 p.m.) There was still no sign of Phil's niece, although he guaranteed me that she would definitely be in by the end of the day to meet me. He had been acting all suspicious again. I wonder what he's up to. He bought us both lunch, which was the inevitable McDonald's. Well, I wasn't going to say no, was I?

(2.15 p.m.) Here are a couple of quickies. These are two incidents that happened one after the other. It was classic stuff.

"No sir, gold-plated is *not* the same as gold."

"Nah mate, it is. I'm telling ya."

"I can assure you it isn't."

"Nah, you is wrong. Me cuz told me..."

And so it went on.

A fella came in with a bit of scrap gold and I offered him £25 for it. He went away to think about it and came back half an hour later wanting to sell it. "How much did you say?" he asked.

Assuming that he knew full well what I offered, I told him "£23."

"OK then," he replied, "£21." Deafness, stupidity or reverse haggling, I wondered?

(3.00 p.m.) There was still no sign of the new girl, but the bizarre little incidents just kept coming. A rather well-to-do gentleman entered to pawn a diamond pendant on a chain. The paperwork was done and the money had been handed over to him. The conversation that followed had me believing that I was unwittingly taking part in a hidden camera show:

Customer: Are you open on Sundays?

Me: No sir.

Customer: Not any Sundays?

Me: I'm afraid not.

Customer: What if it's Christmas?

Me: Especially not Christmas.

Customer: So, if I pawned something and wanted to get it at Christmas, I couldn't?

Me: No, but you could come in on Christmas Eve.

Customer: Hmmmm (pauses), I suppose the same goes for Easter?

Me: (looking for the hidden cameras) You suppose right, sir.

Customer: It's lucky I'll be taking it out before then, eh?

Me: Indubitably.

Customer: Thanks, then.

Me: My pleasure. And Merry Christmas!

Customer: What?

Me: Nothing. Bye.

This is my life, for heaven's sake!!!!

(4.20 p.m.) Phil had a call on his mobile phone. "My niece is here, Pete. She's just parked up. I'll just pop out the front to get her."

"You're keen," I said. There was no reply as he ran out to greet her.

A minute later Phil returned with his arm around

a young lady. He walked her to the back office still with his arm on her shoulder.

"Pete, this is my niece, Selina," he announced proudly.

Selina held her hand out and I shook it warmly. "Hello, Pete. It's very nice to meet you. Uncle Phil's told me a lot about you," she said in a rather seductive voice, head slightly bowed, like Princess Diana. She looked up through her long fringe at me and smiled. Her hand was still holding mine.

"Hello, Selina. Welcome." I couldn't get out my head the similarities between her and Sabrina. Same height, same colour eyes, same ponytailed hair, similar dress sense... and her name is *Selina* for heaven's sake. Sabrina/Selina? You couldn't get much closer if you'd tried.

She finally released my hand, and Phil led her into the kitchen to show her where the tea and coffee was. Priorities. I sat down at my desk with a feeling of disbelief at the irony of the whole situation. She was almost a clone of Sabrina.

A few moments later they came back into the office and Phil announced in a rather sexist and patronising way. "Well, if nothing else, she knows how to make coffee." Selina took it in good humour and said "Black, no sugar?" as she looked at me in the same bashful, but sensual way.

"Yes, that's right," I confirmed and she toddled off back to the kitchen. I didn't expect her to make me a coffee right at that moment, but I didn't say tell her not to.

"I thought so."

Phil looked over from his desk where he was leaning back in his chair, "I think she likes you," he whispered in a cheeky way. "I don't know; you and these young women, eh?"

I hope he didn't expect an answer because he didn't get one. I just gave him an unsympathetic glare, turned around and pretended to look at the list of overdue pawns. I have to say this whole situation had an air of Groundhog Day about it.

(5.15p.m.) The final customer probably summed up the day, if not my career in this shop. It was simple and made me laugh.

Me: Can I have your name, please?

Customer: Angela.

Me: No, your second name?

Customer: Angela.

Me: No, your surname; your last name?

Customer: Angela.

Me: Do you have any ID?

Customer: (Blank expression. Then her friend came in).

Friend: What do you need?

Me: Her last name.

Friend: Kowalski. (Hooray, there's another one!)

Me: So, who is Angela?

Friend: I don't know...

And there, in a nutshell, is my life at this establishment. Catering size confusion.

(12.30 a.m.) Kathy and I enjoyed a nice Indian takeaway this evening before we settled down to watch the televisual event of the year. For over three hours I had been sitting next to her on the couch watching The Olympic Games Opening Ceremony. After months of anti-Olympic rhetoric and general negativity about the whole event, I have a confession to make. It was sensational! I'm not one to freely admit when I am wrong, but expense and propaganda aside, it was a fantastic spectacle, and it cost less than half of what Beijing spent on theirs. It's still £27 million spent on a lot of pomp and circumstance, but it was amazing to witness the precise theatrical display.

I'm not going soft on the whole thing, and I still believe that money could be better spent elsewhere, but I have relaxed my stance somewhat, and I believe that is no little thanks to Sabrina. She showed me that perhaps being bitter and overly political was not the real Pete Dawson, (and that is the only time I will refer to myself in the third person). I'm going to give this a chance. I'm going to try and watch it through the eyes of a sports fan, and I'll reserve my judgment on whether it was a complete waste of money until after the event. It was the lea | st I could do.

When the broadcast finished, I looked at Kathy who took my hand and squeezed it gently. I know I'm a lucky man and really I do have all I want within these walls. Who knows what the future will bring, but in a few months I'll be a grandfather again and that's a fantastic feeling. I guess I'll just keep plodding along. I would say overall that things are looking up.

I turned the TV and lights off and I followed Kathy upstairs to bed.

She stopped on the top stair and asked in a playful voice "Peeete?"

"Yes, darling," I replied without a hint of sarcasm.

"I wonder would you do something for me?" she continued in a rather sexy voice.

"Certainly. What is it, sweetheart?" I responded eagerly.

"Would you... just pop downstairs and put the phone back in its charger for me?"

I just smiled, nodded and did her bidding. It had been on the arm of the sofa for over five hours and she'd said nothing about it for all that time.

Perhaps she does love me after all. Things are certainly looking up.

Glossary of Song Titles and Artists

For those who weren't sure or just needed reminding, here is a full list of all the song titles used in the book along with the artists who, most popularly, recorded them.

Start Me Up	- The Rolling Stones
Food For Thought	- UB40
The Candy Man Can	- Sammy Davis, Jnr.
Piano Man	- Billy Joel
Crime Of The Century	- Supertramp
I Swear	- Boyz II Men
Knees Up Mother Brown	- (Cockney Classic)
Burning Love	- Elvis Presley
A View to A Kill	- Duran Duran
Hurry Up Harry	- Sham 69
Open Your Heart	- Human League
Pennies From Heaven	- Bing Crosby
Paperback Writer	- The Beatles
Can't Buy Me Love	- The Beatles
The Power Of Positive Drinking	
	- Lou Reed
Pyjamarama	- Roxy Music

The Lunatics (Have Taken Over The Asylum)

- Fun Boy Three

Don't Cha — The Pussycat Dolls

Fools Gold — The Stone Roses

Bloody Well Right — Supertramp

Tempted — Squeeze

Gimme Some Truth — John Lennon

Chain Reaction — Diana Ross

Shine On You Crazy Diamond

- Pink Floyd

Land Of Confusion — Genesis

I Remember You — Frank Ifield

Don't Let Me Be Misunderstood

- The Animals

One Moment in Time — Whitney Houston

What A Fool Believes — The Doobie Brothers

Too Many People — Paul McCartney

You Better You Bet — The Who

Here Comes The Rain Again — Eurythmics

Cigarettes & Alcohol — Oasis

Making Your Mind Up — Bucks Fizz

Merry Xmas Everybody — Slade

My name is Elliot Stanton, married with two children I live on the outskirts of North London. I have always enjoyed writing and in my teenage years, even created a fanzine for a friend's band. I had often thought about writing a first book but had difficulty in finding a subject, eventually finding one right under my nose...

I worked in an old, established family jewellers and pawnbrokers and decided to reveal some of the humorous interactions with my customers. Hence, The Not So Secret Diary of a Pawnbroker.

Outside of writing, my interests include history, travel (I particularly love Las Vegas and have been many times), sport (although more as a spectator rather than as a participant), music and quizzing. As a member of a pub quiz team, I enjoy spending my evenings with friends putting my grey matter to the test.

In addition, I have written treatments for three new television quiz shows. So, maybe you'll be seeing my name again quite soon!

Printed in Great Britain
by Amazon